DINO
RIFT

DINO RIFT

DEREK BORNE

DINO RIFT

No part of this publication may be reproduced, stored in a retrieval system, or transmitted in any form or by any means without the prior written permission of the publisher, nor be otherwise circulated in any form of binding or cover other than that in which it was published and without a similar condition being imposed on the subsequent purchaser.

Edited by R.A. Milhoan Book Services
Cover Design and Interior Formatting by We Got You Covered Book Design
WWW.WEGOTYOUCOVEREDBOOKDESIGN.COM
Photograph of Derek Borne by Tara Jeles – So Jeles Photography
Dinosaur Sketches by Awesome ART by Choolee

This is a work of fiction. All characters, names, places, organizations and events portrayed in this novel are a product of the author's imagination. Any resemblance to persons, living or dead, actual events, or organizations is entirely coincidental.

Every song and music artist mentioned in this book is real, including the alexrainbirdMusic YouTube channel.

Published by Virtuoso Press

TO GRANDPA JACK,

Your smile and jokes brought every room to life,
and your laugh was utterly infectious.
I hope to become even half the man you were.
And I wish I could go back in time to when you were my age
so we could be buddies for even longer.

ONE

"COPY THAT. We're armed and ready."

At nine o'clock in the evening, two boys in blue careened past pulled-over cars and sped through stoplights.

In the driver seat, the police chief scarfed down half a burger. Dinner was always a rush when on the clock.

"We may be armed, but are we ready?" The rookie—just over a month into the job—shoved the last few of his fries in his mouth. "Chief, if this really is what they're saying it is, shouldn't we call in an A.C.U. or something?"

"We'll have to assess the situation first." After turning a corner and two bites later, the chief licked burger remains from his fingers. "Probably just an overgrown iguana."

A few minutes later, they arrived at the address of the disturbance, in a rural area on the outskirts of town.

A white two-story farmhouse sat at the end of a long dirt driveway.

A pair of fire trucks had congregated with four other

police cars, which had all pulled off to the sides of the entryway. No one had left the safety of their vehicles but kept their wary eyes focused on the home. The closest officers kept a cautious fifty-foot gap from the residence.

"Didn't think most of a police force would be afraid of an overgrown iguana." The rookie smirked as he placed a hand on the door handle once they'd parked. "When you picked me up, all you called it was 'an *unusual* animal disturbance'."

"Caller was the neighbor." The chief checked over his weapon and protective vest. "Claims that this guy was seen trespassing on the neighbor's property. Had some kind of large pet with him, the description didn't check out, though."

The young rookie, barely in his twenties, gave his superior an odd glance. "Large pets are a cause for complaint?"

The skeptical chief chuckled. "They are when they're reported to have attacked."

A quick, silent prayer later, the rookie exited the vehicle a second behind the chief.

Waves of interchanging blue and red from the multiple squad cars silently lit up the area, bathing the house's siding in their kaleidoscope of color and setting an even stranger mood to the location.

As the two men closed in on the building, the rest of their squad finally exited their vehicles and followed suit.

"Hey, Beninato," the chief called over to a fellow policewoman who approached them. "Why's everyone sitting around?"

The redhead cleared her throat as she kept her stare on the house's front door. "If you heard the noise we heard, you would've stayed in your car, too."

None of the house's outside lights were on.

"'Bout time somebody had the guts to come on out."

The gruff southern drawl came from the right.

"You're the one who called?" The chief shined his flashlight on the man.

"That's right." Tucked under the bearded neighbor's right arm, a hunting rifle tipped the danger meter up a bit more. "Gon' help me put this sucker in the ground?"

The rookie took a quick glance behind. Having eight others watching his and each other's backs helped ease his mind.

"Depends." In hopes of getting more details, the superior officer marched over. "Sheriff Martin Danbury. Can you describe this animal?"

"Unlike anythin' I've ever seen before."

Those six words fuelled the tension in all of the policemen.

Danbury pursed his lips. "How about anything that might help us figure out how to take it down?"

The Southerner revealed a crooked grin. "It's damn quick."

"Uh, that's it?"

"Now that you know, you'll need to make sure you're *quicker*."

Once he'd cleared his throat, Danbury instructed his younger colleague, "Summerford, do a perimeter check."

Already traveling up a stone path to the front porch to survey things, a stench assaulted the rookie's nose. "Dang, did something die around here—"

Squish.

A foot-wide pile of dung enveloped his right foot.

3

With an arm over his mouth, the rookie cursed as he turned his face away from the putrid stench. "You gotta be kidding me."

Danbury called over, "What are you going on about, Summerford?"

Removing his boot from the feces, Kevin Summerford cursed under his breath before responding. "Think I just stepped in a load of—"

"*You need to get off my property, right now!*"

Everyone snapped to attention as the homeowner exploded from his front door in a blur of red hair and quick movements to meet the group of uninvited guests.

"That's the fella right there." The Southerner's overalls straps jostled as he readied his rifle. "His critter shouldn't be too far behind."

The homeowner pointed a finger inches away from his neighbor's face. "Because you shot at it, it sees you as a *threat*."

The Southerner's beard wagged as he countered. "That bloodthirsty *thing* was gonna make a meal outta ma pigs. 'Course I was gon' shoot it."

"You reckless idiot." The redheaded man noticed the chief getting ready to split them up. "I've been trying to calm it down. Since you grazed its leg with your gunshot, it views *you* as a danger to *me* also. You *need* to leave right now."

"Excuse me, sir. I'm Chief Danbury." Martin turned his flashlight onto the homeowner. "We'd much appreciate it if you tell us what kind of animal you're housing, and how potentially dangerous it is."

After some deep breaths, the redhead counted the number

of people around him as he shook his head. "None of you should be here right now—"

A piercing, otherworldly cry came from inside the farmhouse.

Summerford forgot about the dung on his boot. "What on God's green Earth was *that?*"

The redhead's arms slackened. *Damn.*

SMASH!

Glass shattered as a figure tangled up in a mass of curtains had burst through the front window.

Faster than anyone had anticipated, it raced down the front porch steps, knocked over a shocked Summerford, and vanished into the corn crops to the left of the homestead.

"Holy...." Danbury rushed over. "You okay, Summerford?"

Standing at the edge of the crops to the right, the Southerner put his rifle into position, ready for anything. "Told ya it was quick."

"Fine... I'm fine." Summerford hopped back onto his feet. "It just winded me."

"That's because it could smell you from inside." The redhead stayed aware of the crops which surrounded the house from every side except the front. "You're new. Therefore you're nothing to fear. He could have done worse."

"Ain't you boys gon' follow that monster?" The bearded neighbor kept an eye on the corn crop horizon.

Danbury and Summerford stared at each other.

"Heck no." Summerford kept a tight grip on his handgun. "Tallgrass and a crazy animal isn't my kind of adventure."

The southerner stepped forward. "Y'all are a bunch of—
AAAAAAGH!"

In less than thirty seconds, the creature had traveled around the house and snatched the armed man.

A barrage of bullets unloaded on the area where the Southerner had been dragged into the field. Only orders to cease fire from Danbury quieted their gunfire.

Irritation over the unclear situation pushed Danbury to come face to face with the homeowner. "Details. *Now.* What are we dealing with? And if you don't tell me, I'm ordering all my men here to rain down on whatever's out there."

Still hesitant, the distressed homeowner flexed his hands as he sighed. "None of you will believe me."

"After what I saw in Washington a few years ago..." Summerford spoke as if everyone had seen it. "...try us."

"If I tell you...it would be a breach of my contract." The homeowner raised his left eyebrow. "You would all be swimming in red tape."

Done with being kept in the dark, Danbury aimed his gun at the man. "Seems as though you've got some kind of connection with it."

"What are you *doing*, Martin?" Kevin gave him wild glances while keeping an eye out for the beast.

"Either you tell me what this *classified* creature is..." Danbury disengaged the gun's safety. "...or I'll make the classified come to us."

SKREEEEAAOW!

Every policeman swirled around as a dark-skinned creature bellowed from the top of one of the fire trucks. A glow from the moonlight added to its eeriness.

Danbury's jaw dropped. "Holy *mother of*—"

Before anyone could fire off a shot, the beast disembarked the large red vehicle. The odd animal's eight-foot tail whipped past two officers as it put itself in front of the homeowner.

Danbury couldn't believe his eyes.

Teeth.

Claws.

Eyes that could make any man freeze.

"Easy, girl. Hey now." Completely unafraid, the redhead stroked the crown of its two-foot-long head. His fingers rippled down the scales of the nearly ten-foot-tall beast, an attempt to try to calm it down. "They're not going to hurt you."

Summerford fumbled his weapon. "Sir, is that a—"

"Please, don't hurt her."

"Don't *hurt* her?" Danbury aimed at the snouted, reptilian head. Blood dripped from its jaws. "This thing just *killed* someone."

"In all due respect, I've studied this creature for a year," the man rebutted. "I know how it perceives the world. If you—"

"You've had this thing for a *whole year?*" Summerford backed up a step. "And it hasn't taken a chunk out of you?"

"Yes." The redhead raised a hand in hopes of stopping the police from hurting or even killing it. "If you shoot it, you'll be destroying millions of dollars in research."

Gun still pointed at the hissing, man-sized lizard, Danbury shook his head. "Sorry. Can't risk any more...."

An eerie and absolute silence surrounded them, which made the chief peek behind himself over his shoulder.

Every other officer had become incapacitated. Even the firefighters sat limp in their trucks.

Thip!

Summerford's hand slapped against his superior's shoulder for support. "Chief…. Somethi…in my…."

The rookie slumped to the dirt. His head inches away from the dung.

A tranquilizer dart protruded from his neck.

Overwhelmed by the sudden turn in the situation, Danbury's hand tremored as he aimed his firearm back at the intimidating, scaley beast. "What the heck kind of—"

Thip!

"—operation are…you…."

A numbing sensation overtook him. As Martin's left hand discovered a dart in the back of his neck, his legs gave out. Unable to fire off a single bullet, his body met the stone path from the driveway to the house.

Razor-sharp teeth flashed in front of his eyes before the world went black.

TWO

"GOT ANYTHING to say for yourself?"

Stuck at his desk, the student saw no way out.

Six minutes remained until the end of a non-physical phys-ed class.

Kamren fiddled with his folded glasses. "Only that school grading systems are crap."

The pudgy gym teacher, Mr. Richardson, gave his pupil an intimidating stare. Or at least he hoped it would instill some fear. "Trying to be smart with me?"

"There are two things I find unfair." Kamren Eckhardt unfolded his black-rimmed glasses and put them back on.

"*Only* two?"

"For one, art teachers mark grades on what they personally like. And yet, what I paint is probably on par with what an elephant's painting will sell for. Which can sometimes go for a solid grand. Trust me, I saw it on the internet." With only a couple of minutes left, Kamren slid his backpack out from between his legs. "Look it up. They're quite good with their trunks.

"Ultimately, the teacher will try to influence a student in hopes of saying they helped produce an amazing artist, therefore feeding their ego."

Mr. Richardson huffed. "Okay? And the second thing?"

The ash-brown-haired Kamren smirked. "That just like the art teacher, you'll do whatever you can to boost your ego, or *wrestling team*, in your case."

Richardson's jaw tensed. "Excuse me, Eckhardt?"

"You asked me if I have anything to say for myself, and I'm saying it." Eckhardt stood up to match the coach's stance. His grey-green eyes brimmed with confidence. "Sure, I took down Smith, Bradley, and Perry. Three guys over my weight class. Ever since I said no to joining the wrestling team…" Kamren waved his report card in the teacher's face. "…I've seen my grade slip from the nineties to…oh, what's this? An even fifty percent?"

Red in the face, Richardson struggled to form words even though his mouth gaped open.

"Isn't a motto in every school to…what is it now…say *no* to *bullies?*"

Before Richardson could counter, the bell rang.

"I'll be taking this to Principal Crosby." The backpack swung over Kamren's shoulder as he headed for the door. "See you in school court, Richie."

Thankfully, only a quarter of his last semester remained at Carbon High School in Price, Utah. Kamren couldn't wait to be done with the faculty and their politics. More than that, he yearned to finally get a chance to perfect his writing skill and publish his written works.

Whenever he left school for the day, he'd rush home to channel everything into sci-fi, action, and adventures. Sometimes fantasy. *Maybe tonight I'll start on my 'androids vs. aliens' idea. Do I start it on Earth, or in space, though? Or I could spend some time fleshing out backstories for some side charac—*

"Off in some kind of fantasy world again?"

From behind, the slightly raspy voice pulled him out of his creative thoughts.

"Asked the girl who still dreams of one day finding a prince." Kamren arrived at his locker and fiddled with the spinning padlock. After almost four years it seemed to come subconsciously.

Leaning against the locker to his left, she gave him a playful smack on the arm. "One day he'll come for me. Too bad this school is full of jocks and jerks."

"Those words usually mean the same thing, right?" Kamren swapped his backpack for his science textbook and blue binder. "Patience, Princess Vivienne. At eighteen, no one knows who they are yet. All that rules the adolescent mind is what's below the belt."

"Ew." Vivienne giggled, curling mixed strands of blonde and red behind her ear. "Even though that's true, I repeat, *ew.*" Shaking her head in amusement, she'd grown used to Kamren's habit of speaking like her grandpa and learned early on to shrug it off.

He tapped on the earbud in her left ear. "Whatcha

listenin' to?"

"Oh, um…." She pulled out her cellphone and tapped the screen with her thumb a few times before handing over her other earbud. "I found this guy called Cody Fry, apparently he's good friends with Ben Rector."

"Oooh." The mention of the second artist caught his attention since that had been one of his favorites to listen to. "What's his style like?"

"He's kind of indie, but has a symphonic composer aspect, too."

Kam plucked the earbud from her hand. "Now I *need* to hear this guy." He started bopping his head to the tune, then stuck his elbow out to her. "Well, Lady Lancaster, shall we head on to class?"

Vivienne Lancaster looped her arm through his. "Why thank you, Sir Kam."

Being silly had become second nature to them. Awkward stares from the students around them didn't matter.

They'd been best friends since they were two years old. Both families had gone camping in Oregon and through sheer coincidence had lots across from each other. It had been Kam who'd waddled over to the neighboring Lancaster's campsite and struck up kiddie conversation with Viv. They were inseparable for the rest of the trip. Their parents hit it off as well, which led to the Eckhardt's eventually moving to the small town of Price, Utah.

Dinners and get-togethers at each other's houses and movie or game nights became the norm for all of them.

In middle school, their peers had teased that Kam and

Viv would most likely end up getting married. This was due to the world majority's belief that a guy and girl can't simply be friends.

For Kam and Viv, they'd remained friends and nothing more. When things got rough, one would always be there for the other. If any plans were made, one would always make sure to include the other without hesitation.

They became a testament to the phrase: friends are the family you choose for yourself.

As they turned a corner, the science classroom required only a few more steps.

"You *kidding* me?" Viv glanced at him with her teal eyes. "Richardson seriously docked you that much? He needs to be slapped in the face with a chair."

"Metal or wood?" Kamren chuckled as he escorted her to the door. "Ladies first."

The back middle of the room had become their usual desk spot.

"Something interesting happened in math, by the way." She got settled in her chair. "I feel like I already know your answer, but figured I'd see what you think."

"Is this a vague something interesting?"

"Don't be a doofus." Viv cracked a grin as she smacked his darker-toned hand. "We got invited to Amy Kloss's place for a pool party tonight."

It took a moment for the news to sink in for him. "You mean…with *other* people?"

"We don't get invited out often, so I said we'd be there." She tapped her pen on the desk. "Might be nice to get our social on."

With pursed lips, he cracked his neck while deciding. "You sure it's not a trick into becoming the *designated* ones?"

"Or you could give other humans a chance."

"Blegh, disgusting race."

Viv snorted as she flicked his shoulder with the pen. "Whatever."

Hours later, at home, Vivienne had finished picking out an outfit and bathing suit for the pool party. Figuring it would get cool later, she slipped on a light pink sweater. Her hair didn't need much, since it would get wet anyway. Purse. *Check.* Plastic bag to keep valuables from getting wet. *Check.* Cellphone. *Check.* Wallet. *Che—*

"You're wearing *that* to the party?"

Irritating little brother.

Check.

"Who made you the fashion police?"

Arthur, affectionately nicknamed Arty, leaned against the doorframe to her bedroom. "When I was born, it was put in the contract."

"Remind me to ask Mom and Dad to look into the fine print." As she walked past him, Viv ruffled Arty's slicked-back golden blonde hair. "Getting any attention from your fellow minor-niner girls with that hairdo?"

"Do you even need to ask?" Slightly embarrassed, he smirked while following her to the stairs. "So…are you *finally* going to tell Kam tonight?"

"Tell him what?"

"Oh, I see. You're still waiting for the right time."

At the bottom of the stairs, Viv slipped her pre-tied shoes on. "You can stop talking now, weirdo." She peered out the front door window. *Where is he? Save me from this agony.*

Arty had made his way down and leaned against the stairs rail-post. "Love watching you squirm."

Overly annoyed with him, she rested a shoulder onto the door trim. "Mom, Dad, can you get out Arty's leash? He's acting up again."

All they heard from their father who sat in the kitchen was, "Kids, don't make me turn this house around."

Both of the kids had a little chuckle.

A burgundy-red pickup truck pulled up outside and honked.

Arty glanced out the window. "And *Prince Eckhardt* arrives on his steed."

"And the little wart stays home to scoop the dung." Vivienne swung the door open. "See ya, Bro."

"Love ya, Sis."

Halfway down the front walk, Vivienne realized her legs had been moving faster than she'd intended. *Slow down, less eager now.* By the time she reached the passenger door, she saw a busy Kam setting up the Bluetooth on his phone. She made sure to not open the truck door with too much gusto. "What tunes are we playing on the way?"

"What we listen to all the time." Kam pressed play on his cellphone's music app. "Alexrainbird Music just released a new indie playlist a few hours ago."

Viv shut the door and buckled in. "Oh, have you listened to any East Love? Their style is awesome! Nice and folky with a hint of rock. They're on one of their older playlists."

Phone still in hand, he searched for their name. "Any song in particular?"

"Put on *Sweet Arizona*."

"Done and done."

They drove off and headed for the opposite end of town. Amy Kloss's house would only be another ten-minute drive into the country. Though they were together, they didn't need to talk much. Spending years together got them to the point where simply being in a car with great music equaled a good time.

At one point, Vivienne glanced over and noticed he still wore long pants on a hot day. "Are you wearing a bathing suit underneath?"

"Didn't bring one."

She slapped him on the shoulder. "You did remember it's a pool party, right?"

"With a bunch of hormonal child-teens peeing in said pool." He shrugged. "I could tell you really wanted to go, though."

"Wait." The last thing he said made her grin. "The only reason you're going is because...*I am?* Kam, you didn't have to—"

"It's okay, Viv." He held out his fist to be bumped. "If a party will make you happy, then I want you to be happy. Like you said, we don't really go to any."

As her fist bumped into his, it sparked a full smile on her face. *He would do that for me?* After staring at him with admiration for a few seconds, she ran her fingers through her hair while a sign came up on the right-hand side of the road.

The local dinosaur museum notified drivers of being two miles ahead.

SauraCorps had been a popular tourist attraction for six years.

Kam recognized the name of the intersecting road and turned his blinker on to turn right. "All right, almost—"

"Keep going straight."

Her sudden change in destination threw him. "Uh, why?"

Viv angled her body to view him better. "I was just asking myself the same question. More so, why did I want to go to this party? You and I have never quite fit in with the crowd, so why did I think we could be in a pool with them?"

"A pee-pee pool." Kam winked at her as he pulled over onto the road's shoulder. "Viv, honestly, it's okay if we go. More than anything, I just want to people-watch for story ideas."

The last thing he said made her hold back a wince. *More than anything?* She reached over and turned down the volume on the music. "How about…we visit the museum."

"The museum," Kam recalled the sign they'd passed. "You mean SauraCorps?"

Viv pointed to the road. "Make it so, Eckhardt."

"They'd be closed by now."

"Does that matter?"

A surprised chuckle came out of him. "Lady Lancaster, are you suggesting we *sneak in?*"

Her eyebrows danced up and down. "It would make for a good story."

Kamren had never known her to be this unpredictable before. There had been times where they got into some kind of mischief. But this—a whole new level. Either way, she'd made a good point. *People-watch vs. museum break-in.*

Vivienne still grinned as he flicked on the left-hand turn signal before merging back onto the gravel road. "My 'story' line got you, didn't it?"

"It was a good line."

THREE

"FORGOT HOW tall the gate was." Vivienne gawked at the museum's barrier. By now, the sun had nearly set beyond the horizon, which made her enjoy what she wished was a romantic setting.

They'd parked the burgundy truck a couple of stone throws away from the gated entrance. The fifteen-foot thick and formidable wall presented them with second thoughts. The main entrance consisted of the same thickness of metal doors.

"Kinda always wondered why they built this place like an army base or castle." Impressed by its stature, Kamren cleared a nervous scratch from his throat. "Which leads to my next question, how the heck are we gonna climb over this thing? That's gotta be at least fifty feet high, and I left my trusty grappling hook at home."

Viv leaned against the truck's front bumper beside him. "Are you Batman now?"

Adding a gravelly, hard-to-understand tone to his throat,

Kam smirked. *"Wart, hur durd yer knuh? Ers it burcurse I turl ervryom mur secrut urdent—"* The rasp made him start coughing before he could finish.

Busting a gut, Viv smacked his shoulder. "What the heck did you just say?"

A laugh finally came out of him. "Exaaaactly!"

As they assessed their predicament, a white cargo van with a SauraCorps decal on the hood approached from half a mile away.

The teens scrambled into the ditch to avoid detection.

"New plan." Kam flexed his cheek muscles while working out the risky details. "Can't believe I'm about to say this, but when the van rolls by, we'll hop out and each snag a back corner."

"Might work." From her vantage point, she spied the entrance. "There are cameras over the gates. They might catch us."

"You keep saying *might*."

"Yeah, so?"

"That leaves room for a *might not*."

The van slowed down as it neared the truck. The driver stopped to check over the burgundy vehicle's cab only to find it empty.

Kam and Viv scurried out of the ditch and hesitated behind the truck's tailgate.

The driver pressed on the gas pedal.

Both teens dashed behind the van.

Before the white vehicle could gain enough speed, Kam lunged for the back and clamped his fingers onto the righthand-side lip of the roof and one of the exterior hinges. Once he'd found his footing on the bumper, he checked Viv's status.

Her left foot almost slid off the black bumper as she just snagged her fingertips into the left backdoor's rubber weather stripping.

They glanced at each other while thinking the same thing.

This is insane.

The van jerked to a stop.

Both kids almost slipped off due to the sudden halt.

After the driver's door opened and slammed shut, heated footsteps grew louder.

"What the *heck* do you think you're do—" The driver studied their adolescent faces. "Really? A couple of *kids?* Bug off."

Viv sighed. "Guess it wasn't the cameras we had to be worried about."

As Kam dismounted, he noticed the driver was a slender, dark-skinned woman whose super-curly hair poofed out the back of her SauraCorps cap. "Sorry, Miss. We were just hoping to…get a couple of hats like that for ourselves. Got any in the back?"

The woman snorted. "You expect me to believe that?"

"Let's just go, Kam." Viv had already started back for the truck. "It was a decent try."

About to join her, Kam noticed something odd while in mid-step. Instead, he swung his right foot back beside his left. "Hold on, Viv. Don't think we're done here yet."

The hazel-eyed driver's lanyard badge jostled as she

crossed her arms. "Listen, kid, the museum's only open to employees at this time. Come back tomorrow and visit the gift shop."

"Oh, I'm pretty sure you're going to let us in."

Confused as to why he stayed by the van, Viv rejoined him. "She's clearly not going to let us through, Kam."

He chuckled. "Beg to differ."

The stern woman took another step toward the grinning young man. "You must have a lot of nerve, kid."

"And you must have done a rush job on your fake ID."

It took a moment for the lady to clue in.

Kam maintained a nonchalant expression. "Your, uh… face is sliding off."

Lifting the badge to check it, the lady cursed under her breath. "Never using that glue again." Once she slipped it out of the sleeve and repositioned it, she looked back at the two teenagers sticking around. "And I suppose you want something from me?"

Still uncomfortable, Viv grabbed her friend's arm. "We should just leave, Kam."

"Nah, we're so close." He stepped forward and matched the woman's stance. "Tell you what, Holly Reynolds, if that *is* your *real* name. My friend and I are going to stow in the back of the van."

The woman scoffed. "Or you could just head on home."

"All right, fine." Kam pulled his cellphone out from his pocket. "But nine-one-one are such easy numbers to push."

Maybe-Holly's eyes flared up. "You wouldn't."

"We won't call the cops on you if you let us through."

Impressed by Kam's checkmate—since he was horrible at chess—Viv glanced back and forth at them. *Even if we don't get in, this is amazing.*

Tapping her foot, Holly weighed her options. She'd traveled all the way there and couldn't wait another day. "One condition."

Kam returned the cellphone to his pocket. "Which is?"

The woman leaned in, making sure they could see the determination in her eyes. "If we make it through the gate around back and into the building—and that's a *big fat if*—I'll direct you to the museum portion and you'll be on your merry way. Got it?"

Vivienne's heart beat a little faster.

As for Kamren, he saluted. "Loud and clear, Holly-bo-bolly."

While pointing a finger at the young man, Holly met eyes with Viv. "Is your boyfriend always this aggravating?"

Vivienne snorted, also trying to hide an awkward smile. "Um, there's…good days and bad days."

"This has been fun, but can we get going now?" Kam purposefully bumped into the woman's finger on his way to the back of the SauraCorps van.

After a long, heated sigh, Holly shook her head as she opened the vehicle's rear doors. "Can't believe this is happening."

Unsure of what to say as she hopped in the back after Kam, Viv simply smiled at the driver of their trojan horse. A hard object poked her as she sat down on a green tarp. "Ow, feels like something boney just stabbed—oh, right.

Dinosaur museum."

"Even though you've blackmailed me into doing this, there are some ground rules." Exasperated and rushed, Holly's voice remained firm. "Rule number one, no noise. Number two, don't steal any of these dinosaur bones because, yes, they're real."

Kam threw his head back with a sigh. "Four *hours* later."

Holly blasted an 'excuse me?' glare at him. "The most important rule, *don't* get in my way and *don't* irritate me."

"We understand." Ready to carry on, Viv nodded. "All we wanted to do was check out the fossils in the dark. Night safari style."

"Wait," Kam thought out loud. "Do you consider that all one rule? 'Cause it sounded like it was technically two rules."

"*Shut up*, Kam." Having enough of his antics, Viv shoved him, making him roll into the vehicle's inner metal wall.

"You, I like you. You're not irritating." Holly continued pointing her finger. "Him, not so much."

A few minutes later, Holly pulled the van around back to the shipping and receiving gate. A high-tech metal tower with a speaker and scanner greeted her window. Holly checked her ID once more before holding it up to the facial scanner. *Face is on straight.* Thankfully, a hacker contact had assisted in inputting a fake profile in the SauraCorps database weeks before.

Similar to the front gate, the back one opened inward with a buzz after an eternal moment passed.

"And we're *in*." Pleased by the first stage of her entry, Holly's anxious fingers touched the beak of the cap, swiveling it back and forth to scratch her forehead.

Kam whispered loudly, "Are we allowed to ask why *you're* also sneaking in?"

She rolled her eyes at the boy's inquiry which came from behind her through the dividing grate. "No noise, remember? And no."

"It's a legitimate question."

"I said *no.*"

"How do we know we're not in the back of an *actual* thief's van, or whatever you are?"

Swerving around to back up to a bay door, she pressed on the brakes. Two kids in the back of her van amounted to the biggest wrench to ever be thrown into her plan. "Don't think you want to get wrapped up in it. Even if I tried to explain, I doubt you'd believe me."

Kam exchanged curious glances with Viv. "Huh, sounds pretty intense."

Since she perceived to be on the lady's good side, Viv came at the situation from a caring perspective. "Is there anything we could maybe help you with?"

Holly backed up toward the overhead door. "Trust me, kid, you *don't* wanna mess with these guys."

The ominous reply made Kam tense up.

Beside him, Viv began picking at her thumb.

A certain tone in Holly's voice didn't sit right with Kam. "It's just a museum. You make it sound sinister or something."

Parked outside of the bay door, Holly bent down, unzipped a duffle bag, and stuffed an object inside her windbreaker jacket. "If only you knew." She exited the van and marched over to the man-door beside the overhead. The barcoded ID badge met another scanner.

It took her a moment to realize she'd been subconsciously tapping her left foot. *Keep calm. Don't mess up.* Her spirits lifted when green lights of success lit up beside the handle. *Here we go. No turning back.*

In the back of the van, the teenagers heard a heavy metal door slam closed.

"She isn't *leaving* us out here, is she?" Viv had moved on to picking her other thumb. "Hate to say it, but that pool party sounds real good right about now."

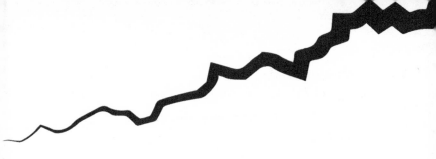

FOUR

INSIDE THE complex, Holly slid the overhead door's metal security bar into the unlock position and reached for the chain.

"Didn't know we were expecting a delivery."

The voice from behind made Holly glance back while unwrapping the hoist chain from a wall hook. "Yeah, uh, sorry. Kind of a last-minute thing."

The Latino guard strolled over. "Where's Phil? Haven't seen you deliver before. Got your papers?"

"Um, yeah." About to pull down on the chain to raise the door, she turned to address the guard. "On the passenger seat."

"Hey."

While trying her best to stay calm, she couldn't stop the adrenaline surge when that single word entered her ears.

The man took hold of the chain. "Let me help you with that."

Holly put on a relieved grin. "All yours, bud."

Once the bay door had opened to human height, she slipped back outside and hopped into the van. The tense situation almost made her forget about the stowaways. "Hang tight back there. If you were having thoughts about turning back, it's too late now."

The vehicle lurched forward, swaying the teenagers back and forth.

Vivienne braced a hand on her friend's shoulder for support. "Will we have to go through all this again to get back out?"

Kamren rocked into the van's inner wall before giving her a cheeky smirk. "*If* we get out."

"Not helping."

"Quiet," Holly called back to them with a lowered voice. "Pulling in now."

Once the van had parked inside, the guard decelerated the slide of the chain as the overhead door closed.

"Through the second checkpoint." Holly snatched her duffle bag before leaving the driver's seat. "Give me one more minute."

Interested in seeing what had been delivered, the Latino man arrived at the rear doors before she did. "Is this a fossil delivery?"

From inside the van, the man's outline could be seen through the tinted window.

Viv gripped Kam's wrist.

"Wait!" Hand tucked into her jacket, Holly hoped the man would take his hand off the handle. "Don't you want the packing slip first?"

"We'll get to it either way."

"No, *really*, I can get it for you."

The guard removed his hand from the rear door handle. "If you insist."

"I do."

Pthew-thip!

The man took a step back before collapsing to the concrete floor.

After a quick inspection of the area, Holly threw open the van's back doors. "All right, folks, entrance to the public museum is on your right."

As soon as Viv hopped out, her hands shot to her face as she whispered in trepidation, "Oh my God! Did you just… *kill* that guy?"

Exasperated, Holly threw her head back. "He's not dead, I just—"

"That's it, I'm calling the police." A shaken Kam fished his cellphone out of his pocket. "This has gone way too far—"

"He *isn't* dead!" To show them how she operated, Holly knelt by the body and pointed to a dart protruding from the man's upper chest. "I tranq'd him."

"Guess that makes me feel…a little better?" Viv's breathing sped up as her trust in their break-in helper wavered.

"Okay, so you're not a killer." After returning the cellphone to his pocket, Kam pointed at the unconscious person. "But this? I mean, what's your deal?"

Back on her feet, Holly got in his face. "You better get lost before this problem becomes your problem."

Kam didn't back down. "And what if you turn out to be the *real problem* all along?"

Holly threw her arms up in the air and growled at the industrial ceiling. "Boy, I got you and your girl in here. This is where we part ways."

"Now I'm not so sure we should leave you unattended—"

"Uh, guys." As stubborn Kam and annoyed Holly bickered, Viv noticed movement through the windows of double doors. "Wherever we go, we should get *moving*."

The other two stopped talking immediately.

To their left, a grey metal door led to a stairwell.

"Fine then." Holly took charge. "That's the next checkpoint. Stay close."

The unlikely group hurried over.

With the duffle bag still slung over her shoulder, Holly pulled out a gadget and hooked it up to the code reader. It broke the sequence within six seconds.

Impressed by the resourcefulness, Viv chuckled. "First a tranq, now this? You're pretty badass."

"Cool, huh?" Holding the door open, Holly checked behind for followers as everyone entered the stairwell. "Head down. Since we're sticking together now, might be good if I get your names."

"Can we use fake names like you?" Kam referred to the ID badge once more. "We can keep with the Reynolds names. Call me Captain Malcolm."

Holly cocked her head. "Firefly reference?"

The catch surprised Viv. "You've seen the show?"

"Only the best show to be canceled way too early." As she

passed the kids on the steps, Holly checked the next flight for security with the tranquilizer gun. "And you're right, by the way. Holly Reynolds isn't my real name."

Another flight of stairs down.

Still no guards.

The watchfulness of the mysterious woman made Kamren keep an eye on things behind them. "So, who are you?"

The woman stopped at the next level. "My real name is Emily-Ann Lewis. E-A, if you'd like. You two?"

"I'm Vivienne." She waved a hand over to her friend. "And this is Kamren."

E-A pulled out the code reader again for the door. "Funny, thought his name would be Irritator."

"Hilarious." Kam's face stayed deadpan.

Desired lights and a beep signified entry, allowing E-A to stash the gadget in the bag again. "Oh, you got the Cretaceous period dinosaur name reference?"

Kam squinted. "Excuse me?"

"Ah, good." E-A opened the door for the tag-alongs. "Thought you were a constant know-it-all."

They started down an empty hallway with taupe walls and speckled linoleum floors, passing marked rooms where scientific work happened.

Other than some domed ceiling cameras, the group hadn't noticed any kind of human security whatsoever.

The deeper they traveled into the complex, the more Viv's worries grew. *How are we going to get out of this place? More importantly, what kind of trouble are we getting into?*

Moving at a decent pace, E-A set her sights on an

intersecting hallway up ahead. Skinny signs stuck out from the corners indicating particular areas in each direction. In yellow letters, the left led to 'Fossil Restoration'.

Going straight, 'DNA Extraction'.

To the right, 'Supplies & Cleaning'.

E-A's back met the corner to their right as she held up her left arm to stop the others. "Hold up. Let me take a look."

After glancing at the sign, Kam spoke up. "Supplies? Why would they guard—"

"Listen." E-A's eyes belied a fierceness which she couldn't mask anymore. "What I'm trying to do here is—not to freak you out— but it's a matter of *life* and *death*. The more you talk and ask needless questions, the less I can focus on keeping *us* all *alive*."

The vague seriousness of the situation finally kicked in for him. This woman meant business. For the first time in his life, a truly frightened Kamren swallowed down a scratchy lump in his throat.

E-A poked her head around the corner.

An elevator door stood at the end of the fifty-foot section of hallway. Another camera hung right in the middle of the ceiling above it.

"This should take care of you." E-A pulled out a handheld object half the size of a television remote. Her hand by the floor, she snuck the remote around the corner and pressed the main button for five seconds to distort the camera's view. "Almost there. Go."

The three rounded the corner. It didn't take long for them to reach the next point.

"You've got all this tech and weapons..." Something about the whole break-in seemed off to Viv. "...but we've only run into one person this whole time."

"Yeah." The same thought had been niggling on E-A's mind. "Worries me a bit." About to crack another access code, she unzipped the black bag. "But I *have* to—"

Ding!

The elevator opened on its own.

Kam raised an eyebrow. "You...didn't even use that thing, did you?"

"No." E-A tensed her jaw as she entered. Inside, thoughts about turning back started a screaming match with others telling her to march on. "We've come too far to turn back now." Stepping inside didn't shut up her inner protests. "Get in."

Even though the events kept getting stranger, Viv stepped inside with Miss Lewis.

In disbelief, Kam's eyelids flared open. "Viv, what *are* you doing?"

"She's our best chance of getting out of here." Vivienne's eyes met his. "I trust her."

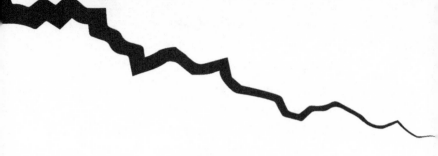

FIVE

AN AWKWARD silence filled the four-floor descent.

The teenagers stood next to each other on one side of the elevator.

On the other, Emily-Ann reloaded her tranquilizer gun.

Vivienne needed answers. The woman they'd inadvertently joined didn't seem like a bad person. And yet, E-A's vague nature still kept her on her toes. Viv couldn't judge, though, since they'd also broken in and entered alongside her.

As for every time Kamren wanted to inquire more, he opted to bite his tongue.

Ding!

The ominous elevator door slid open.

Another barren hallway stood before them.

E-A took the first wary step out. "Should only be one way to go from here."

"How do you know this place so well?" Viv took it upon herself to learn more. "Did you work here before?"

"Not me, but someone in my family used to." E-A broke into a brisk stroll as the duffle bag bounced against her hip. The closer they got to the end of the single hall, the faster her pace became. "Took me three months to prep for this."

"We definitely ruined things for you then," Kam quipped, keeping up with her.

E-A chuckled at the ridiculousness of it all. "I mean, Viv's fine. Could've done without you and your smart mouth, though."

"Okay, that's *enough*." Viv came to a halt. The banter had finally reached her threshold. "Somehow, all of us have to find a way to get along whether we like it or not."

A few feet ahead of them, a reluctant E-A also stopped.

On Viv's right, Kam gave her a sheepish glance.

"And now we're all on some insane, random mission under some dinosaur museum," Viv summed up, getting more riled up as she spoke. "Now, I for one had hoped to make it to my graduation." She turned toward the still somewhat secretive E-A. "But the more we head toward—whatever it is you're bent on getting or doing—the more I feel like Kamren and I may not even get to see that day."

With his fingers folded behind his neck, Kam removed his left hand to point at his friend. "She makes a fair point."

"*Kamren.*" Viv whipped her gaze to him next. "You're my best friend. Having said that, you need to tone it down. At least until we get out of this mess."

It had been a long time since he'd seen her so stressed out. As soon as her anxious teal eyes bored into his, he almost became speechless. "Uh… Okay."

Ready to keep moving, E-A raised an eyebrow at them. "You two have something really special."

Kam whipped a denying glare at E-A.

Viv, on the other hand, blushed and looked down at her shoes.

E-A put her hands up in defeat at their different responses. "Sorry, thought you guys were a thing."

"We've known each other since we were toddlers," he explained, giving Viv a one-armed squeeze. "But we're not *together* together."

"Gotcha." With the more pressing matter returning to priority, E-A swirled back around and continued marching. As they passed by more security cameras, she couldn't shake an increasing worry in the back of her mind. *Something is wrong, but what?*

It wasn't until the halfway mark down the hall that Kam noticed another odd thing.

Other than double doors at the end, no other doors lined the taupe walls.

No windows either.

He turned to Viv on his left. "What do you think they do down here?"

"Who knows." What E-A had warned about earlier kept ringing in her ears. "All I hope is that we get home safe."

"Maybe they're trying to bring dinosaurs *back to life*, mosquito-in-amber-style."

She smirked. "I've been waiting for a Jurassic Park reference."

E-A came within ten feet of the end.

Once the double doors became clearer, her eyes opened wide. "No."

The single word made Kam and Viv snap to attention.

"No, no *no!*" Jittery hands opened her duffle bag as E-A plopped it on the floor beside the righthand door. "I need…blueprints. They must've…changed the setup from the original blueprints."

Viv came to her side. "What's the problem?"

"There's…no code to read…." E-A's voice shook, having no idea of what to fish for in her bag. "There should be a-a-a code activator, but there's nothing here."

As he surveyed the doors, Kam stepped forward. "Maybe there's another way in." He referred to his movie knowledge. "Is there a floor tile that looks off from the others?"

Viv rolled her eyes and chuckled. "Check for a candle to pull out and put back, too."

"If only Gene Wilder were here," Kam chuckled in reply.

"You two…need to…." E-A couldn't finish as tears took over her face. She'd come so close. "Please, *stop* with the *stupid* references."

Both teenagers refrained from making any response.

Viv's empathy kicked in as she crouched beside her. "Emily-Ann, what's *really* going on here?"

Sniffles preceded E-A's reply as she wiped her cheeks. "They… I came here to fi—"

The double doors unlocked from the inside with a heavy, mechanical click.

As if in slow motion, what seemed like the end of their journey opened up into a room the size of an airplane hangar.

Electrical noises crackled from somewhere inside. Though they couldn't see the source from behind a reinforced, mostly solid steel gate with foot-tall bars lining the bottom of it. The bars allowed brilliant flashes of blueish light to trickle through.

"What the...?" Completely bewildered, Kam glanced down at the ladies in trepidation.

"This...." E-A rose to her feet. "Wait, I wasn't expecting this."

Viv squinted at her. *"Wasn't?"*

The unknown of the room pulled all three of them into its clutches.

None of them could take their eyes off the odd gate which spanned the entire width of the chamber. Large bolts kept it upright and attached to raw rock walls which lined the entirety of the area. A thirty-foot wide door sat in the middle of the stainless steel that reached up to the fifty-foot ceiling.

"What exactly were you expecting?" Viv somehow pulled her full attention away from the zaps and pops from beyond the steel.

"I...." E-A went over everything in her head. The plan had been set. She'd made it to the end. "I thought—"

"Miss Lewis."

A man's voice came from behind them.

"It's about time you arrived."

SIX

SECURITY GUARDS rushed in and took up positions along the entrance wall.

They pointed their rifles at the three intruders who huddled together.

Dressed in a navy-blue suit and matching blue necktie, the man who'd spoken also wore a devious grin. "And who are your two little friends?"

"Get behind me," Emily-Ann instructed the teenagers. Duffle bag still slung over her right shoulder, she held her tranquilizer gun up in defense. "Leave them out of it."

"Oh, I'm not so sure I can do that." Hands behind his back, the man took a few intimidating steps closer. His dark beard had been trimmed with crisp lines. The thirty-something's sharp style made him out to be a man of image and power. "Now that they've seen this room, they may just have to suffer the same consequences as you."

Vivienne shoved herself into Kamren's arms.

"Hey." Kam gave her a reassuring squeeze. "I've got you."

"You would do something to a couple of *kids?*" E-A scoffed, disturbed by the idea. "Who do you think you are?"

A sinister chuckle came from the suited man, who combed his fingers through his coffee-brown hair. "You study this place for three months, yet you don't research the ones who built the empire?"

"Don't like to spend too much time on scum."

The man burst into disturbing laughter. After being entertained, he rubbed his hands together. "Name's Sharpe. Sebastian Sharpe."

Kam couldn't help but smirk. "Did he just…introduce himself like Bond?"

"*Quiet,* Kam." Viv didn't want things to get worse.

Recollection came over E-A as she gripped her gun even harder. "*Sharpe,* you *disgusting* piece of—"

"Whoa, Miss Lewis, not in front of the children, now." Sebastian brought his hands up. "Especially if these are the last words they ever hear."

E-A stepped forward. "If you even *touch* them—"

"You'll tickle us with that tranquilizer gun?" Mr. Sharpe strolled a few more feet toward them. "You don't have a killing bone in your body." With crossed arms, he took in a deep breath while looking her up and down. "But…you've got a *fire* in you."

"Only because of what SauraCorps…. What *you* did." Extreme revulsion dripped from her lips.

At this point in the confrontation, Kamren and Vivienne only had more questions. Now wasn't the time to start asking, though.

"What *I* did?" Sebastian's right hand went to his chest. "What I *did?*"

E-A finally blurted it out. "What did you do to *my father?*"

Kam and Viv stared at each other in shock.

Sharpe stared E-A down as his words came out smooth and precise. "Your...father." Instead of walking toward her, he started to head to the left. "Theodore Lewis. What a brilliant scientist, so full of... what word do kids say these days? Spunk, among other things. Unfortunately, it was that which cost him everything."

"He saw what SauraCorps was willing to do with what they'd found," E-A countered, wishing she had brought a more harmful weapon with her. She could never bring herself to kill anyone. Right now, though, being so close to one of the heads of the company responsible for ruining her family's life, she toyed with reconsidering. "Take me to him, *right now.*"

"Ah." Staring up at the ceiling as he leaned against the reinforced stainless steel, semi-cage-like gate, Sebastian bobbed his head side to side. "That may be a tad difficult."

Tired of his games, she spit out, "Stop stalling."

"Absolutely, I can point you in the right direction." Sebastian pulled out a keycard from the left breast pocket of his tailored jacket. "As for finding him, well, that's going to be all on you."

Kam shouted, "Watch out!"

Smack!

41

E-A shrieked as the tranquilizer gun flew out of her hand as two of the guards seized her by the arms. She immediately responded with flailing kicks and trying to wrench herself free.

Mr. Sharpe's chitchat had distracted her from watching her back.

"Viv, no!" Kam's fingers slipped away from hers as they were ripped away from each other by SauraCorps security.

"Kamren!" She screamed while being dragged away from him.

Infuriated, E-A jerked her body to hopefully slip out of the guards' grasp. "Leave…those kids…*alone!*" Her left foot swung back, forcefully striking the man's kneecap. As the guard on her left crumpled, the other's face met with her left hook.

Unable to break free from her captors, Viv ceased struggling as she whimpered. "Please… Please, let me go."

Getting docked marks by Mr. Richardson had annoyed Kam. But seeing his best friend helpless and crying sparked a rage inside him. "If you hurt her, I swear I'm going to—"

Thock!

Wind left his stomach, no thanks to the back end of a rifle.

E-A turned to save the others.

"Don't even try, Miss Lewis." Still standing by the large metal gate, Sebastian Sharpe flicked the keycard between his fingers.

Four more guards encircled her with their weapons pointed and ready.

"What are you going to do with them?" E-A couldn't see a way out.

"I said it before," Sebastian countered, nonchalant as he touched the keycard to the reader beside the massive door. "The same fate as you."

On cue, the steel door buzzed. Once unlocked, it took two other guards on either side to pull it open. The teenagers were hauled over as E-A got prodded with the ends of rifles as if she were a farm animal.

The three unlikely allied victims passed the threshold whether they wanted to or not.

A fascinating sight nearly paralyzed each of them.

The source of the weird crackles of electricity had been revealed.

Vivid blueish voltaic light snapped and swirled in a fifty-foot circular frame. Limbs of lightning burst outward and inward to its core, creating an ethereal yet threatening aura.

Still ensnared at their arms, Kam and Viv managed to gaze over at each other. The fear and awe in their eyes told them they were thinking the same thing.

What the heck is *that?*

In between the two teenagers, E-A went from taking in the amazing glow of the churning border of voltage to what seemed to be just beyond it. *Dad was right all along.*

Flora.

On her side of the indescribable entity, rock walls, concrete floors, and guards were the environment.

Yet, when she gazed through the window-like thing, she noted ferns, trees, and a pristine lake off in the distance.

"Beautiful, isn't it?" Six feet behind the captives, Sebastian wore a boyish grin. "Every time I come down here, it never ceases to amaze me."

"Is this…what I think it is?" By now, a woodland scent had reached E-A's nose from the other side of what they were viewing.

"Here at SauraCorps, we simply refer to it as 'The Rift'." Mr. Sharpe drew in a deep breath of delight. "We unearthed this anomaly about eight years ago. While blasting through all of this thick crust around us in the name of archaeological discovery, who would have thought one of our explosions would rip a hole in… Well… The highly-theorized space-time continuum."

"You gotta be kidding me." Overwhelmed by it all, Kam toed the line of belief. "It's *actually* a real thing?"

Sebastian nodded. "Sure is, kid." As he paced back and forth, he continued. "The other thing we didn't expect…" He paused for dramatic effect. "…was how far back into the past it would take us."

Though the rift still made her nervous, E-A stepped toward it. "My father, he told me all about this."

"He told *you* about this *classified* information?" With his hands in his pant pockets, Sebastian sighed with disappointment. "All the more reason to have banished him those five years ago."

E-A's heart dropped. *Banished.* Small steps turned her around to face the despicable man. "How could you?"

"Oh, poor Theo. He simply knew too much and tried to stop greatness," Sebastian continued in a monotonous tone.

"We gave him one last shot on a little experiment, and it backfired. Someone died, police got involved, we had to clean up the whole thing. Should've known it was a bad idea in the first place, but oh well. It's too bad we couldn't use a rift to go back to that moment and stop it all from happening."

Fury engulfed E-A's stare, removing all care about the guards as she marched forward. "I'm gonna kill you—"

"Throw them in." Mr. Sharpe ordered with a raised index finger swirling around in a circle. "All of them."

"What?" Vivienne's feet shot to life as the guards worked their way toward the window-like rift. "You can't—*no!*"

All of Kamren's strength couldn't break the security guards' grasp. "Take your hands...*off* me!"

Each of the four guards that separated Emily-Ann from Sebastian took one of her limbs. As she yelled and screamed, she couldn't accept the fact that her whole plan had fallen apart so quickly. All her research, acquiring equipment and the vehicle—all for nothing.

A hard heave sent Kam flying up and over the rim of surging space-time electricity.

Next in line, Viv's last squirm failed to thwart her captors.

Another toss. Another one through.

Defenseless, E-A wished she could close her ears as the insidious crackling noise grew louder. Not only would she become a victim of them, but she had also sent two young people into the rift's otherworldly clutches.

"One more thing before you go." Sebastian strolled over, calm and collected. "Watch out for the bugs."

SEVEN

"AM I dead?" On her back, Vivienne stared up at the canopy of tree branches. "Are we all dead?"

To her left, Kamren lifted himself to his hands and knees. "This can't be happening. We were just...." His mind couldn't compute the events which had just unfolded. "And now we're...where exactly?"

Snaps and pops of electricity preceded Emily-Ann getting spit out of the rift beside them. Her breathing sped up as she glanced all around while wobbling to her feet. "No... no no *no!* This... We *can't* be!"

Crouched a few feet from the rift, Viv combed her hair back with both hands. "E-A, you said your dad told you about this place? Where are we?"

Kam recalled another clue. "That jerkwad Sebastian, he said something about 'back into the past'." On his feet, he turned to a fern beside him and rubbed his fingers along one of its gangling fronds. "Are we where I think we are?"

"You're using the wrong word." E-A kept her head on a swivel. "Don't ask where, ask *when*."

Viv squeezed her eyes shut. "This is a dream. Tell me that I slipped in the museum, hit my head, and this is all a dream."

"Sure, let's go with a cliché story ending," Kam quipped, picking up on E-A's nervousness.

A buzzing came from his left.

Before they could even look in that direction for the source, the sound zipped over to their right. Then up above.

"What's making that noise?" Still unable to come to terms with what had just happened, Viv struggled to keep herself calm as she gazed upward. "Sounds like a small lawnmower."

E-A sunk her hand into her duffle bag. "I think we're about to find—look out!"

The source of the noise whizzed down like a hummingbird.

Kam jumped out of the way. "Holy, is that a—" he ducked his head. "Jeez, it's quick."

As the creature zipped over to check out E-A, she whipped out a machete. "This thing's huge." After admiring the size of it, she swatted the sharp weapon back and forth.

On a dime, it backed up ten feet from them.

"It's a *giant* dragonfly," Kam remarked with wonder. "Gotta be a foot and a half long."

Out of the three of them, Viv seemed to lock eyes with the oversized bug. "It's kinda cute, in an ugly sort of way." Out of curiosity, she held out her palm.

The shiny green, inquisitive insect darted back and forth with its nearly two-and-a-half-foot, transparent wingspan before making a gentle landing on her forearm. Its twiggy six-jointed legs twitched, unsure if she would be a friend or foe.

"Must be close to five pounds." Wanting to inspect even further, Viv brought her left hand up nice and slow. "Hey, little guy. Well, guess you're not so little now, are y—"

The dragonfly jumped off her arm and onto her hair.

"What the flip, get off me!" In a frenzy, she batted her hands at it. "Get *lost!*"

Like a hair-clip, the bug's mandibles pecked away at her head. Its feet crimped strands of her hair and tried to fly up. The only thing it could do was cause her discomfort.

A chivalrous Kam shot over and seized the bug's skinny segmented abdomen. "Come on, she isn't food, you dumb thing."

In a split-second reaction, the dragonfly let go of her hair and bent into a C shape to defend itself.

"Yee-ow!" Kam let go, allowing the giant insect to escape and leave them. "That stupid thing *bit me*." Thankfully, the bite didn't pierce his skin. "Should name it Charlie."

E-A gave him an odd glance. "Why Charlie?"

"You haven't seen that YouTube video?" Kam chuckled just thinking about it. "Two little boys, the baby brother bites the older one's finger—ah, I'll just show you." After pulling out his phone, he tried to access the internet. "Wait, I've got no bars."

A realization sunk in for Viv. "You mean we have no way of contacting anyone?"

"First world problems, right?" Kam smirked. "Gen Z

would lose their minds."

Up ahead of them by the edge of the forest, E-A tightened the strap on her duffle bag in a make-shift way for a backpack. "You two still haven't figured it out yet, have you?"

Viv shook her head. "I'm still trying to wrap my head around the fact that we all just got tossed through a time rift. Then I got attacked by a giant flying bug." By now she had rearranged her hair into a ponytail since the dragonfly had acted like a crazed hairdresser. "Guess I can scratch those off my bucket list."

The second thing she said made Kam angle his head at her. "Getting *attacked* was on your—"

"You know what I meant."

On their way over to E-A's position, Kam looked over his friend. "Are you okay, by the way? Doesn't look like it did any damage."

"It just frazzled me, that's all." Hearing his compassion made Viv grin. "I'm just happy it wasn't strong enough to whisk me away."

"I would've chased after you," Kam responded, a measure of manliness in his tone. "No bug hurts my girl and gets away with it."

Speechless, she kept walking alongside him. *My girl. He* actually *said that?* It became difficult to keep her grin from getting any bigger. *If we're going to be stuck here, maybe it's time I finally say somethi—*

"You guys are going to want to see this," E-A called over as they came within five feet of her. "Should clear things up for where and *when* we are."

Kam countered, "Or you could stop being vague and just...." The edge of the forest passed him as his feet moved on autopilot. "Just...." His jaw dropped. "*Damn.*"

Awe shook Viv to her core. "Are those...?"

A massive creature arched its long neck to take a drink from the freshwater lake. A reddish-brown, thirty-foot-long creature of the past with a double row of spikes running down its neck noticed the humans.

"It's a...." The eight-year-old in Kam bubbled to the surface. "*...dinosaur.*"

Finally able to form a sentence, Viv's breath escaped her mouth in amazement first. "Is that a brontosaurus?"

"Brontosaurus aren't called that anymore, turns out they were just a different type of Apatosaurus." E-A pointed out, enthralled by seeing one in the flesh. "But this guy is an amargasaurus."

Kam squinted at E-A. "How do you know how to pronounce it?"

"Back when my dad used to work for SauraCorps, he made many trips back and forth to this time." As she explained, E-A swung the duffle bag off her back and searched inside of it. Then she presented a worn, leather-bound notebook. "He left this for me. Everything he ever saw and experienced here, it's in there. He even added dino name pronunciations."

The fondness E-A radiated for her father made Kam understand her a little bit more. "Do you mind if I see it?"

The book met his hand.

A moment of hesitation made E-A hang on, but not for long. "Page three. He met these sauropods pretty early. They must graze close to here."

♀ amargasaurus

10 m

Kam found the section. "A-mar-guh-sawr-us. Believed to be alive in the Cretaceous period. Whoa, and an average weight of *six thousand* pounds." His eyes snapped back to the graceful dinosaur ahead. "This journal should come in handy. You could be like our tour guide."

She laughed. "A tour guide of a place I've never been before."

"You've got the hat for it."

"Forgot I'd been wearing it." After slipping the cap off, she worked her hair into its normal curly style. The SauraCorps logo sickened her. "That name doesn't deserve to be worn." E-A whipped it back into the forest like a frisbee. When she turned her attention back to the scaley beast, she pointed.

"Looks like Viv's getting close and personal."

Having been distracted by the book, Kam lifted his head. "Viv, be careful."

Every time Viv had ever gone to a zoo, she'd always wished she could hop the fence and walk right up to an elephant. But of course, unless you knew someone at the zoo who could take you behind the scenes, security would most likely take you down if you tried.

Here, in this time, no fence had been built.

No security.

As she came within five feet of it, the amargasaurus craned its neck to bring its curious head closer to her. Trickles of lake water spilled from its mouth.

Only one thing came to Viv's mind. *Please, be nicer than the dragonfly.*

Kam called over as he handed the book back to its rightful owner, "Make sure it doesn't sneeze on you."

Standing still as the dinosaur inched its face even nearer, Viv giggled. "Now I'm thinking of dino snot."

"You're welcome."

Viv's fingers trembled a bit as she reached out.

With eyes on the sides of its head, the amargasaurus gave her a sideways stare and vocalized with a low bellow—resembling whales singing.

"Oh, you're gorgeous." Her hands shook even more as her palm patted the smooth scales on its cheek and snout. Her ooh's and ah's were reciprocated by means of mild, curious honks from the beast's toothless mouth. "Guys, this is the most *amazing* thing I've ever done."

"Think it likes you," E-A remarked as she came to the other side of the head. "Treat any creature with kindness and they'll do the same." She backed up a step as it flared its nostrils like a horse. "Something mankind has forgotten how to do."

At Viv's side, Kam had plucked a handful of long grass from the ground and waved it near the end of the amargasaurus' snout. "Better than any pool party."

Amused by his reasoning, she traced one of the beige stripes from the edge of its mouth to the back of the cheek. "Still not thrilled that we're trapped here. That said, I'd rather spend time with this big lug than a bunch of weirdos." She squealed as the herbivore sniffed the grassy gift and bit down on it.

"Huh, it doesn't have any teeth." Kam beamed with excitement. "Hey, there you g—*whoa!*"

The dinosaur yanked and lifted its head, bringing the teenager along with the green snack.

"Let go, Kamren." Viv laughed at the ridiculousness of it all. "You're gonna fall."

The creature focused its brownish-yellow eye on the strange being holding onto the grass.

When Kam realized how high up he was, he reached over and hooked his fingers onto a neck spike closest to its head. Similar to rock climbing, he pulled himself over and up to sit on the creature's crest.

E-A went into responsible mode. "What do you think you're doing?" Her hands rested on her hips. "It may be an herbivore, but if you make one wrong move, it can still hurt or even *kill* you."

"Chill, Amadeus is fine." Kam leaned forward and rubbed his hands on its crown. "See? No harm. Hey, Viv, take a picture."

E-A smirked. "Did you just *name* it?"

"Yep. Amadeus the amargasaurus." He patted the side of the wide neck like he was on a horse. "Has a nice ring to it."

"What if it's a girl?" E-A gave him a doubtful stare.

Kam chuckled. "Why don't you lift its tail and let me know."

Nervous for his safety, Viv still took out her cellphone and snapped a shot. "No one's going to believe us. If we make it back, that is."

Their predicament hadn't been fully realized until now.

Emily-Ann had tried to infiltrate a devious, corrupt archaeological corporation to try and find out what had happened to her father.

Kamren and Vivienne had simply wanted to be reckless teens for a night.

Nothing could have prepared any of them for getting tossed through a time rift and possibly being trapped in the dinosaur age for the rest of their lives.

A silence had set in, which made Viv uncomfortable. "Sorry to bring down the mood. Is there even any chance of seeing my family again? *Our* families again?"

Still perched on the amargasaurus' head, Kam met eyes with E-A. "Did your dad ever write about the rift itself in that notebook?"

"Only about its discovery." E-A flipped through the pages,

though she'd almost had the whole thing memorized. "A lot of the space-time continuum stuff just goes over my head."

"And if we jump back through where we came out of, we'd just be trapped behind that metal gate," Viv added, becoming more despondent. "Basically, we're screwed." The high of being beside a real, live dinosaur soon faded. "My parents will be worried sick. I'll never be able to annoy Arty again." The more she thought about her family, the more her eyes brimmed with tears as she sniffled.

The weeping caught the amargasaurus' attention. It lowered its head once more, bringing its nose close to her shoulder, and made little whines.

"Aww." E-A could see something in its eyes. "I think it knows you're sad. Like when a dog or cat can tell when something's wrong." She remembered some of the things her father had told her those few years ago. *My dad was right again.*

Since he'd come closer to the ground, Kam slid off the leathery scales to the grass.

Arms wrapped around Viv, who opened her eyes to find a comforting Kamren who pulled her in close. As she continued to cry, her heart swelled.

"We're going to figure something out," he whispered in her ear. "Don't give up. This isn't the end of the story."

E-A's attention turned back to the placid giant lizard. "There's a good chance my dad could still be alive."

Still consoling his friend, Kam gazed over at her. "In this time? Whatever they did to him happened *five years* ago."

"It's still possible."

Kam broke the full embrace but still kept an arm around Viv. "Okay, so say we do find him. First of all, how?"

The notebook still sat in E-A's hand, so she wagged it for emphasis. "Like you said." She pointed a thumb at herself. "Tour guide. Everything he recorded in here is like a map of where he's visited and studied." The more she spoke, the more she couldn't wait to get going.

"Secondly, *if* we find him, what will we do then?"

E-A turned around to view the time rift through the trees. "Five years is a long time. Maybe it's given him enough time to come up with a plan."

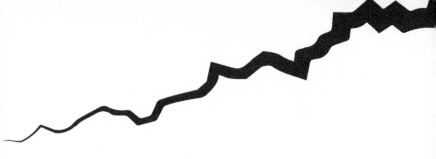

EIGHT

SEBASTIAN SHARPE rubbed his clammy hands together while on his way to a meeting.

What had happened earlier replayed in his mind.

Every step he took in his high-priced designer shoes distanced himself from the choice he'd made. At the same time, something about the decision followed behind him, poking him in the back of the head.

It had to be done. He nodded while repeating it to himself. *It had to be done. Too many people, too many problems.*

The environment around him faded away as he got lost in thought.

Buzzzz. Buzzzz.

Vibration in his jacket pocket pulled him back to the here and now.

Sebastian noted the contact and brought the phone to his ear. "Has a date been selected yet?"

"Sorry, Sebastian, your ex-wife is being rather proficient at

delaying things."

"Are you kidd—" Stopping in his tracks, he raked the fingers of his free hand through his hair. "All she's proficient at is being a total...." His hand left his hair before he could rip a section out. "I am *not* playing her game. She's only delaying what could be a civilized settlement."

"Well, as your lawyer, I suggest you still don't contact her. We don't want anything you may say to her to potentially be used against you."

Heated breath shot out of his mouth. "Surprised you haven't recorded that yet to play it on repeat every time we talk." A glance at his fifty-grand watch told him he'd be late if he didn't get moving. "What did you call me for, Preston?"

"Julia's people informed us that you won't be able to see your son this weekend. Something about a play date."

Before turning a corner, Sebastian closed his eyes as he leaned against the frosted glass wall with his free hand and grit his teeth. "She knows I've been planning something special for him for a month now."

"Remember, there needs to be no contact—"

"I *need*...." Sebastian's fist came at the glass but slowed down on contact. His next few words came out with a whimper. "I need to see Aiden. I *need* my son."

"I'm sorry, Sebastian. I'll keep you posted."

Without a goodbye, he hung up.

The battle to simply see his son Aiden had been going on for close to two years now. Not being able to see his four-year-old had taken a toll on him. *Julia's working her manipulative strings yet again. As long as I have money to drain, she'll never change.* He recalled all the times she'd complained that he wasn't focused on them as a family when everything he'd done had been for their benefit. More than that, his teenage daughter Olivia had also been turned by her mother's lies to not want anything to do with him. Sebastian's fingers seemed to be slipping from the edge of his children.

The cellphone buzzed again, still in his hand.

A text message from his boss:

We're about to start the meeting.

His whole body shook out of its numbness as he raced down the hallway. A right turn brought deep-red stained wood doors into view.

Before entering, Sebastian checked his hair in the slight reflection of the frosted glass pane in the middle of the right-hand door.

"Sorry I'm late, Felicia," he announced while marching in and sat down in the end seat. "Had to take a call from my lawyer."

"Glad you could finally join us," his co-worker remarked from the other end of the conference table. Felicia Voorhees shifted her red lizard-scale framed glasses and curled a strand of wavy black hair behind her ear. "And to the rest of you here, thank you for being able to make it tonight. I know it took a fair bit of travel to be here."

Sebastian rested an elbow on the table and kept his head propped up with his hand. *Oh, Felicia, you'd be prettier if it weren't for those ridiculously bright glasses.*

Behind her on the wall, a large flat-screen television displayed the SauraCorps logo.

"Are we any closer to locating more *giganotosaurus?*" a French woman inquired closer to the middle of the table. "There had to have been more than only twenty-sree, no?"

"We still have a task force on the search, Nadine," Felicia remarked, almost as disappointed as her co-worker. "As long as they have the highest price on them, I assure you we will search all of Pangea until we do find more." Then she addressed the man on her left and two chairs down. "How about you, Mr. Tómasson? How are things in Iceland?"

"We are very pleased with our discoveries." With a flick of his finger, he transferred a video from his tablet to the bigger screen. "Four months ago, we pinpointed another potential mark deep in the *Surtsellir* lava cave in *Kalmanstunga*, North East of Reykjavík. Once we blasted through a section of rock, sure enough, the explosion unearthed another rift."

The Icelandic time rift appeared up on the screen.

"We have no idea why, but notice the difference in color of the space-time energy from the one located under us here. This one has more violet characteristics."

Others around the table had been eager to see the official report.

"And what of the discoveries beyond the rift, Kristjan?" Miss Voorhees identified a lush environment through the anomaly's window. "What assets do we have access to?"

Tómasson continued. "For so many years it had been

believed no ancient beasts had roamed the area of Iceland in its Pangaea state…well, let me show you."

The next slide showed a caged, greyish-green dinosaur with burnt orange stripes down its back and tail.

A caption at the bottom identified the creature:

LOPHOSTROPHEUS (LOW-FOE-STRO-FEE-US)
SPECIES: L. AIRELENSIS

It measured over sixteen feet long and stood on its hind legs. Two red crests ran lengthwise along the top of its crown, which banged and rattled against the bars of the cage. Clawed arms also clashed against the metal.

"Weren't those only supposed to be found in Normandy, France?" Sebastian recalled a particular detail, pointing a pen at the screen. "That's a Triassic species."

"And a *rare* species," Felicia added with weight in her words. "I already have a long list of buyers who've been waiting for this one."

The recording showed a man walking up to the fierce

creature with a raw whole chicken in one hand and an electric shock stick in the other.

"Here's your lunch!"

Zaaaap. Zap. Zap.

Scared screeches like an eagle mixed with a hyena came from the animal's tense throat.

As the lophostropheus cowered into a corner, the worker lifted a small metal door near the base of the enclosure and tossed in the meal.

"Come on. Gonna eat it or what?"

The dinosaur bent down and sniffed the bird carcass.

One swift kick sent the meat into a corner—away from it.

Most of those in the meeting room couldn't believe it.

Felicia sighed. "More evidence to what we've seen so far." She swiveled her chair back around to talk to the blond Icelander. "Any others?"

"Of course." He sent another snippet to the television. "Our very first expedition confirmed the theory that there were many lakes and rivers so long ago. Here's documentation of another finding."

A petite British woman in hiking gear and a SauraCorps cap turned to the camera. "Is... Is that what I think it is? Look over there, to your right!"

The cameraman panned over.

Emerging from the river, a salamander-looking amphibian twice the length of the average man pulled itself onto the bank. Olive green skin covered the body, leaving the rims of its mouth more yellow. Small fangs slipped past its lips.

Another caption had been added:

CYCLOTOSAURUS (CY-CLOT-OH-SORE-US)
SPECIES: C. ROBUSTUS

"Didn't think we'd see a cyclotosaurus this early into the trek." Excitement overflowed in her tone as she hurried over for a closer look. "Aren't you a gorgeous thing?"

At first, the dinosaur scooted backward, wary of the unknown being approaching it.

"Oh, I'm sorry. I'll go slower for you." The woman dropped to her hands and knees, making herself smaller. The closer she got to the prehistoric amphibian, the more it made a purring noise of sorts. "Do you guys hear that? Wonder what that means."

Everyone in the meeting room leaned in closer to the flat-screen.

The lady's fingers stretched out, then brushed against the animal's skin. "Wow, my goodness. Like a salamander, it has that icky sliminess to it—"

Crunch!

The cyclotosaurus spun and dove back into the river.

Blood gushed from the woman's stubbed arm as she screamed, notifying those with medical knowledge to tend to her.

A board member from China near the end of the conference table by Sebastian commented, "It is *carnivorous?*"

"Piscivorous, Mr. Xing." Tómasson turned the video off. "We believe it had been more skittish than anything."

"Aren't those quite rare?" Sebastian crossed his arms, working out the possible figures it could go for. "I'd like to claim a pair, male and female."

Tómasson glanced back at him. "They're going for sixty million each."

Sebastian chuckled. "An easy investment." He typed a note into his cellphone:

Two cyclotosaurus @ $60 mill each.
Double markup = $240 mill.

Mr. Sharpe rubbed his mouth and scratched his beard, amazed and ecstatic at what he could make on them. "I know just the buyers too."

NINE

ORANGES AND pinks weaved through the sunset sky.

Cries of other sauropods in the distance created an ethereal symphony which filled the air almost as much as the clouds.

The time spent with the gentle giant still made Vivienne smile. Each one of the amargasaurus pack that they came across among the grassland lowered their heads in curiosity. Of course, three humans in this time were a rare sight for the dinosaurs.

"Should probably make camp for the night." Emily-Ann let her duffle bag drop to the ground. Since they'd made it to the edge of another forest, she figured it would give everyone time to recoup physically and mentally. "First things first, let's gather stones and enough wood for a good fire."

"Viv and I can work on that." As Kamren stepped in among the trees, he scanned the area. "Doesn't look like any dragonflies are in here."

"Never gonna let that go, are you?" Vivienne shoved his shoulder.

E-A grinned at the sign of affection Kam had just been given. "Actually, if you do find some smaller bugs, we'll need some food."

"Blegh." Grossed out, Viv cringed as she turned back to E-A. "Just the thought of that…. *Ewwww*. Makes my skin crawl."

"We'll need some kind of protein."

"I'd rather eat grass."

"Sorry, I lied." Kam marched out of the brush with a large twitching dragonfly in each hand. "They must sleep hanging onto the trees."

"No, no. *Nope*. Nu-uh." Viv closed her eyes. "You're *really* going to eat that?"

"Remember that one Lion King scene?" Smirking, he made a slurping noise. "Slimy yet satisfying."

"Barf." Saying it out loud even made her stomach turn. "Firewood. That's my focus."

E-A laughed at the reaction. "Might just taste like chicken."

"Not listening!" To avoid the teasing, Viv entered the woods.

Chirps and squeaks echoed from all around. Nighttime always seemed to bring out more life, whether in the present or the past. Careful steps took her deeper as she asked herself, *What kind of creatures will I find? Or…will they find me first?*

Along the way, she collected random sticks into a bunch

under her left arm. What she thought was a growl from somewhere else turned out to be from her stomach. *Gonna need a lot of grass. Could totally go for some ice cream. Baskin Robbins. Aw man, cookie dough. Unless…. Wonder what kind of vegetables grew in dinosaur times.* Vivienne glanced around and hoped something edible would appear. *Should probably be some fruit trees somewhe—*

Kraaaakew!

"What the?" She spun around.

The high-pitched cry only came once.

Thankfully, she could still see the makeshift camp through the trees from her location, in case she needed to book it back. "Easy, Viv." A deep breath made things somewhat better. "Probably just a bird. If…there are birds yet."

Kraakew! Kraakew!

It came from behind again.

"Jeez!"

One of the bushes rustled to life.

Multiple cries emanated from the foliage.

Her eyes opened wide as she took a step backward.

"Found some firewoo—"

"*Baskin Robbins!*" Viv tossed the bunch of sticks into the air as she flailed into Kamren. "You…. Don't sneak up on me like that!"

Unable to hold back cheeky laughter, Kam managed to ask, "Did you…just scream: Baskin Robbins?"

"That's not important right now," she shot back before pointing at the commotion. "Something or *things* are over there. It's freaking me out."

Before either of them had time to move, three animals emerged.

Chicken-sized, slender lizards hopped on their hind legs out from behind the bush. The inquisitive forest green creatures cocked their heads back and forth, gazing up at the two foreign humans in front of them.

♀ compsognathus

0.25m

"Aww, they look kinda cute." Kam knelt to the dinosaur's level, unafraid. "Wait, I know these ones. Yeah, I did a project on them in school. Comp-uh... Compsog... Compsognathus. These guys were thought to be scavengers."

"Doesn't make me feel any better about them," Viv countered, undecided on whether to pick up all the sticks again or not.

"I don't think they're interested in eating *us*."

The trio of compsognathus' preferred to chase and nip at

the fireflies. A little clumsy, a couple of the four-foot-long animals tumbled after jumping a little higher than usual. The teenagers couldn't help but chuckle at the creature's unintentional theatrics.

"They're like little Larry, Curly, and Moe—whoa!" Kam backed up as one of the compy's scurried past them to gobble up another juicy firefly. "Quick little things."

An unsuccessful chomp led one of the little green dinosaurs to Viv's left leg. "Oh my gosh, *seriously?* Get lost."

The compy climbed her leg and up the front of her like a squirrel eager for a treat

"What the flip?" She froze like a statue. "What is it with things wanting to *touch* me?"

Up by her shoulders, the smallish dinosaur could finally reach the bug with its goose-like neck and snapped it up with its small snout.

Kam took a picture with his cellphone. "Look at you, you're a Disney dinosaur princess." The compy almost looked happy to be with her. "Who knows, maybe you'll find your prince out here."

Other than the weird sensation of having lizard claw feet clamped into her shoulder and its tail curled around the back of her neck, Viv relaxed. That was until the curious dinosaur's face entered her personal space and chirped at her.

"This could be like your dino-frog." Kam grinned. "Kiss him and see."

"I'd rather kiss someone else." Viv wanted to be annoyed with his joke, but she couldn't deny his charm. What she'd said out loud registered in her brain. *Crap.*

It took a moment for him to replay her words in his mind. "Some*one* else?"

As if she were a pirate with a parrot, she bent down with the lightweight compy still attached to her. "Um, can you…help me collect these sticks again?"

Minutes later, they returned to camp where E-A had collected some large leaves from the plants around them. She'd laid them out in three single bed formations on the grass. "About time you guys got back. Did you—oh, I see you've made a friend."

Viv glanced at the compy which had switched shoulders. "Mo here has decided to claim me. Not sure why."

E-A brought a finger up and stroked its smooth beak-shaped head. "Lil' cutie. Mo?"

"Like the Stooges." Kam dropped the kindling bundle into the middle of stones set out in a circle. A couple of flat stones sat beside the campfire, which he assumed E-A had gathered to act like a flint.

"Except, I think this is a girl, so Mo with no e." Getting more attached to it, Viv leaned her head into it. Mo ran its head through her blonde-ish hair, making her giggle.

For Kam, hearing her joyous chuckles had always been music to his ears. After seeing her stressed earlier, he grinned, pleased to see her more laidback.

"You gonna keep staring at your girl, or do you want me to light the fire?" E-A asked in a lowered voice to keep it out of Viv's earshot.

He snorted while squinting at her. "W-what?"

"I see the little looks and things." E-A took the stones

70

from him. "Whether you want to deny them or not, they're there."

Uninterested in the topic, he picked at one of the make-shift bed leaves. "Think you're a bit mistaken there."

Four strikes with the flint landed among the dried leaves under the kindling. E-A blew on it until the flame took. "A fire doesn't know it's a fire until the spark has been lit."

"Are you going all Confucious on me?" Kam pursed his lips, then took a quick glimpse at Viv. "That's a good line, actually. Mind if I use that in a book?"

E-A shook her head in response to his deflection as she repositioned some of the firewood for better airflow. "Knock yourself out."

Meanwhile, Vivienne had traversed along the line of trees in search of any kind of fruit. It wasn't until she made it about forty feet away that she found something edible.

"Looks like we've got ourselves some apples, Mo," she remarked to her new scaley friend. Her thumbnail broke the skin and she scooped out a small chunk. "Wanna try some?"

Mo sized up the bit with its little black eyes, sniffed it, then snatched the chunk away from her fingers. Between crunches, the compy made little chirps.

"You like that, huh?" Taking a bite herself, she savored the crisp, sweet, and tart flavor. "Oh man, you dinos have better tasting fruit than what we have in our time."

As if part of the conversation, Mo squeaked twice before finishing its morsel.

With two apples in one hand, she plucked a couple more with the other. "Yup, be glad you don't have GMO's in this time. Nasty chemicals." She made her way back to the others with arms full of the fruit. "Found some apples just over there."

"Really?" Curious, E-A met her at the edge of their small makeshift camp. "Huh, it makes sense that apples of our time had to come from somewhere." Inspecting one up close, she nodded. "Remind me to store some in my bag before we leave tomorrow morning."

Kamren just finished shoving a stick through the thorax of one of the giant dragonflies. "Sure you don't want some barbecued bug-on-a-stick?"

"That's a *major* pass." Viv took an exaggerated bite into the red and green fruit. "Oh yeah, so juicy. Mmmm."

Her lip-smacking intermingled with yummy sounds of glee made him smirk. He liked seeing her cheery despite the circumstances.

She handed another scrap over to Mo before continuing. "Man, I'm glad I found these. Soooo delicious."

He held the lifeless bug over the flames, its black, bulbous eyes staring back at him. "You're such a tease."

"I know."

TEN

HALF AN hour later, everyone's bellies were full.

Vivienne had made herself as comfortable as possible on her green, leafy bed. The number of times she jumped due to some unfamiliar noise lessened as the day went on. As for the night, she wondered what else may be lurking around them.

Little Mo pranced around the campsite. It kept most of the bugs at bay by snapping them up in its mouth. The fire glistened off its smooth greenish scales.

"Have to say, I'm just happy we haven't come across any carnivores yet." Kamren roasted a couple of apples on his stick for dessert. "Maybe we should take turns keeping watch tonight." After saying it, he gazed up at the treeline and began studying every inch of it.

Every dinosaur movie Viv had ever watched came to mind. "I'd rather not wake up to some T-rex teeth. Or worse."

"We might be all right." Emily-Ann spoke without any reservation. "Judging by my dad's research, that is."

The mention of her father made Viv roll onto her side. "That's horrible what they did to him. Although, we can kinda relate now."

Figuring the fruit had been cooked long enough, Kam removed them from the flames. "What did he do? Take a dinosaur home with him or something?"

E-A chuckled. "Actually, he did."

"*Seriously?*" Flabbergasted, Viv's pulled her head back. "Did he put people in danger?"

"That's pretty hardcore," Kam remarked, impressed. "And unfair. I want a dino pet."

"There was no danger, at least not until the police showed up." E-A tossed a pebble into the fire. The fire's flames reminded her of how that situation had ended. "Things went from bad to worse."

"Are you gonna leave us hanging, or are we getting storytime before bed?" Ready for some dessert, Kam blew on his apple and took a bite. "Ah-ha-how, dangit! *Stinkin'* hot."

Viv laughed at his pain. "Well, it did just come from a fire."

"Guess a little backstory wouldn't hurt." As the memories came back to her, E-A took a deep breath. Emotions flooded back. Her chest tightened. "My dad…. He immersed himself in this time of dinosaurs as much as he could. Even though I lived over on the East Coast at the time, after every trip through the rift he would call me to tell about his findings." Talking about him made her even more determined to find him. "Although he wasn't supposed to. Shady SauraCorps wanted to keep everything classified."

As more became revealed, Viv sat up. "Sounds like you were close with him."

"He always said if he ever discovered a new dinosaur out here, he'd name it Em-ann-osaurus," Emily-Ann mentioned with a chuckle. "Anyway, with every trip, more and more archaeological theories kept getting debunked."

Kam handed over the roasting stick for E-A to take her apple, then swallowed down a juicy bite of his own. "Theories are only theories until proven."

"Exactly." E-A tucked her legs in and folded her arms across her knees. "First off, ever since man has dug deeper and deeper into the earth, we've classified dinosaurs as living in different periods from each other. Triassic, Jurassic, Cretaceous."

Viv's interest grew even more. "Man, I just flashed back to early grade school."

"Now, what we first encountered—and some of us just ate—the giant dragonfly, was thought to have lived in what's called the Carboniferous period. Now that's supposed to be millions of years before the Cretaceous, which is when the *amargasaurus'* were believed to have lived." Then E-A glanced over at the tiny dinosaur still chasing little flying bugs. "As well, compsognathus was believed to live in the late Jurassic, *before* the amargasaurus."

As more details were brought to light, Viv caught on. "But…they're all here together in the *same time.* How can that be?"

"Don't know for sure." A quick test of piercing her fingernail into the fruit's flesh told E-A the apple had reached her desired temperature, and she took a bite. "Mmm, you were right, Viv. That's the best damn apple I've had in a long time."

"Right?" Viv kept wondering about the reason for the time discrepancy—a welcome distraction from their predicament. "I've always thought it was kind of ridiculous to keep tacking on more and more millions and millions of years. Like they want it to be impressive or something."

"We still have no idea of how old the earth is," Kam pointed out. "I do remember reading, though, that radiocarbon dating is highly inaccurate. A physicist did about ten years of testing and concluded that radioactive carbon atoms didn't exist in the earth's atmosphere in large amounts before... before, uh—"

"Two-thousand B.C.E.," E-A finished for him, recalling the study. "That was Physicist R. Brown of Andrews University. How do you even know that?"

Before taking the last bite, Kam responded, "Did some research when I wrote some historical fiction. Still unpublished."

Nodding, E-A held out a fist for him to bump. "Impressive, Kam."

Her compliment took him by surprise. "Thank you." About to take the bite, he smirked. "Did we just have a little *bonding* moment—"

"*Don't* push it."

After laughing at them, Viv asked, "What does all that mean, exactly?"

Ready to explain, E-A glanced over at Kam. "Do you

want the floor?"

As he began, he tossed the apple core into the campfire. "It means nothing can be accurately carbon dated past two-thousand B.C.E. What's super interesting, is Brown stated that sometime around that date, a major atmospheric change had likely occurred."

E-A kept nodding. "Like something was *blocking* the sun's radiation."

"Oooh, ooh! I actually know this!" Vivienne put her hand up. "Miss Lewis!"

The on-the-spot teacher chuckled. "Yes, Viv?"

"What is: the water canopy theory?"

Kam put on his best announcer voice. "The lady wins 'double jeopardy'!"

Even more astounded, E-A looked at them back and forth. "Look at us, a bunch of nerds hanging out together nerding it out."

Viv explained herself. "I only know that because of a school project on the water cycle, and I got a little lost down the Google rabbit hole."

"Haven't we all?"

A low, resonating groan carried over the grassland behind them.

The hairs on the back of Kam's neck stood up.

As Viv turned her head to try and see where it came from. "What was that?"

E-A's gaze went straight to the fire. Maybe it had become a beacon of sorts.

Or a lure.

Anxious, Viv didn't know whether to make herself smaller or stand up and bolt. "Sh-should we put the fire out?"

Out of nowhere, Mo skittered back to the campsite making a frenzy of chirps and squeaks. Cries of distress.

Since their camp sat at the bottom of a small hill, Emily-Ann took it upon herself to check things out. "Stay here." She dropped into a hands-and-knees crawl as she neared the little summit. Setting her chin low to the ground, she spied something that didn't belong in that time period just as much as them.

A large militaristic vehicle slowed to a stop halfway across the grassland.

Attached to the hitch, a long flat trailer carried chains laid on top.

Off to the right, six men grappled with taut ropes.

The other ends of the reinforced cords disappeared into the trees and brush, swaying back and forth in quick jerks.

The source of the distraught grunts.

"What's happen'n' cap'n?" Kamren appeared and plopped himself beside E-A.

Startled, she turned her head to him. "Thought I told you to *stay put.*"

"Teenagers never do what they're told," he countered, deadpan. "Just keeping up the stereotype. Are those SauraCorps guys? What are they—"

"Think we're about to find out."

More bellows came from beyond the trees.

Some of the men engaged every muscle and heaved, while others were jolted to the ground face first.

Crackles preceded young trees toppling over.

The oblong head of a lively dinosaur barely poked through the forest as another tree came crashing down. Multiple lassos had been slung around its neck.

"Almost got it, men!" A built, weathered man stood to the right of the eight-wheeled armored vehicle that resembled a tank without the cannon. "If you take it down faster than the last one, you'll make your wages count tonight."

Another yank pulled the frightened creature further into the open.

Close to a thousand pounds, the greyish-brown, bull-sized dinosaur dug its heels into the ground. With a small horn at the end of the snout, its tusked head tugged from side to side, wailing out into the night for help.

None of the men ventured close enough to the fully-armored animal to identify frightened tears running down its face.

Unfazed, the leader leaned against the vehicle as he yelled out, "Save some of your strength to grab another one of these Scuto's. We only get paid if we get the pair."

The nickname given to the creature helped Emily-Ann recall. "Scutosaurus? Really? My dad mentioned these guys, too."

"That poor thing." Kam had never witnessed any kind of animal cruelty in person before. "Looks like a bullfrog mixed with a rhino."

E-A had already pulled out the journal. "This guy is supposedly from the Permian period. *Before* Triassic."

The scutosaurus dragged one of its front paws through

the dirt before charging at the group of humans at full speed. A flick of its tusked head sent one man crunching into a tree.

As other men scurried to gain containment, the scutosaurus knocked over another operative and grabbed onto his leg with its flat-toothed jaws. An abrupt shake roughed up the man, sending bones out of sockets and other appendages snapping.

"Take it *down*, men!" their superior roared as he fired up a heavy-duty stun stick.

Still crying out in fear, the herbivore reared up on its hind legs in a last-ditch effort. The force hoisted two of the men up into the air.

By the campfire, Vivienne jumped as gunshots echoed.

As the scutosaurus came back down, armor-piercing tranquilizer darts in its weaker underbelly took effect. A couple of SauraCorps employees leaped out of the way as the dinosaur lurched forward, losing all sensation of its limbs.

The leader laughed while pulling out a walkie-talkie. "All right, get the forks out here. *Be careful* with the package. Bosses are saying we're getting sloppy, getting too many scratches on the skin. *Whatever.*"

A forklift emerged from behind the armored vehicle. The forks dug into the ground a few inches below the scutosaurus' belly. Ten minutes later, the dinosaur rested on the flatbed trailer as chains were tossed across the bed and cinched it down tight.

Those who had been injured were assisted to the safety of their vehicles.

"This one shouldn't be too far from the herd." The grey-haired leader barked to the others. "Let's grab that second scuto. Hopefully it doesn't put up as much of a fight."

Once the people drove off, E-A and Kam returned to camp.

"What happened out there?" Viv used the poking stick to keep the fire going. "Was it…. I heard gunshots."

Instead of going back to his leafy cot, Kam plopped down beside her. Before even saying anything, he put an arm around her. "Nothing died. Although, what those SauraCorps men just did…" He looked over at E-A, shaking his head. "…that wasn't right either."

Like the fire in front of her, E-A's sense of justice burned within. "They treated that scutosaurus like it… like it wasn't a living breathing creature." Her voice trembled. *I should've done something.* "That was utterly *disgusting.*"

What Kam had just seen made him realize a sad truth. "There's something to be said about money and prominence." His unreasonable gym teacher also came to mind. "It makes people suck."

"Amen to that." As much as Viv received warmth from the campfire, she more than welcomed Kam's body heat beside her. "Are they coming this way?"

He caught the fear in her tone and squeezed her arm. "No, I think they were far enough away that they didn't see us and went off in another direction."

E-A tsked as she re-evaluated a thought from earlier. "Maybe the dinosaurs aren't the ones we need to keep an eye out for."

Snap!

In the middle of the night, Vivienne cracked open an eye. *What was that?* For a moment, she'd forgotten where she was. The day's events replayed hazily in her head until the flattened grass underneath her reminded her that she'd been sleeping out in the open.

Crack!

More alert than she'd ever been before in her life, Viv froze and jerked her head back and forth as her gaze danced around the area. What had sounded like a twig being broken made her zone in on the forest beside them.

The darkness of the brush provided perfect cover for whatever had caused the disturbance.

Her eyes washed away cloudiness with rapid blinks. Once she adjusted to the night, she noticed some tree branches protruding out from the treeline, swaying in the slight breeze. *Of course, it's nothing.*

As she set her head back down, Viv glimpsed back at the branches.

Something about them seemed off.

Three of its smaller twigs twitched.

Twitched.

Moonlight allowed some clarity to what she tried to identify.

The twigs—talons.

Attached to sleek, muscular arms.

Snouts with nightmarish fangs peeked just beyond the treeline.

Four of them.

"Ka-Ka-*Kam*." Viv reached over to tap his foot. "Kamren, wake—"

Seconds after she'd taken her gaze off of the creatures, she looked back.

Gone.

Whatever had been lurking had retreated into the foliage.

"Urmph." Kamren turned over, putting his back to the forest. "What, Viv?"

"I thought I saw…."

Still, nothing had returned to watch them.

Viv sighed as she hugged a large leaf blanket. "Nothing. Sorry."

ELEVEN

EARLY THE next morning, Sebastian woke up to his alarm. Sitting up, he swung his legs over the edge of the bed.

His index finger and thumb scans turned on the display of his cellphone on the bedside table. No calls or messages. A couple of work e-mails had come through.

Rather than spend more time with the phone, he picked up the picture which sat almost right beside his bed. A photo of his son Aiden. The most recent one he could get. *Can't call Julia to ask for an updated photo, of course. The whole damn world would come crashing down.*

Sebastian placed it back on the side table and stood up.

A few minutes later, he'd made it to the kitchen, his bare feet slapping against the cold granite floor. Breakfast entered his thoughts as he came between the island and his stainless-steel fridge. He opened the fridge door, surveyed his food supplies, and mulled over his options.

Tap-tap-tap-tap-tap.

Without even looking up from his fridge, Sebastian grinned at the quick footsteps.

Raaaawr-skree.

Tap-tap-tap.

"I know you're out there."

Raawr-krrrraoww.

He grabbed the jug of orange juice. "You coming over to see me, girl?"

An orangey, snouted reptilian head popped up over the door. *Skree-kow.*

Sebastian chuckled as he gave the underside of the creature's head a scratch. "Oh yeah? And did you sleep well, Trudy?"

The fridge door swayed closed.

A cheerful, slender juvenile troodon chirped in response. By species, it resembled a slightly larger version of a compsognathus.

"Guess you're wanting some breakfast, too, huh?" Sebastian opened the fridge once more and reached into one of the lower crispers where fruit would normally be kept. Instead, he removed a dormant dragonfly. "Still love these things, don't you?"

Trudy's eyes went into predator mode.

"*Hey.*" Sebastian raised his food-holding hand higher and snapped his fingers with the other. "Watch the *fingers* this time."

The dinosaur stayed put while flexing its little arms, anxious to tear into its meal.

"Good girl." He set the insect down on the pristine

white, granite-countered kitchen island. Then he placed his left hand on top of the dinosaur's head. "*Wait.*"

About to snag the bug, Trudy jerked its head back.

Sebastian couldn't help but chuckle. "Ah, you're too cute. Go ahead."

Teeth flashed as the insect left the island within a second.

Like a squirrel coveting a walnut, Trudy clutched the dragonfly in its clawed hands and strolled off to dine. *Kree-ow!*

"You're welcome." Sebastian served himself some orange juice and hopped onto one of the barstools. Taking the first sip, he turned on his tablet.

Ding-dong.

Trudy turned its head to acknowledge the visitor. *Krrreee.*

"This early in the morning?" Sebastian slid off the stool as he pressed the security app on his tablet. "Who does that?"

Video surveillance showed Felicia Voorhees standing on the porch dressed in her usual business attire.

Still in pajama pants and shirtless, Sebastian sauntered over and squinted as he opened the door. "You do realize I'm not on the clock for another couple hours, right?"

"Don't care." She entered his home without asking and peeked at his muscular form. "We have a problem to fix."

"Okay?" The abrupt entrance put him on edge. "Wait, Felicia, can't we take care of whatever you're here for at work?"

Once she made it to his kitchen, she glanced around. "Pretty sure you don't want others to learn of what you did last night."

"What *I* did?" He feigned innocence with a hand on his chest. "Not sure if I follow—"

"Sebastian, this is *very* different from what was decided upon concerning Theodore Lewis." Felicia remained serious as she sat on a barstool and straightened her beige jacket and black skirt. "At least that was a decision made by the organization as a whole."

All he responded with: another sip of orange juice.

"Fine, if you're not going to talk about it, I will." From her purse, she pulled out a manila envelope and removed pictures. Felicia spread them out for him. "First of all, why was there a truck parked outside our facility here in Utah?"

He shrugged. "Must've run out of gas or something."

"*Dammit,* Sebastian!" She held up another photo, this time of the two teenagers with an African American woman. "Did you really think I wouldn't see the security tapes? Especially when it comes to them going *into* the rift area, and somehow *not* coming back out with you?"

As she raised her voice, Trudy the troodon poked its head around a corner and cooed.

Felicia placed one hand on her forehead to rub it and pointed at the dinosaur with the other. "And then there's still *that.*"

"I've always kept an eye on Trudy," he countered, fully aware of the weight of having a dinosaur in his possession. "She can't escape this place."

"And I've kept your little 'secret pet' from the rest of the board," she spit back, unbridled weightiness in her tone. Though her piercing eyes bored into his, she turned back to the pictures. "But this? Two kids and…some woman?"

Sebastian rubbed the back of his neck. "Emily-Ann Lewis. She's Theo's dau—"

"Theo's *daughter?*" Overwhelmed, she slid off the stool and began pacing. The situation had just turned into a potentially worse one. "This isn't happening." She stopped and stared him down. "Tell me you didn't do what I think you did."

After finishing his juice, he shrugged again. "People go missing all the time."

Still holding a picture in her hand, she crumpled it up and shook her fist. "If the police or detectives come knocking on our doors, you can forget about me bailing you out." As she bored her gaze into his eyes, she shook her head at him. "We could have let them go. Even if they tried to tell anyone anything, who would believe them?" Felicia began chewing on her bottom lip. "I mean, a couple of *kids,* Sebastian. Of all people, I thought you would be better than that."

The last comment slammed into his hardened exterior.

Smash!

Trudy screeched as she ran from the room.

The empty drinkware traveled from the island to the backsplash on the wall. Cracked tiles and shattered bits of glass littered a section of his countertop.

His outburst made Felicia jump.

"*Don't you dare* play that card on me." Sebastian's words came out hot and furious. His chest heaved up and down as he threw a finger in her face. "They found the rift. It was either keep tabs on them for the rest of their lives or remove them from the equation. I saw it as no different than the Theo incident."

"Mhmm, and what would you do if Olivia, or even *Aiden* found the rift?"

Mouth open, Sebastian could only find silence to retort with.

After waiting a few seconds for a reply, Felicia headed for the front door. "That's what I thought."

Before she reached the door, he called down to her, "That's different."

"To you it is," she fired back. "Better figure out your statement for the police now."

The door closed behind Felicia.

Tension remained in his chest.

That's different.

Sebastian wiped sweat from his face. He braced himself against the island as a whimper shuddered out of him. He'd made his decision. Now, he had to live with it.

The ringtone on his cellphone sang its tune.

He fished it out from his pajama pant pocket.

A deep breath exited his lungs as he swiped the green indicator. A business tone readied itself in his voice before he brought the phone to his ear. "Mr. Bartelloni...good morning. How are you today?" Calmness finally took over him as his nasal airways opened up. "Yes, I've got just the dinosaurs to add to your aquatic collection. Have you ever heard of a cyclotosaurus?"

TWELVE

SCRAAAAAAPE.

Emily-Ann's head rolled to the side.

Scraaaape.

Strands of grass brushed against her cheek.

Scraaaape.

Hissss.

Scraaaape.

"What?"

Dazed, she squinted as she realized dawn had come.

Hissss.

Scraaa—thump—aaape.

A rock had skidded under her back.

One of the large plant leaves of her bed slipped out from under her.

Scraaaape.

Once E-A's eyes adjusted, she noticed tree limbs above her seemed to move past in some kind of interval.

It hit her.

She was moving.

Scraaaape.

Hissss.

Instead of glancing side to side, her head snapped up.

She was being dragged.

"Oh my *God!*"

Mandibles the size of barbecue tongs were crimped around her left foot. A reddish-brown, round head hissed with determination once more.

E-A screamed, "No! Heeeelp!"

An eight-foot-long body with multiple legs glided backward. From one end to the other, the legs themselves moved up and down in a smooth motion like twisted, grotesque piano keys.

"Giant…millipede!"

Over by camp, the shouts woke Vivienne up into a groggy state. It took a moment for the yells to sink in. Her vision cleared as she glanced around. Where E-A had slept sat empty but had left an imprint in the grass. *Where did she—*

"Someone *help me!*"

Though frightened, Viv shot to her feet. "E-A, where are you?" *Is it what I saw last night? Or was that just a dream?*

"In the forest," E-A shouted back, grunting and trying her hardest to wriggle free. "Being dragged by a *freaking* bug!"

Kamren sat up with one eye open. "What's going on?"

"Emily's in trouble." Viv rushed over to their captured friend's duffle bag. "Maybe the tranq gun would work?"

Up and hobbling over to the edge of the forest, Kam

rested against a tree. "Tranq's may not penetrate. Might need something…" A yawn cut him off. "…a little stronger."

Not wanting to waste time, Viv tossed the tranquilizer weapon to him. "Try it anyway, we can't lose her."

From further into the woods, E-A called out, "Vivieeeene! Kamreeeen!"

He stared at the gun in his hands. "Nothing like a surge of adrenaline in the morning with a side of firearms." He set his gaze on the inner forest. "We're coming!"

Leaves and sticks brushed past E-A as she continued to thrash. "Get off me."

Thwak!

Her free foot walloped the giant millipede in the head.

The oversized arthropod hissed at her. For the most part, it remained undeterred. All its focus remained on keeping hold of the morning human meal.

A flick of its strong body rammed her into a boulder.

Her ribs struck the hard rock. E-A gasped in shock and for air.

This thing's gonna kill me.

Another jostle knocked her clambering body onto her back.

As she rolled onto her right side, she managed to glance down to the back-end of the huge bug. The rear began disappearing into the ground just before a mossy log.

Oh God no. Its burrow.

A low-lying cycad tree with palm fronds and a trunk resembling a pineapple came up on her right.

Like a fish out of water, she lurched her body over

and clasped her hands onto the bumpy tree trunk. Every muscle in her body engaged—inducing searing pain due to what must have become a cracked rib on her left side. *I can't die this way.*

Meanwhile, Kam hoped he'd been heading in the right direction. "Hey, I need your voice for guidance."

Another tug from the millipede made her suck in an agonizing gasp. "Over—*gaah, frig*—here!"

Thirty feet at ten o'clock from his position. "Almost to you." As he took off, he glanced back for a moment. *Where's Viv?*

The roughness of the plant's bark scuffed against E-A's palms.

Determined, the giant bug planted its back half and lifted the front half higher into the air.

E-A's fingernails dug into the tree until shooting pain flared up from under the nails. If she held on, the possibility of her nails getting ripped from their respective fingers would cause even more agony. Otherwise, she'd continue to be at the mercy of the monstrous vermin.

Pthew! Pthew!

Two tranq's glanced off the insect's armor-like exoskeleton.

After firing the shots, Kam stood there. Shock set in. "Crap, tranq's are useless."

"Then try…" E-A's arms and hands grew tired as the millipede lowered its front half and yanked once more. "…something else."

Face to face with danger, he became paralyzed. "I…don't know what to do."

"Do…" E-A grinded her molars together. "…*anything!*"

A war cry sounded.

From behind a tree, Vivienne sprinted and leaped onto the back of the millipede. Positioned behind its head, she raised a knife and slammed it down with a yell of exertion. Once. Twice. Three times she sunk the blade in.

The giant insect writhed, giving in to a slow death.

Its mandibles drooped.

Finally able to take her half-worn hands off the tree, E-A tucked her feet away from the enormous bug. "Flippin' heck. That…was…insane." More than happy to no longer have to fight for her life, she turned and smiled at her rescuer. "Viv, you *saved* me."

Viv stared wide-eyed at the dagger still in her hands. "Can't believe I just…did that." Slime from the innards of the millipede's head dripped from the blade. "Eh-heh-heh-heeewww." She cringed, almost to the point of puking as she tossed the knife to the side. "That was *absolutely* disgusting."

"No, that was amazing." E-A hobbled over and gave the teenager a tight, appreciative hug, within her parameters of current searing pain in her side. "Didn't know you had all of that in you."

About ten feet away, Kam stared at his best friend. Mouth open. Arms slack. *Holy mother of…. She just* did *that.* Her assault on the bug amazed and almost scared him. Seeing the intense side of her also unlocked something within himself, creating uncertainty of how to deal with it. *That was…kinda hot.*

The two ladies stepped away from the dead bug.

E-A placed a thankful hand on the side of her savior's face, hoping to lessen Viv's worries. "Are you good? I mean, you went all badass 'Xena: Warrior Princess' on that thing, but are you okay?"

It took a few seconds for Viv to process it all. "I stabbed that thing." After swallowing down a lump in her throat, she shook her head in realization. "No, I just…. I just *killed* this thing."

"Yes, but you saved my life, Viv." As the adrenaline wore off in E-A, she winced when the palms of her hands rested on her friend's shoulders. "As much as this hurts, I'm happy to still be alive to feel the pain."

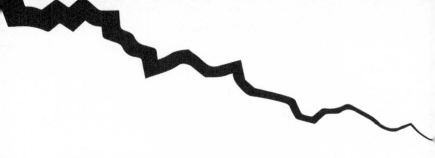

THIRTEEN

ONLY EMBERS remained of the fire as they left camp.

They'd taken some time to collect more apples in her duffle bag. From now on, they agreed to keep an eye out for any other sources of food. The more food they could find, the less cranky they would become.

Emily-Ann took the lead with her father's journal in hand. Traversing among the rich foliage and having seen dinosaurs up close made page six became more real to her now.

Day Two:

Since we spent probably too much time among the amargasaurus herd, today will be more focused on getting better acquainted with the lay of the land. This may be difficult because every rustle from the forest and every deep bellow off in the distance begs to be discovered.

Once we passed the grassland beyond the rift, a twenty-minute walk through a section of the farthest woods brought us to a freshwater lake. Smaller theropods like compsognathus (*komp-sog-nay-thus. Late Jurassic.) and troodon (*tro-uh-don. Late Cretaceous) like to dart around among the trees. Some are more curious than others, coming about thirty feet away from us. [Note: Observing Jurassic and Cretaceous dinosaurs together is fascinating. Those in the archeological and paleontology fields would lose their minds.]

Keith Archer tried to lure a compsognathus closer with a chunk of his roast beef sandwich. Only one compy was brave enough to make it five feet away from us. Strangely, the morsel didn't seem to entice the little guy in any way. For a dinosaur thought to be a carnivore—a scavenger, even—more time and study will be required to determine their preferred source of food.

As awe-inspiring as it is to venture deeper into the world of this time, only one thought remains at the forefront of my mind: I wish my Emily-Ann could be here to experience this with me.

The last paragraph of his words seemed to wrap around her heart and made her tear up. After taking a beating from the millipede, she fought back a wince every time she breathed in. *Possible cracked rib. Sore ankle. Am I going to make it to you in one piece?*

Behind her, Kamren strolled alongside Vivienne.

"Should I be calling you Lara Croft from now on?" He grinned as he reached over and squeezed her bicep through her light sweater. Realizing he'd become fascinated by her muscle, he coughed himself back into a relatively normal headspace. "Have you, uh…been working out and not telling me about it?"

The intensity of the experience still gave Viv's hands a slight tremor. "Didn't think you needed to know, but for the past year, I've been trying my best of getting into a morning workout routine. Mostly bodyweight stuff."

"Well, you're a beast, just saying."

His compliment made her smile, as well as give his left shoulder a shove. "I'd rather be a beast than a popsicle."

Kamren stopped marching and gave her a puzzled look. "What's that supposed to mean?"

"You *froze* back there."

Back in step with her, he stared at the ground, sheepish. "Yeah, well, when you're ten feet away from a massive insect…."

Vivienne glanced over and noticed his embarrassment. For encouragement, she brushed a finger against his chin to tilt it back up. "Hey, no one's blaming you. We get it, this is all new." By the time she'd finished, she discovered that her hand had gone further than expected, rubbing his arm for extra reassurance. *Crap, did I just do that to him? Quick, change the topic.* She pulled her rebellious hand back. "For the record, I hope we never have to deal with another freaking millipede ever again."

He smirked. "You've got experience now, though."

"Doesn't matter." Her next words came out with added abhorrence. "Big or small, I officially *hate* bugs."

Ahead of them, E-A turned around. "Sorry to say this, but the next possible checkpoint is a twenty-minute trek straight through the forest."

The mere thought of another possible millipede encounter made Viv tense up and close her eyes on the spot. "Do we really *have* to?"

In tune with her thinking, Kam added, "I for one would rather not find out if there are more I.O.U.S.'s in there."

E-A scrunched her eyebrows at him. "I.O. what now?"

"Insects of unusual size." A nerdish grin formed on his face. "Like the R.O.U.—wait, have you never read or seen *The Princess Bride*?"

"Sorry, bud." E-A turned back to examine the woods. "Must be in the minority."

As both teenagers came to her side, Kam shook his head. "You haven't lived."

"Excuse me?" E-A snorted, somewhat offended. "Pretty sure being tossed around by a gigantic, *horrifying* insect counts as living."

About to make a reply, Kamren read the 'I don't need your attitude right now' look she'd been sending his direction. Instead, he glanced side to side before backing away.

Before stepping in among the new section of forest, E-A addressed the other teen. "You going to be okay there, Viv?"

A deep breath seemed to help calm Viv's nerves a bit. "I'd

be better if I could have the knife back."

The group entered the unsettling woods.

Bird-like screeches resonated from the tree-tops.

As Kamren kept a wary eye on the environment above, Vivienne examined every inch of the forest floor. Both of them now had a better understanding that only when something terrifying happens, people become much more aware of their surroundings.

Emily-Ann kept the notebook tucked under an arm as she navigated through the brush. The sting in her side reminded her of the potential lurking threats. *Only twenty more minutes of this.* On high alert, she didn't pick up any large beast movement within a fifty-foot radius.

Ferns brushed against their legs as they trekked. Roots jutted out from the ground, acting as nature's steps throughout the terrain.

A couple of minutes in, Kam glanced more and more at his best friend. All his life, he'd only perceived her a certain way. Glints of sunlight snuck past tree branches to illuminate her blonde hair with red highlights. *Her hair. It's...gorgeous. Like rose gold.* The moment she displayed her strength replayed in his mind. *Never realized how strong she was.*

One of the tree roots tripped him off balance for a moment.

A little ahead, Viv checked on him. "You all right, Kam?"

"I'm...good. Yeah." Back on track, he exercised more caution on where he stepped. "Just got thinking—" *Maybe shouldn't say that out loud.* "—um, kinda got distracted is all."

"What'cha thinking about?"

He winced. *Think fast.* "Well, I…s-s-started wondering… what happened to Mo. Thought you'd bonded with the rascal."

She held back a younger tree's flimsy branch for him. "It wasn't meant to be. It must've preferred staying with its posse."

Kam chuckled. "Don't want to break up the Stooges now."

In a flicker of a moment, she noticed something foreign in his eyes as he passed her. *That's a new look. Wonder what's going on in there.* For a little test, she halted and slipped off her bug-gut stained, light pink sweater and tied the arms around her waist before carrying on.

Out of his peripheral, Kam had noticed the slight clothing change. It took everything he had to stop himself from glancing over. *Crap.*

Vivienne pulled a scrunchie out of her back pocket and raised her arms, putting her hair into a short ponytail.

Again, he couldn't help taking a quick peek. *Dang, she's been working out.* He noticed the sweat on her arms glistening among the rays of sunlight breaking through the trees. Then he snapped his eyes forward. *Dammit. What's wrong with me?*

Once she'd fixed her hair into place, she caught little twitches in his facial expression. One of her eyebrows arched in unison with a grin sneaking onto her face. "Kam, you keep looking at me."

"Wh-what?" Trying to act cool, he scratched the hair on the back of his head. "I mean, I have eyes. We look at each other all the time."

"True, but you're *looking* at me."

"So?" He pulled another sentence out faster than he had time to think about it. "I'd rather look at you more than E-A."

Viv decided to go a little more forward with her approach. "Ah, so you think I'm prettier than her?"

"I... Wait, *what?*" A nervous chuckle overtook his throat. "You... I'm not gonna answer that."

She gave him an expectant stare. "So you *don't* think I'm prettier than her."

Her last statement made him stop in his tracks as his brain seized up. "Vivienne, what's going on with you?"

"Nothing." She smirked, not missing a beat. "Come on, popsicle. Can't have you freezing up twice in one day."

A couple of wide tree trunks created a narrow passage.

Since they'd been busy talking, their arms brushed together as they assumed the opening would be wide enough for them both.

The warmth of his skin brushing against hers made Viv blush. A breath shot up from her lungs and hitched in her throat.

For Kam, the sensation lingered on his forearm. "Sorry." In gentlemanly fashion, he held his arm out all chivalrous to let her go first. "After you, Lady Lancaster." Though it had been accidental skin contact, for some reason he wanted more of it. Perhaps it was because she was the only true friend and the closest thing he had to family among the current dilemma. Every other reason seemed to make his veins pump blood a little quicker.

Everyone traveled in silence the rest of the way.

No creature crossed their path. Only odd chirps and shrieks reminded the humans that they weren't alone. Few trees remained, allowing everyone to gaze past to the freshwater checkpoint.

It wasn't until the picturesque water came into view that Kamren realized how thirsty he'd become. Plus, his newfound view of Vivienne scratched away at his insides. The awkward moments and his nerves seemed to suck all the moisture from his mouth and throat.

E-A reached the edge of the forest. "This is the next—"

"Water." Kam blew past her, craving a drink.

As she reached out for his shirt, he'd already gone too far. "We should check for—"

"This is freshwater, right?"

"It is, but we—"

"Got any straws in that duffle bag of yours?" Already at the water's edge, he turned right and stepped up onto a pier-like fallen tree trunk.

"Nope, we're entering a new biome, though," E-A called out to him with a warning tone. "Might want to check for dinosaurs around here."

At the border of the woods, Viv joined her. "He's a little...*preoccupied* right now."

E-A considered taking off her shoes to walk on the stretch of sand and stones. "Didn't realize thirst could be so distracting."

With a giggle, Viv countered, "Pretty sure it's not the water."

Perched near the end of the collapsed tree, Kamren held onto a small branch as he lowered his mouth to the water.

Sluuuurp.

Refreshing liquid entered his mouth and replenished his parched throat. The drink helped him to clear his head until new questions arrived. *Does she actually have feelings for me? Did she mean to touch my arm like that?* Another gulp of water didn't do much for his throat on the next question. *Do I… Should I have feelings for her?*

Viv called over, "Are you sure you should be drinking that? Might be some weird stuff in there."

Sluuuurp.

He wiped his chin with the back of a hand. "Compared to the chemical-riddled water of our time, I think it's safe."

Sluuuurp.

Splash!

Still a fair distance from her friend, Viv's ears perked up as she turned to E-A. "Did you hear that?" Her gaze darted over to Kam, who hadn't fallen in the lake. "Swear I heard something hit the water."

E-A yelled over as she came closer to him, "Eyes up, Kam. Something's out there."

After another slurp, he pulled himself back up a bit. "This water is so clear and delicious. I can even see right to the…."

Below the surface, piercing amber eyes with black, diamond-shaped irises glared up at him.

Every single muscle of his locked into place.

From Viv's position, she could read his expression.

"What's wrong, Kam?"

On the log, he opened his mouth only to hesitate. *Do I say anything?* So far, it only sat at the bottom of the lake. *Will it attack if I speak?*

Vivienne marched toward him. "Kamren?"

The crunch of her shoes on the rocky shore made him glance up. "Viv, don't come any closer to—"

Hissss!

Ker-splash!

FOURTEEN

"KAMREEEEN!" VIVIENNE dashed over to the log's gnarled base.

One of his legs flailed out of the water and back down.

Seconds later, a slender, dark-blue tail thrashed above the surface.

"Should've checked the damn environment." Emily-Ann dropped the journal and swung the duffle bag off her back before sloshing into the lake. As her cargo pants became soaked, she didn't let it deter her from possibly making a difference in a life or death situation.

Underwater, Kamren somehow managed to keep the creature within arm's length. The odd thrust of a hand or foot kept it at bay. Both feet struck the animal's side, propelling him away and up to the surface.

Ten feet out from the tree, he popped up and gasped for air.

"*Kamren!* Oh my God, are you okay?" An agitated Viv had

made it out to the end of the tree and extended a shaky hand out to him. She'd never thought that she'd be trying to save people twice in one day. Then again, Kam's best friend status added more tenacity to her efforts. "Come to me, Kam!"

His weakening arms stroked through the cool water twice. "I can't—"

A clawed foot pulled him under once more.

Shoulder deep, E-A dove in.

The dinosaur's head brushed against Kam as he sank.

Steak knife-like teeth zoomed past his face.

A long and slender crocodilian form allowed the aquatic dinosaur to twist and turn with ease. Once the head shot by, a couple swift twists garnered enough momentum for it to turn back and rocket toward him.

Kam tucked his arms into his core for protection.

The snout poked and prodded at his upper body.

Eyes still open, he noticed it stop, check on him with its amber eyes, then return to its nudging. *What the heck? This thing's friggin' weird!*

Talons nicked his jean pants as the creature growled. Water swirled around them. The tip of the snout inched closer to the teen's face.

The look it gave sent shivers down his wet body.

Kam closed his eyes.

This is how I go.

Flashes of all the times he'd hugged Viv entered his mind. Though his eyes were closed, it seemed like they had finally opened for the first time on his true feelings.

How did I not—

A gargled snarl two inches away snapped his mind back to the chilling situation.

Dark hands wrangled the end of the dinosaur's tail.

Its head snapped to the left as it eyed up Emily-Ann.

A flick of the strong tail sent E-A further toward the lake bottom. Unwilling to let go—even though her hands had nearly been rubbed raw from earlier—she stayed for the ride.

The distraction allowed Kam to scramble for the surface. Popping up closer to the fallen tree, he thrust his hand out with a loud inhale.

Vivienne snagged his wrist. "I got you!"

Drawn further out into the lake, E-A needed air and released her grip. She hoped her assistance had worked, while another part of her feared to discover what else could be waiting in the depths.

Two heaves later, Kam rolled over onto his back on the safety of the tree trunk beside one of his rescuers. "Thank… Thank you, Viv."

"Of course, Kamren." A sweetness saturated her voice. "Are you hurt? Did it bite or cut you anywhere?"

His chest heaved less as he returned to normal breathing speed. "I don't…feel hurt." After a forceful cough, he picked up on the signals his body sent to his brain. "Nope, no pain. Weird."

"Really?" She leaned over him, checking over everything to make sure. As well, she didn't mind checking him out in the process. "What was that thing doing to you then?"

E-A swam up to them. "It's gone. At least I hope so."

Still letting his body recuperate, he only lifted one arm

with a thumbs up. "Thanks for your help down there, Emily. Did it hurt you?"

"Nah, I'm fine." By his feet, she patted him on the shin. "Hopefully this means you'll listen to me the next time I tell you to check the area."

His thumbs-up turned into a pointed index finger. "It's *definitely* noted for future reference."

Viv smirked at him. "Sure got more than your feet wet with these dinosaurs."

The joke made him choke with laughter. "Oh, that's a good one."

Minutes later, everyone reconvened on the beach.

As the adrenaline depleted from him, Kam gave his clothes a once-over. "A couple of small tears, but nothing major. No bleeding or anything."

"So weird." Viv let her eyes dawdle on how his wet red shirt stuck to his handsome frame before finally shifting her gaze away. "E-A, does your father's notebook say anything about what they may have found out here?"

Sitting cross-legged on the beach, E-A opened the book. "If my memory serves me right, he didn't spend too much time here." When the page came up, she perused the notes. "Says here they could only see dinosaurs on the opposite side of the lake with binoculars. Some they assumed to be nundasuchus or postosuchus."

"Can I see?" Kam took the book. "Noon-dah-soo-kuss. Reminds me of a crocodile." As he neared the edge of the lake, he came to terms with almost becoming the dinosaur's prey. "That thing, it looked at me as if…." As terrifying as it was, he closed his eyes to relive the instant its reptilian eye connected with his own. "I don't think that was an attack."

nundasuchus ♂

Perplexed, Viv gave him an odd stare. "Sure looked like one to me."

He closed the book and used it to point at the lake. "This could be totally off, but I think it was...*playing*."

An explosion of water by the lake's fringe revealed the aquatic dinosaur.

Before he had any time to react, Kam's back hit the rocky shore as it bowled into him.

The notebook flew from his hand.

Both ladies screamed and backed away.

Slow and threatening, the nundasuchus stepped over the teenager with its lean legs.

Helpless, Kam's heart raced when he peeked at the muscular, greyish underbelly of the fierce beast.

Stripes of citrus and lavender colored its sides, popping

against the deep blue.

Compared to earlier, the sleek dinosaur seemed more interested in a meal this time. Its hissing snout inched closer to the teen's nose.

"Get outta here!" E-A yelled, waving her arms around to make herself bigger. "Scram!"

About to join in shooing it, Vivienne jumped as the nundasuchus snapped its jaws at her, followed by a menacing hiss.

Kam remained petrified on the sand. *Please, don't kill me! I'm too young to go.*

Unaffected by the other humans, the dinosaur's nose rubbed against its prey's face. A low growl formed in its core and reverberated up to its toothy jaws. Saliva dripped from its chops to the young man's left cheek.

Seeing no way out, Kamren whimpered. Frightened tears squeezed past his shut eyelids.

The nundasuchus' nostrils flared, ruffling tufts of his hair.

Viv swirled around, throwing her hands over her face. *I can't watch.*

As the dinosaur's mouth opened wide, E-A couldn't look away.

Something warm and gooey rubbed against Kamren's forehead. His trembling voice blurted out, "Oh...*jeez.* Just...eat me already."

No jabs of sharp fangs came to his head.

E-A's stare of shock turned into amused disbelief. "Um, Kamren."

"Is it bad?"

"It's just...*licking* you."

As soon as the commentary registered in her brain, Viv turned back around to see for herself. "What the heck?"

"Did you just say..." Kam opened his right eye a smidge. "...*licking?*"

"Seems like you were right." E-A stayed put, crouching to the beast's eye level. "Either you taste really good, or you've just been adopted by a dinosaur."

Hoping the nundasuchus would respond well to it, Kam brought his hands up to protect his face. "I mean, when I was nine, sure—blegh, dead fish breath." His trembling hands steadied as he placed them on the sides of the dinosaur's head.

"It's...not eating you." Bewildered, Viv shook her head. "I get *attacked* by a freaking dragonfly. Emily gets *dragged* by a gigantic millipede."

"Still fresh," E-A quipped.

"Sorry. It's just..." She laughed at the ridiculous circumstances. "...you only get *licked.*"

Kam sat up, pushing the nundasuchus back a bit. "Yeah, but be glad your face doesn't smell like rotten fish now." He wiped his face with the short sleeve from his shirt before standing back up. Moments ago, his life flashed before his eyes while underwater. Only now he could truly comprehend the playful curiosity in the reptilian eyes. "You're like a little croco-dog, aren't you?"

"This is crazy." Still a bit on the nervous side, Viv came closer. "I would've never thought that—"

Hissss!

Her hand whipped back to her chest. "For the love of…. Are you *kidding* me?"

The nundasuchus placed itself between her and its new friend. All water had dried on the layer of crocodile-like armor which stretched from the neck down to the tip of the tail. The armor made little pops and cracks as it curled into a defensive stance.

A few feet away, E-A brushed some sand off the notebook and chuckled. "Think you've got yourself a little guard dino there, Kam."

Calmly, Kamren knelt to the nundasuchus' level. "Hey, now." Half of his brain still couldn't wrap around the fact he'd bonded with a dinosaur in some weird way. "Uh… Nandy, you be nice to Viv, okay?"

"Nandy?" Vivienne raised an eyebrow at him. "Really? You're gonna name that nasty thing that hates me?"

"Mo chose you, and Nandy chose me." He scratched the dinosaur's rough chin. To him, it seemed like the dinosaur smiled back. "Plus, Nandy the nundasuchus. Gotta keep with alliteration. A non-gender specific name, too, since I don't feel like lifting its tail to check."

Far enough away from Nandy to keep it from hissing, Emily-Ann savored her first bite into another apple. Light spray from the juice landed on a page of the notebook. Something about the lake area jogged her memory. "Hey guys, this lake turns into a river off to the northeast. Going off my dad's notes, we should follow it."

"We're getting closer?" Viv hoped the journey wouldn't take much longer, even though they were only a day into the impromptu dinosaur safari. "How much more is there?"

"There's a lot of notes on what they found along the way." Pages flipped by as E-A skimmed through. Past the dinosaur discovery notes, she came to a particular page and tensed her jaw. *Oh...right.* "Let's...eat something, then be on our way."

FIFTEEN

GRAVEL CRUNCHED under the wheels of the car.

An hour's drive through the countryside did two things for Sebastian. For one, he enjoyed the serenity. For another, it gave him time to think to himself. The choice he'd made to remove the three infiltrators from the SauraCorps facility stared him down as if it were sitting in the passenger seat of his car.

On top of that, Felicia's words echoed in his head during the trip.

What would you do if Olivia, or even Aiden found the rift?

Her voice nagged.

He hadn't noticed how tight he'd been strangling the steering wheel. *How dare she? It would be* completely *different.*

Another question presented itself.

But, hypothetically, if anyone else on the board had found out either one of them discovered the confidential anomaly...?

Lost in his thoughts, Sebastian almost missed a driveway. Grand iron-barred gates stood out of place among the dense forest. A speaker and camera hub greeted his window.

He ran his fingers through his hair, hoping it would help to sift Felicia's words out of his head. Once he collected himself, he rolled down the window and pushed the intercom button.

A voice came after the buzz. "Mr. Sharpe, you're early."

"Early means I'm not wasting anyone's time, Mr. Bartelloni."

"Always admired that." Another unpleasant buzz came from the gates as they unlocked and proceeded to open. "Plus, you bring me presents."

Sebastian drove his sleek silver Mercedes-Benz through the entrance. A fifty-foot-long, reinforced SauraCorps cube van with holes in the sides followed.

It always excited him to visit one of his best clients. Mostly because he didn't get many chances to go in person to view the connected biodomes surrounding Mr. Bartelloni's estate. From the front gates, one of the tempered-glass structures stretched to just behind the Victorian-style home.

Sebastian made it halfway across the bridge driveway and slowed to a stop. Taking a moment for himself, he hopped out of the car. He straightened his favorite navy-blue suit while approaching the railing. The breathtaking view made him grin. *This never gets old.*

Underneath the bridge, a man-made lake stretched one-hundred feet out from his position. A pair of crocodilian dinosaurs sun-bathed on a small island in the middle. Two iguanodons took a drink from the water's edge. Three of their younglings pranced around them, playing among the field. Primeval trees and ferns grew throughout, adding to the authenticity of the environment.

"Tours aren't until noon."

Sebastian turned his head as Mr. Bartelloni pulled up on a personal golf cart. "Sorry, Anthony. Didn't mean to keep you wait—"

"No worries, Seb." Dressed in a black pin-striped suit, Anthony Bartelloni strolled over. "It's not every day you get to gaze upon a prehistoric paradise within the modern world."

After a handshake, Sebastian focused back on the baby iguanodons. "I'm more amazed at how your animals are thriving here. Those baby iggy's are adorable."

Bartelloni wore a perfect smile. "Once we deal with our business, I'll take you down to see the clutch."

As Sebastian turned around to head back to his car, he paused. *Babies lead to more dinosaurs, which lead to more babies.* "You've been a three-year client, correct?"

About to return to his cart, Anthony nodded. "Three and a half."

"Surprised I haven't asked this before." Sebastian crossed his arms as he glanced left to right, viewing the dinosaurs on either side. "As your creature population increases, do you expand their biome? Keep them onsite?"

Anthony broke into a pretentious laugh. "Twenty acres per biome at five biomes is big enough. It's comfortable."

"These *babies,* though." Sebastian pointed a finger in the iguanodon's direction. "What do you do with them when they're adults?"

With a narrowed gaze, Anthony let out a defensive chuckle. "Once they become *my* property, does it matter?"

"It matters if you're operating outside of our guidelines."

"You're poking where you shouldn't be." Bartelloni hesitated before giving into a proud grin. "SauraCorps truly has no idea of what it's sitting on."

"Enlighten me."

"You look at those creatures as assets." Anthony pulled a handkerchief out of the inner breast pocket of his suit and wiped off a section of railing before leaning on it. "These creatures are much more than that. These are *investments*. Guess you could say I even consider myself a breeder of sorts."

Sebastian stepped toward him. "We didn't give you the proper credentials for that. You're supposed to apply for a license from us. Unreported selling of—"

"Are you that naïve to think all of your clients play by the rules?" Anthony closed the gap even more as he laughed at him. "Or have you forgotten how the world works, Sharpe?"

A crack of the neck loosened Sebastian's tension a bit. "Anthony, we need to—"

"SauraCorps scope is way too small." Settling into an air of bravado, Bartelloni continued. "Did you know a stegosaurus steak tastes even better than beef? Especially the younger ones when their meat is nice and tender, with some garlic butter rested on top."

It took a moment for Sebastian to realize his mouth hung open. "You're…*eating* them?"

"I've had some, sure." Anthony remained indifferent.

"There's even more of a demand for it overseas with our Asian friends. They go crazy for the stuff." He squinted at the businessman. "If you're not convinced, I may have a couple of steaks left in my freezer."

What Sebastian had been told almost didn't compute. "You…. You *slaughter* dinosaurs."

Still casual about it all, Anthony leaned in and shook his head. "Cows, pigs, chickens. What's the difference between those and some stego-steaks, or pterodactyl thighs? A family of five can be fed with one iguanodon egg for breakfast. They make exquisite omelets, too."

"That's…." Sebastian struggled to find the right words. "How can you even—"

"Hey, don't go starting on *ethics* with me, Sharpe." Self-justifying passion poured out of Anthony's voice. "I wasn't the one who discovered a time rift and exploited it for monetary gain. You've made your profit, now I'm making mine."

Sebastian clenched his jaw. *Profit.*

Just like earlier with Felicia, Sebastian's chest stiffened as he glanced back at the cube van. Two cyclotosaurus' had been flown in overnight by priority. Male and female. "I can't believe this. This…. I have to report you."

"After all this time of sending me dinosaurs two by two like I'm a modern-day Noah?" Wearing smugness as if it were another accessory, Anthony closed the gap to a foot between them. "Plus, I've already paid half upfront for these new ones."

"Anthony, I… I can't let you do this."

"These dinosaurs are my property." Anthony folded his

arms together. *"End of discussion."*

Cellphone in hand, Sebastian's thumb hovered over the screen. "I can transfer your funds back to you—"

"And what would your board think if you return empty-handed?" Anthony fired at him without hesitation. "Especially considering I just bought some SauraCorps shares earlier this week."

Sebastian almost dropped his phone. "You…*what?*"

"No one told you? I bought shares, and worked out a deal to own part of the company." With an intense stare, Anthony didn't back down. "Which also entitles me to a twenty percent discount, correct? Or should I deal through someone else from now on?"

"That's…" Sebastian sighed, defeated. "…correct."

Pleased with how the conversation went, Mr. Bartelloni grinned as he returned to his golf cart. "Excellent. Now, let's get all paid up and unload the cyclotosaurus pair." Once he sat down behind the wheel, he gazed over at a motionless Sebastian. "The tour offer still stands."

"Uh…s-sure."

"And remember, Sharpe, it's all just business."

SIXTEEN

VIVIENNE SAT cross-legged on the beach, chewing her last morsel of a peach from a nearby tree. Thanks to Nandy wedging itself between them, she had to sit away from Kamren. Considering how their interactions had gone back on the forest trek, she'd hoped to attempt more flirting with Kam. For now, she had to settle with the current company of Emily-Ann beside her. "Should we collect some water before we carry on?"

"Don't have anything to collect it with," E-A replied, wishing she did. "Only packed this bag with the intent of a break-in, not a safari."

Kam snorted. "And yet you brought a machete with you."

E-A shrugged. "Hey, you never know when you might need one."

As time had gone on, Viv let the fullness of the situation sink in. "All this time, we thought SauraCorps was a simple chain of dinosaur museums."

"Looks can be deceiving."

Viv nodded while gazing over at Kam, who continued to make friends with the intimidating nundasuchus. "Just like how that thing looks like it could rip Kam's face off at any moment?"

E-A chuckled. "Believe it or not, I've seen behavior like Nandy's before."

With a stick in his hand, Kam wagged it in front of the inquisitive dinosaur's face. "Wanna learn how to play fetch? Huh?" He tossed the hunk of wood off to the left, which landed about fifteen feet away.

Uninterested, Nandy watched the stick fly away. Instead of chasing, it stared back at him as if he was an idiot and snorted.

"Uh...." Kam scratched the back of his head. "Guess we'll need to work on that."

After chucking her peach pit into the woods, Viv gave her full attention to E-A. "How've you seen that before? This *is* your first time through the rift, right?"

"Through the rift, yes." By now, E-A had removed her shoes and socks, letting her toes wiggle into a patch of sand. Fond memories came to the fore. "Remember when I said my dad brought a dinosaur home with him?"

"Right."

"It was a species of raptor."

Kam perked up. "Did you just say *raptor?* Like, *super-violent* velociraptor, raptor?"

E-A responded, "It's called a utahraptor."

"Oh, that's the one on display right near the front of

our museum, because it was the first raptor discovered here in Utah." Viv's eyes lit up, thrilled to have recalled the information. "If *where* we are, here in the *when,* is still Utah, that is."

Kam laughed. "That's the most wibbly-wobbly timey-wimey sentence I've ever heard."

E-A squinted at him. "Doctor Who line, right?"

"Your nerdiness continues to impress," he replied with a grin. After admiring the orange spots around Nandy's eyes, he glanced back over at E-A. "So, your dad...raptor... continue."

"Right. He'd gone against protocol and brought a juvenile utahraptor back to his home out in the country. My parents were split by then, so I would drive in and see him whenever I could." As she related the details, E-A spoke with even more enthusiasm. "One weekend, about six years ago, he told me he had a surprise waiting for me down in the basement. Dad covered my eyes once I'd made it down the creaky stairs. Thought it was an early birthday present.

"Noises I'd never heard before came closer and closer. I kept wanting to pull his hands away from my face, but he just laughed and kept telling me to wait." While retelling the memory, she couldn't hold back a fond smile. Yet, part of her also wanted to cry. The urge to rise up and continue searching for him seized her entire being. "It took a moment for me to realize something down there was... *alive.* It wasn't until something nudged me under the chest that he revealed the utahraptor right in front of me."

"And it didn't attack or try to *kill* you?" Viv soaked the

story in with wonder.

"No, but I did freak out, which made it leery of me." E-A pointed to the nundasuchus. "Kind of like how Nandy is with you, Viv. The utahraptor had spent about two weeks with my dad before I came around. Eventually, my dad had discovered something that would shake the paleontology world to its core."

By this point, both of the teenagers leaned in.

"Judging by my father's research, it's possible that nearly all dinosaurs were herbivores."

Perplexed, Viv wondered if she'd misheard. "That…goes against everything we've been taught about them."

"But there's carnivores and herbivores within the animal kingdom in our day," Kam reasoned, trying to make sense of it all. "Why would dinosaurs be any different?"

"Maybe it's more than what science can tell us," E-A mentioned in a philosophical manner. "My dad said biblical analysis wasn't out of the question. Whatever the reasoning, every dinosaur SauraCorps has encountered so far—other than the insectivores, piscivores, and scavenger bugs—has only been found to eat vegetation."

A certain odor remained on Kam's face. "Is that why Nandy has *fish* breath?"

"Exactly. Aquatic dinosaurs ate what came from their environment." Confident from what she'd experienced with the utahraptor, E-A stood up and made her way over to the nundasuchus. "Nandy never intended to hurt or eat Kam. If anything, she just wanted to see what you were and if you would maybe play."

Viv chuckled. "Good thing you don't resemble a really big fish then, Kam."

As E-A neared the young man and creature, Nandy tensed up and let out a low growl followed by a little hiss.

"Hey, now. It's *okay*." E-A lowered into a crouched position and extended her right hand forward.

Still wary of her, the nervous dinosaur remained defensive. *Hissss!*

Nandy snapped its toothy jaws at her but didn't bite.

"Okay…all right." E-A kept her voice composed. "I'm friendly."

Wondering if it would help, Kam placed one of his hands on the side of the dinosaur's neck for comfort. "Don't worry, girl."

A quick side glance at him reminded Nandy that he wasn't a threat. Maybe this other human wouldn't be either. A tad timid, Nandy bowed its head and closed its eyes to slits.

A probable sign of submission.

Without making any sudden movements, E-A placed her warm hand on the top of the cold-blooded creature's smooth snout. "There, see? That's not so bad." Her tone remained soft as she cooed, "You're all right. Did you know, Kam, that even modern-day alligators can form social bonds?"

Curious to see if she could follow E-A's lead, Viv strolled around the back of Kam at a non-threatening pace.

Though Nandy had allowed another human being to touch her, it kept an eye on the young woman.

E-A let her hand remain on the dinosaur's scales. "Go slow, Viv."

"H-hey, Nandy." Nervous, Viv crouched all slow and careful. "It's okay, I'm not gonna hurt you." *Please, don't bite my hand off.* Her hand trembled slightly as she reached out. "Don't be afraid." *Crap, they can probably sense fear.* Shaky fingers made it an inch away from the nundasuchus' blueish armored top plate. "Can I be your frie—"

Growl! Snap!

Tumbling backward, she yanked her hand away just in time and kicked up sand. "*Stupid...freaking...lizard!*" As she scrambled back to her feet, she didn't take her eyes off Nandy in case it decided to attack. "Great, apparently I'm unlovable."

Surprised by Nandy's actions, Kam stood up and stepped over to his friend. "Viv, don't worry about it, okay?" To comfort her further, he placed his hands on her arms and gave them a gentle squeeze. "Once we're done here, I'm sure Nandy will run off to its pack, or something."

Still unimpressed with how the dinosaur reacted to her effort at being kind, Viv looked up at him past her furrowed brow. "Or I could give it a little send-off."

"Huh?"

"With a *swift kick.*"

"Now, now, Lady Lancaster."

SEVENTEEN

"AT LEAST these babies look healthy." After learning about all the shady business his client had been up to, Sebastian held a handful of berries.

Juvenile iguanodons cocked their heads side to side as they neared the humans. Inquisitive green eyes checked over the bunch of fruit.

One out of the clutch of three worked up the courage to step forward.

Sebastian smiled as the playful iguanodon honked. It seemed to grin at him before scooping a mouthful out of his hand. He chortled at how it had a cute, black stubby beak for lips. "Oh, you're a greedy little guy."

"These have been a fairly frisky bunch." Bartelloni stood about five feet away, admiring his animals. "They've already been purchased by customers of my own, too."

The size of a large dog, another dark green iguanodon with racing stripes of golden yellow came forward for some food.

Sebastian opened his mouth. *No, better not say anything.* He scratched an umber brown spot on the dinosaur's crown. "Do you spend much time with the babies? Are they handled at all so they get used to humans?"

A callous Anthony crossed his arms. "I don't get overly attached to commodities."

The third iguanodon juvenile swallowed down the berry snack and stuck around to lick the juice from Sebastian's hands.

Sheer joy warred against the disgust which had been cooking from deep within Sebastian. *Commodities? These precious animals? Guess I've been viewing them the same way, but still....* It took everything in him to focus on the positive happening right in front of him. *Keep your cool, Seb.*

Bartelloni continued. "Especially when parts of them may end up on your plate."

"Okay, you're a frigging sicko."

"Excuse me, Sharpe?"

Sebastian's hands balled into fists. "How you're treating these animals, they don't deserve it." His sudden outburst sent the baby dinosaurs galloping back to their parents. "Selling them for pets is one thing. And sure, I can overlook the whole unlicensed breeding part of it all." A burning sensation surged through his core and swirled around inside of his chest. "But *eating* them? *Actually* listing dinosaur by-products on a menu as...as...a *delicacy?*"

"What are you saying, Sebastian?"

"I'm saying..." He steadied a tremor in his throat. "...I

can't be an intermediary to this."

Anthony brushed his hands down his suit jacket. "Are you thinking straight?"

"I'm not the one who needs to be asked that question."

"Sharpe, come on."

Completely done with being there, Sebastian marched back toward the sliding entry door for the cube van. "The cyclotosaurus pair are yours now. This is our last meeting."

"Not even going to shake my hand goodbye?"

"Have a nice life."

"Too bad, Sharpe." Anthony shook his head and sighed. "They thought you were going soft on them. Sounds like they were right."

Sebastian halted mid-step. Topsy-turvy alarm bells and sirens created chaos in his mind. "What did you just say?"

Like a fishing line, Anthony arched an eyebrow as Sebastian turned around. "A businessman with a heart. Maybe...*half* a heart?" He snorted in disbelief. "Thought your breed was going extinct."

"Rewind." Sebastian narrowed his gaze. One thing had to be set straight. "Who are the 'they' you referred to?"

A few steps brought Bartelloni within a couple feet away from him as he snickered. "They? Who else would I be referring to?"

Thip!

"You...." Every muscle in Sebastian's body weakened from his neck down to his feet. His unsteady hand reached behind his neck, grasping at a small needle stuck in his skin. It dawned on him.

A tranquilizer.

Damn.

Voices resonated all around.

His ears perked up as his mind fought against the darkness of sedation.

Intermittent flashes of bright light washed over him.

Blackness overtook him.

Someone tugged at his arm.

Who....? Get...off...me.

Two unidentifiable beings grasped both arms.

He barely had the strength to fight back as he slipped into unconsciousness once more.

Electric hums and crackles assaulted his ears, waking him up again.

What's happening to me? "Let go of—"

A masculine voice came from behind. "He's coming to."

"We're still doing this," another responded from the side.

Limp and helpless, Sebastian recognized the feminine voice. "Fe...*Felicia?* That you?"

Weightlessness.

The hands on his arms had released.

Blurred blue and white light whooshed by Sebastian's face. His limbs sprang to life just before he landed on hard ground surrounded by grass, leaves, and trees. Dirt rubbed into the skin of his left cheek, making him wince. *No.*

Rich, clean oxygen filled his lungs after the wind had

been knocked out of them. To push himself back up, his right hand pressed down on a fern sprout. *No.*

Patches of dirt had soiled his suit pants. *What's happening—*

The last bit of sedative wore off.

Realization sunk in as Sebastian turned around and gazed forward.

The Rift stood in front of him.

On the other side—the future side—Felicia Voorhees stared back.

"Felicia." There had been times when Sebastian had crossed the rift willingly. As for right now, dread and bewilderment collided together inside of him. "Why am I… Can't we discuss this?"

"Judging by our chat this morning and how you handled Bartelloni, there will be no discussion." She stood there motionless, reserved. Her distant eyes made it clear that all ties were being severed in this moment. "Your judgment on issues continues to falter. Too many slips down the slope, Sebastian."

"Are you honest to God *kidding* me right now?" At a loss of how to compute and react, his entire face tensed into a desperate glare. "Thanks for telling me about Anthony buying up shares—my own client—by the way. How can you not even care about what he's doing with his dinosaurs?"

"Maybe you care a little too much," she rebutted, still nonchalant as she stepped closer to the anomaly's frame of time-space energy. "SauraCorps has and always will be *a business*. You've lost sight of that."

His tongue pressed against the inside of his bottom teeth. All moisture had nearly disappeared from his mouth. "This... This is insane."

On his side—the past side—of the rift, an unnerving screech echoed through the trees.

In reflex, Sebastian's feet started for the rift. "Seriously, Felicia, let me—"

"Not another step."

Armed guards came to her sides, rifles pointed at him and ready to protect.

Sebastian backtracked. "Okay, all right, just.... What will everyone else on the board think when they notice I haven't shown up in a while?"

Mr. Tómasson stepped into view from the left.

From the right, Mr. Xing also joined the group.

Dumbfounded, Sebastian forgot to blink. "Kristjan? Yin? Guys, can't we...."

The rest of the board members congregated together in the cave-like room underneath the SauraCorps building. Some wore looks of disappointment. Others displayed distant pride along with displeasure.

Those faces of whom Sebastian had worked the closest with for a few years seemed like strangers to him now. It took him a couple tries to swallow down a hard, uncomfortable lump in his dry throat. "This is it, then." A blaze of resentment ate him up as he pointed at his former workmates. "Are you all happy with yourselves? *Huh?*" In his enraged state, a single tear rolled down from his right eye. "Sitting in your *overpriced* cars and live in houses *full* of empty *things* as you all lose your sense of *humanity?"* His voice grew louder as he continued, suddenly aware of his hypocrisy concerning his past thoughts and actions. "You disreputable traitors are making a huge mistake."

"We are correcting the mistake, Mr. Sharpe," Xing countered, his voice uncaring. "And we are cutting it off at the head."

"Xing, you piece of—"

"Goodbye, Mr. Sharpe." Mr. Xing walked out of sight.

The rest of the board followed suit.

Sebastian's breathing sped up. "No, please. Tómasson? *Miller?* Carey?" *They're shells. They're nothing but shells of what they used to be.*

As the rest exited the caged wall section of the underground room, only one member remained by the rift.

Felicia closed her eyes for a few seconds.

"Please, *Felicia.*" Sebastian's voice tremored the worst it ever had as tears streamed down his cheeks. "*Aiden* and *Olivia.* Let me leave m-my *kids* a voicemail, or-or-or... *something.*"

"I'm..." A flash of a wince showed up on her face before she turned rigid once more. "...sorry. I'll take care of it."

"And T-Trudy?" Sebastian's voice cracked when he mentioned the troodon which would be waiting for him at home. "There's dragonflies in the fridge for her."

Felicia had already started for the large metal door when she turned her head, but couldn't look at him. "She'll be transferred to Bartelloni's care."

Hearing the Italian's name sparked more rage inside of

Sharpe. "That *disgusting* excuse of a man? How *dare* you."

As Felicia stepped through the doorway back to the SauraCorps building, her voice carried back to him. "Take care of yourself, Sebastian."

EIGHTEEN

BACK ON track to finding Emily-Ann's father, the trio of humans followed along the bank of a rushing river. They'd left Nandy behind at the lake. Of course, they wondered what other ancient creatures they might encounter on their trek.

The beauty of the area made Kamren think of a photo opportunity. After pulling the cellphone from his pant pocket, he stared at the black screen. "Crap. My phone got wet when Nandy pulled me in." Pushing the power button did nothing. "Hey, Em, got a jar of rice in that duffle bag?"

E-A called back, "Was going to save it for making sushi later."

"Don't play with my emotions like that."

Vivienne checked her phone. "I've still got a fair bit of battery."

"Want to take a picture of us here?" Kam smiled at her. "I'm still a little wet, but this spot is gorgeous. Then we'll post it on the 'Gram when we get back."

"Sure, why not." More than happy to be in a picture with him, she tried to reserve displaying it. "You've got the arm for the shots." She shivered as their fingers brushed against each other's as he took the phone. Pink immediately colored her cheeks.

After everything that had happened so far in the day, a moment to slow down had sounded like a good idea.

Without warning, Kam's arm cradled her back. "Get in here, Princess."

Like a race car roaring to life, Viv's heartbeat sped up as she got pulled in closer to his body. *Oh gosh, he's really warm right now. Should I…wrap my arms around him?* She acted on her thoughts and cleared her throat to cut off her giggle. *Okay, play it cool.*

Kam caught himself looking down at her too much as he extended his arm with her phone in hand. *This will make a cute shot. Cute? Should I say that?* He put on a smile and hovered his finger over the touchscreen button. *No, don't say it. Just take the pic, idiot.* "Ready?"

As she smirked, she gazed up at him with a wanting stare and a half-bitten bottom lip. "Ready when you are, hon."

Snap.

The picture saved itself to the cellphone.

"Wait." Viv's blood pumped in double-time as she realized the pining face she'd been making. "Can I see the pic first?"

"Can we look at it together?"

She reached out for her phone. "Please, Kam, it's *my* phone."

"And did you…." He couldn't keep a smirk at bay. "Did you just call me *hon?*"

Viv swung a hand for her phone again and missed. "I've called you 'hon' before."

Keeping it out of her reach, Kam switched the mode on her phone from 'camera' to 'album'. "True, but it's more in *how* you said it." He brought the screen closer to his face.

Defeated, she stopped fighting for it.

The yearning on her face in the picture stirred something within him. "Viv, I've…." *Whoa. I've never seen her look at me like that before.* It shocked him like a barrage of lightning, yet warmed him as if bathing in lava.

Mortified by him discovering her expression, she backed away a bit. "You've…what?" Unable to lock eyes with him, she glanced left and right while picking at one of her thumbs. She considered running away, but there was nowhere to go. "It's not what you think, Kamren."

Mouth open, he mulled over what his response should be. *Don't want to embarrass her further. Wonder what she'll say.* He handed over the phone. "Viv, you know you can talk to me about anything, right?"

For her, thoughts and emotions swirled around in her head like newspapers stuck in a tornado. *I can't lie to him.* None of what she felt toward him were lies, anyway. "You really want to know?"

Kam read from her scratching the insides of her wrists just how uncomfortable she'd become. It hadn't occurred to him until now that he'd considered it an adorable tell. "Only if you truly want to say, Vivienne."

His soothing voice uttering her name warmed her heart as if he'd just wrapped her up in a cozy blanket. Eyes closed, she grimaced at the ground. "Before we knew Nandy the ninja dachshund—"

"Nundasuchus."

"Whatever. Anyway, before we knew she wasn't a carnivore and you got pulled under, I…." Her voice almost threatened to leave her. "I thought I'd *lost* you."

Her words blasted him in the chest. True, he'd seen his short life flash before his eyes at the time. Never once did he consider what she'd been going through in that alarming moment. It made more sense now considering the picture he'd just taken of them together. "Sorry. I didn't mean to be a jerk about the pic."

"You're not a jerk." Finally looking back up, she let her teal eyes connect with his. "It's just…." Everything started to tingle in her body as he kept his gaze locked into hers. A quiet gasp of air hitched in her lungs before she continued. Her hands wanted to give in to their own minds to reach up to the sides of his face and pull his lips to hers. "It all happened so fast, between you getting yanked under, Nandy coming out of nowhere on the beach, then you getting distracted by that dinosau—"

"What are you getting at?" He placed a gentle hand on her left arm in the hopes of calming her down.

The simple touch almost made her go up on her tiptoes. *Just pull me in.* "As soon as you disappeared into the water, my knees almost gave out."

"Oh, Viv." Kam didn't wait another second to slip his arms

around his best friend. The cracks in her voice broke his heart. He'd never had any doubts that she cared about him.

The recent close call intensified those emotions.

Enwrapped in his toned arms, Viv soaked it all in. Including some of the water that hadn't dried from his clothes yet. "I never really got a chance to hug you once I knew you were safe."

Having her so close, he welcomed the rush of affection in all its being between them. "Hopefully now makes up for that."

She nuzzled her face into his taut, comfy chest. "More than you know." Lost in his solid yet tender embrace, she wished for time to freeze. For all the years she'd been waiting to have a somewhat romantic moment with him, she hoped that this would be the beginning.

Every other time they'd hugged, it had been more like buddies. Simple and nothing more.

This time, Kam found himself getting more energized than expected. For a moment, he thought he could sense the pounding of her heart against his torso. In response, the rhythm of his own heart sped up to match hers.

Enjoying every bit of it, Viv wondered what was going through his mind. *Hope this isn't getting weird for him.* He hadn't said anything negative about it. *We have been hugging for a bit now. How long is too long?*

Kam gazed off into the distance, then pursed his lips in worry. "Um…where'd E-A go?"

Viv had been too into the embrace to truly comprehend his concern. "Hmm?"

"E-A, she's gone." He stepped away from her as blood and adrenaline surged through him due to distress. "I don't see her anywhere."

"Did she fall in the river?" Viv joined him in fretting over the new friend they'd made. "We would've heard a splash, though, right?"

"E-A!" He cupped his hands on the sides of his mouth. "Emily!"

An unnerving thought overcame Viv. "Hope she didn't come across the first carnivorous dinosaur."

Newfound bravery helped Kam to start marching along the river. "*Eeeemilyyyy!*"

"Kamren, should you be yelling that loud?" Though a measure of panic came over Viv, she stayed close to him. "What if whatever found her *finds us?*"

"Viv, she's risked her life for us." He gave her a firm stare. "We owe it to——"

"Stop yelling, guys." E-A's voice carried out to them. "Sorry."

Viv turned her gaze to the right. "Is she…in the forest?"

Unable to pinpoint E-A's position, Kam started for the trees. "Em? What are you doing in there?"

"*Don't* come looking for me," E-A called out.

Viv and Kam exchanged confused glances.

"*Seriously.*"

Nervous and perplexed, Viv called back, "Is everything okay?"

In innocence, Kam wanted answers. "What's the matter——"

"Listen." E-A's serious tone came from behind a wide tree. "We're trapped in a time where *bathrooms* haven't been invented yet and I didn't want to interrupt your little moment. All right?"

"Ooookay then. Loud and clear," Viv yelled back, fully understanding the human body's needs. *Thank you for not ruining the moment.*

Kam stayed put. "Do you…uh…need some leaves or anything?"

"Ewww!" Viv shoved his shoulder. "Dude, so gross."

"Nah, I think I'm good." E-A finally emerged from behind the wide tree trunk. "And just a heads up, I think our digestive system doesn't like prehistoric dragonfly meat very much."

A snort-laugh erupted from Kam. "Noted."

Flexing her fingers in disgust, Viv added, "Another reason for me to hate bugs."

NINETEEN

"SO, DO you have any idea of what we're heading toward?" Kamren called up to their leading lady. Other than wondering about the journey, he scanned the trees on either side of the river for other sources of food. "Surprised we haven't come across any other fruits, like bananas or something. Haven't seen any clues for vegetables either."

A moment of hesitation preceded Emily-Ann's answer. "There's some notes. Not sure how long it will take to get there."

As Vivienne traversed among the vibrant, ancient world, her mind wandered in another. The embrace she'd shared with Kamren lingered on her mind. *That was the best hug we've ever had. Wonder if he's thinking about it too.*

"Should totally put on some tunes."

Oblivious to what had been said, Viv remained lost in her thoughts.

"Your phone still works, right, Viv?"

A little rock got kicked to the side as she strolled along.

Kam spoke louder. "Pangea to Vivienne, come in, *Vivienne.*"

"Huh? W-what?" A sudden fluster came over her. "Sorry, um—"

"Where'd you go off to?" His shoulder gave hers a slight nudge. "Back to your daydreams again?"

Butterflies in her stomach emerged from her mouth as anxious giggles first. "Something like that. And it's not like you don't get lost in your head when you're writing your stories." Even so, she'd always loved seeing him in the creative zone. The way his mind worked fascinated her.

"Touché."

"What were you saying about my phone?"

"You should put some music on for the walk." Kamren patted his dried pant pocket. "Seeing as my phone is still waterlogged."

"That's why you always go with a waterproof cell like mine," she remarked with a cheeky smile. "You never know."

"Riiiight, because you never know when you'll get pulled into a lake by a playful dinosaur." Kam caught a glimpse of her little grin, which made him follow suit.

"Exactly."

"It's weird not checking my phone as often, considering there's no service in this place."

Viv poked his arm. "In this *time.*"

Up ahead, E-A sighed with relief. "I'm loving that fact."

As Vivienne put on a playlist of indie music, she started it off with *Colors* by *Honest Men.* One of the songs she'd put on repeat at home while thinking about Kamren. *Let's see if he picks up on this upbeat* love *song.* "Why do you say that, E-A?"

Slowing down to be closer to the teens, E-A explained further. "To be honest, I'd rather take this time over our own to some degree. No technology, no phones, no being inundated with reports of politicians with empty promises and corrupt companies that sponsor illness research programs when *they're* the *cause* of the illness in the first place."

Kam chuckled as he bent down to pick up some small stones. "You don't harbor any resentment at all, do you?"

"The time we're from is riddled with stress."

Viv arched an eyebrow. "Can I just say, being here does stress me out a fair bit. That's not just because of the giant creepy crawlies."

Emily-Ann sensed the uneasiness in the young girl's voice and turned around. "Don't lose the bravery you had earlier, Vivienne. Bravery and determination go hand in hand." For added support, she rubbed the teen's back. "Don't take this as an empty promise, but we *need* something to hope for. I'll do everything I can to get you back to your families."

"The further we get…" Kam skipped a stone into the river. "…from the rift we came through…" Another stone made it five skips. "…how do you expect us to even have a smidge of a plan to get back?"

The optimistic moment weakened due to his attitude.

No one knew how to even begin planning an attempt to return to their own time.

Beyond the rift itself, SauraCorps guards would be armed

and ready. As well, the reinforced, cage-like metal barrier separated them from the prehistoric time and theirs. The odds didn't look great by any means.

"And I just brought the party down, sorry," Kam continued, a level of shame in his words. "Reality and hope rarely work together well, is all I'm saying."

Viv crossed her arms as E-A returned to the trek.

"That didn't help either, did it?" After a deep sigh, Kam pulled his arm back to whip another pebble into the river. As he followed through with the toss, he added, "Just forget what I—"

A noise like incredible bass in a theater pierced them to the bone.

Trees swayed as their leaves jittered to life.

The ground vibrated beneath their feet.

E-A turned her attention to the forest. *Stampede?*

Tremors worked their way up Vivienne's body. "Kamren, what's going on?"

Just as distressed as her, he glanced all around. "Earthquake?"

CRRRRACK-ACK-ACK! ZAP! CRACKLE! SNAP!

Everyone looked to the river.

Blueish electric energy burst to life from thin air, forming a giant circle in the middle of the waterway. A third of it swirled and fizzled under the river's surface.

"Oh my God." Vivienne's heart jumped at the possibility of a way home.

Jogging back to the teenagers, E-A's mouth hung open. "Another rift?"

From their vantage point, only the dinosaur world could be seen through the rift window.

"Come on!" Kam pulled his friend by the arm. "Maybe we can see where the other side leads."

As much as the time-space quake of sorts had shaken them, their legs became flooded with adrenaline as they backtracked.

"Should we swim for it?" As the words came out of Viv's mouth, her urge to do so brought her closer to the riverbank's edge.

A FEW MINUTES EARLIER – PRESENT DAY

"I gotta head inside, this stupid machine won't take my credit card." Evan Eckhardt left the white SUV and headed for the gas station building. Only one thought plagued his mind as he scratched an anxious itch under his ash-brown hair.

Kamren hadn't returned home the previous night.

They had assumed he'd slept over at the Lancaster's. Failed text messages and phone calls later, Evan had called Andrew Lancaster to find out Vivienne hadn't shown up either.

Something uncharacteristic of the both of them.

By now, the police force and respective parents searched every nook and cranny of the town. Phone calls had been made to the Kloss family concerning the pool party, only to be told their kids had never arrived.

Halfway to the building, Evan pulled his buzzing

smartphone out of his windbreaker jacket's inner pocket. From the moment Evan had gone into search mode, every notification from his phone caused his anticipation to skyrocket. "Anything yet, Andy?"

"It's Denise, Andrew's driving." Everything considered, her voice managed to stay strong. "We got a call from Detective Fischer. Kam's truck has been found."

Evan almost dropped his cellphone as the news sunk in. "Text me the location. Gotta pay for my gas first." He ended the call as he rushed through the door.

The lady at the till smiled. "Hey, Evan, we heard about Kam and Viv—"

"Pump number six, Heather," he spit out as he almost threw his credit card at her. "Sorry, I-I-I'm in a rush." He fidgeted with his hands. "They found Kam's truck."

"Oh my, I hope those kids are okay."

"Me too."

Heather pulled up his pump information. "Forty-four thirty-seven."

"Credit, please. Can I tap?"

She slid the terminal toward him.

Evan's card touched the screen.

Beeeep!

CRRRRACK-ACK-ACK! ZAP! CRACKLE! SNAP!

The inside of the building lit up.

Lightning force coursed in a half-circle. The bottom tore up some of the tile floor as cool water spilled into the snack stands and gushed toward the till area.

Outside, those who'd been filling up their vehicles gazed

in bewilderment over the arch of electricity ripping a hole in the gas station's roof.

Back on the dinosaur side of the rift, the anxious gang stood on the riverbank and gazed through it.

Vivienne's eyes grew big. "That's…our local gas station."

As water gushed through the opening, Kamren ducked to spy under the ceiling. A familiar face got overtaken by the diverted river. "Dad? I think *my dad's* in there!"

Inside the station, the force of the liquid began pushing past the front doors and into the lot. Some who'd made their way over to the building backed away from the out-of-place stream in confusion.

Pinned against the customer side of the till, Evan struggled to fight back against the current. "What the heck?"

Eager to act, Viv grabbed Kam's arm. "Let's jump!"

"Hold on, let's assess the options." Emily-Ann headed back into the forest to search tree limbs. If they were going to attempt something, she wanted to be ready for anything. "The river's running fast, help me look for some vines to tie around our—"

Splash!

Something hit Kamren's shoe as he stopped watching E-A and turned. "Hey, Vi—"

Gone.

Her cellphone sat beside his foot.

Fear zapped him to his core. *"Vivieeeenne!"*

Soaked blonde hair broke through the water's surface as Viv swam for the space-time anomaly. Water entered her mouth, but she coughed it out while speeding up her breaststrokes and kicks. *I need to get back*, she repeated to herself. *We need to get back.*

Still standing on the bank, Kam nearly screamed, "Viv, what are you doing?"

Ten feet out from the rift, Viv swirled her gaze back to her friends. "Come *on,* Kam! We can all make it!"

E-A froze. The rift showed them a way home. On the other hand, she hadn't even found her father yet. If he was even still alive.

"She's gonna make it." Kam couldn't take his eyes off her.

Six feet soon remained between Viv and her goal.

For a second in present day, Evan Eckhardt's head popped above and recognized the face on the past's side before slipping under again. *"Vivienne?"*

A level of excitement entered E-A's eyes. "Come on, Viv!"

Three feet.

Fingers outstretched, Viv gasped for air.

Z-Z-ZAP! ZZZZEEEEUUUU-POP!

Before the tips of her nails could even pass through, the rift disappeared into nothing.

Particles of water heated up by the time-space gateway misted into the air.

"No!" She flailed her arms. "No, it can't—"

Back on course, the rushing river shot her forward like a cannonball.

"Oh crap." Kam pushed past E-A. "Help me save her!"

Among the swirling water, Viv fought hard to try and make it back to the bank. She'd already expended much of her strength trying to exit the prehistoric pain of a time.

Up ahead, Kam spied some vines draping down from a tree. He snagged one of the hanging, rope-resembling plants and dove into the river.

"Ka—" Viv accidentally swallowed some water.

Something nudged against her legs.

A log? She stiffened. *Please be a log.*

Determined to reach her, Kam made every swim stroke count.

Pulled under for a moment, Viv caught sight of a scaley tail slip past her face. *Oh God. This is how I die.* Helpless, she continued down the river's current. *I haven't even kissed him yet.*

"Viv!" Kam reached for her. "Grab…my hand!"

Her fingers clasped around his wrist. "Ka-Kamren."

"I got you," he assured with confidence. "Just hang on."

Moisture between their skin added to the dilemma.

Viv's hand slipped an inch, causing her to yelp in dismay. "There's…s-s-something in the water. It *touched* me."

"I'm gonna get you out of here." As the words came out of his mouth, a surge of courage made him grip her hand and the vine tighter.

A force yanked on the cuff of her left pant leg.

After screaming, Viv did all she could to lock eyes with her best friend. "Kam, something's got my leg. *Something's got my leg!*"

With a strong heave, he managed to throw his hand a

few inches up the vine. "Keep your eyes on me, Viv. We're gonna make it."

Another yank made him slip back to where he was before. *Snap!*

Emily-Ann shot a hand out as the last few feet of the broken vine whipped past her face. "Oh no you don't." Digging her heels into the ground, she engaged every muscle in her body. Her rib injury from earlier made her howl in agony.

When the slackened vine became taut once more, the shudder didn't help Kam's grip. Less than a foot of vine sloshed in the water past his hand.

Another yank.

The creature below hadn't given up.

Only a few inches remained.

On the riverbank, E-A wrestled with the vine to pull them in. Though she'd injured her hands earlier, she fought to keep her pain at bay.

"Kamren…I can't—" Viv coughed out another mouthful of river water as her fingers lost their strength. "I can't hold—"

"You can do it, Viv!" he called back with a fire of determination in his eyes. "I'll *never* let go of you."

Their fingertips interlocked into each other's.

Neither of them wanted to believe that they would lose each other. They'd only just begun getting acquainted with their true feelings toward each other.

She couldn't hold her grasp any longer.

With two fingers left, Kam yelled, "Noooo!"

As every ounce of her strength became depleted, Vivienne called out to him, "Ka-Kamren…I love—"

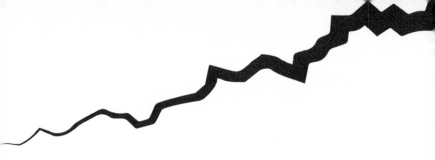

TWENTY

EMILY-ANN SUCKED in a sharp breath due to her bruised rib as she hauled Kamren back up to solid ground. "Hey, you okay?"

On his hands and knees, he cleared his throat. "No."

"Are you hurt?"

"No."

His short answers didn't need any further explanation.

"Listen, Kam," E-A began, hoping to sound as reassuring as possible. "It's not your—"

"She…slipped *right through* my fingers." Staring at the ground, Kam became numb to his surroundings. Not even a tingle flowed through him. An emptiness threatened to consume his being. "She's…*gone.*"

"We don't know that for sure yet." With all things considered, E-A placed a hand on the back of the boy she didn't quite gel with.

Once his breathing returned to normal, Kam gazed up at

her. "Where does this river lead?"

Worry in her eyes, she glanced away. "Viv could've ended up downstream. If we keep moving—"

"Emily." An ache found a home in his voice. "Don't think I haven't noticed you skirting the question." Back to standing, he stared at her. No injury had come to him. At the same time, no Vivienne by his side resembled having lost a limb—an analogy he'd never related to before. E-A's harboring of information had been likened to an insult to injury. "From what I understand, rushing water usually means something bad. Am I wrong in this case?"

With closed eyes, E-A flared her nostrils. "It leads to a waterfall."

"Frig sakes." A wave of nausea made him want to scratch at his insides. Picturing a helpless and frightened Viv going over the edge assaulted him. "So, you're saying I may have just let her fall to her *death?*"

"She might have washed up further down before even reaching that point," E-A hypothesized, trying to veer things to a hopeful point of view. "We'll keep our eyes open as we keep going."

Like a statue, he stood there. The moment she slipped away from him replayed slow and excruciating in his mind.

The terror in her eyes.

Her face filled with dread.

More than anything, the last two words echoed in his head. *I love—*

"Kamren."

Fingers snapped in front of his face.

"You have to get with me here, Kam." Ready to continue on, E-A brought her eyes to his level. She gave his right shoulder a firm squeeze. "She's your best friend and means something to you, I get that."

Unable to verbalize, he simply nodded his head.

"Every second spent sitting here is time wasted trying to find her." After releasing his soaked shoulder, she left her hand out in front of him, open and ready to be taken. "Are you with me?"

Two deep breaths later, Kam looked up at her. "Let's go save my girl from this dinosaur world." When his hand clasped into hers, the comradery invigorated him.

"Knew you had it in you."

"You're a good motivational speaker."

E-A shook out her aching hands as they strolled at a faster pace. "This place is going to be the death of my hands."

Kam smirked as a detail came back to his mind, making him backtrack. "Or, you know, death in general."

"You could use some work on the motivational stuff." Sliding her arms back through the straps of her bag, E-A gave him an odd stare. "Where are you going?"

About thirty feet away, Kamren bent down to pick something up. "Viv left her cell behind. When we find her, I'm sure she'll want it back."

E-A grinned at the sign of positivity. "That's more like it."

TWENTY-ONE

DRESS SHOES *are the worst for this.*

Already past the grassland, Sebastian Sharpe entered the cover of forest. Some of the terrain he'd recognized from the few trips he'd taken to this time.

Other parts appeared exotic and mysterious.

Thankfully, every dinosaur SauraCorps had encountered so far posed no predatorial threats. Even those assumed to be carnivores. They simply roamed the land like the wild herbivores of present day.

Don't bother them and they won't bother you.

Always checking his surroundings, he kept himself alert for the only potential threat.

Bugs.

Sebastian had never encountered them before.

For those who'd trekked into the primeval time period, some returned injured. Some came back on stretchers. Others didn't return at all.

Once he'd made an awkward hurdle over a fallen tree, he took a moment to catch his breath. Dirtying up his favorite suit didn't worry him. Neither did the fact he was now out of his business element.

Two things waged war in his head for primary concern.

The first left him bruised and battered on the inside. *How could they do this to me?* Once he'd stretched his legs out in front of him, he pulled them in close to his chest, wrapping his arms around the knees. *Seven years. Seven whole years of loyalty and they ship me out without a second thought.*

More than that, another thought stabbed him in his heart. *I might never get to see Aiden or Olivia again.*

Sebastian's forehead rested on his knees. Overwhelmed by everything piling up in his brain, the turmoil of it all forced tears past his clenched eyelids.

Light taps skittered onto his left elbow.

Instead of jumping and causing a stir, he raised his head.

A pair of coffee-bean-sized insects—likened to a cockroach and praying mantis hybrid—cleaned themselves with their forearms.

Manipulator modificaputis. Sebastian remained still. *Prehistoric cockroach. Scavengers.*

One of the first expeditions into the dinosaur time came back to him. Two of the men had taken watch around the perimeter of their camp. The next morning, the rest of the team had woken up and found their protectors on their backs.

Covered in the little cockroaches.

Pictures had been taken and sent back. The disgusting images flashed in his mind.

Then he lifted his head even higher. *There must be more than two.*

On either side of him, more of the roaches scurried out from under the log, joining the mass of their brethren which surrounded him.

His eyes went back to the two on his arm.

They stopped cleaning, angling their little brown heads with bulbous eyes and fidgety mandibles to study him.

"Crap."

Smack! Slap! Thwap!

As he sprang up from his position, Sebastian did everything he could to knock the insects off and check himself over. Every time he placed a foot back down on the ground, he heard cracks as he stepped on some and had others latch onto his pant leg.

"Get off me, *damn bugs!*"

He kicked his right foot back and forth, shaking off a few.

Quick stomps of his dress shoes on the ground knocked some out of the inner pant legs.

A frustrated roar emptied his lungs as he balled his hands into fists.

The cockroaches scattered.

"That's right. Get *lost*, little freaks."

When the last roach returned to the nest under the log, Sebastian straightened his suit. On turning around, he discovered the true reason why the insects had taken cover.

Bigger bugs.

Pincers snapped as tails arched with stingers.

Scorpions.

Three jet-black scorpions—the size of small dogs—sat a few feet out, twitching their hairy walking legs.

Ready to attack.

Pulmonoscorpious, Sebastian growled on the inside as he tensed up. *The place where the bugs try to squash you.*

TWENTY-TWO

BURNT TO a crisp.

Kamren's truck had been found smashed into a wide tree which had caused a fire to destroy everything.

Cassie Eckhardt flew out from the passenger door of their white SUV as soon as they'd parked. She pulled her bronze-brown hair into a ponytail as she hurried over to Denise Lancaster, who had been sobbing for a while.

One of the few police officers at the scene finished tying off a border of caution tape.

Andrew Lancaster hugged Evan as everyone congregated on the safe side of the gruesome scene. Dampness from his friends' shirt soaked into his own. "Did you take a dip in your pool before you came here?"

Evan shook his head as he glanced around. "Story for later. Probably won't believe me either."

"Add it on to this, then," Andrew stated with a mix of defeat and grief. Since he'd arrived, a twitch had taken over a corner of his mouth. "It doesn't look good, Ev."

After coming out of the hug, Evan couldn't tear his eyes away from the scorched vehicle. Even after what he'd already seen, many questions bombarded his mind as he subconsciously scratched the side of his face. "Are they saying it was an accident?"

"It's looking like it." Andrew ran a stressed hand through his caramel hair. "Ambulance is coming to take the… the, um…."

Denise continued to cry behind them. All day, she'd been twisting her blonde, shoulder-length hair between her fingers. Now, part of her wanted to rip it all out of her head to feel a different kind of pain. Any pain other than the loss of their daughter.

Trying to console her friend, Cassie turned her head to ask, "They didn't get out?"

"No." Andrew fought to stay strong as he sauntered back to the wives. "They…didn't."

"Does Arty know yet?"

For a moment, Denise managed to calm her shallow breathing. "He's… My sister is with him. We haven't… told them."

Evan marched over to the police chief. The incident at the gas station had been running through his mind. *What was that…swirling thing?* More importantly, *What was* Vivienne *doing on the other side of it? That was definitely her.*

"Mr. Eckhardt, I'm sorry for your loss." The chief shook hands with him. "It's never easy losing a child. Especially in this fashion."

"Thank you, Chief Watson." Arms crossed, Evan studied everything involved. From his vantage point, he could make out two charred, unidentifiable bodies. All things considered, something didn't seem right. "Mind if I ask who found them?"

Chief Watson pointed off to the right. "That lady over there is finishing up giving her statement to Detective Fischer. Says she came through on her way to work—that dinosaur museum just down the road there—when she saw roaring flames and called it in."

"Did you question her at all?" Evan asked with noticeable suspicion.

The dark-haired woman marched away from the detective, opened the door to her Porsche, and drove on to work.

"We chatted when I arrived here. Guess she's on her way now." The chief examined the eyes of the father in front of him.

"Am I allowed to talk to her?"

After glancing over at the heartbreaking accident, Watson looked back at the tense Mr. Eckhardt. "Technically, nothing's stopping you, if you need some closure."

Evan turned around to head back to his SUV. "Think I might do that."

Chief Watson raised his voice to grab Evan's attention. "Mr. Eckhardt, an old book once said: There's no word for a parent that's lost a child. That's how awful the loss is."

"What are you saying, Chief?"

"I'm saying, don't let the emotion of all of this get out of hand."

Evan took a moment to reflect, then nodded. "I'll keep that in mind."

On returning to the other parents, he grabbed Andrew's forearm. "Come with me."

"What?" Surprised by his friend's vague demand, he yanked his arm out of the grasp. "We just discovered that *our kids*...." Unable to keep himself stable, Andrew's voice shook as he brought his face closer to Evan's. "Our kids have just *died* in a horrifying crash..."

"Andy."

"...two kids who've never once given us a day of grief..."

"Andrew, listen to me."

"...and now they're dea—"

"No, *they're not.*" Barely any doubt resided in Evan's intense eyes. "I mean, I think... As crazy as this is going to sound, I think they're still alive." Evan had stepped even closer and lowered his voice so only his friend could hear. "After what I saw earlier, *Vivienne could still be alive.*"

Words failed to form in Andrew's mouth. He glanced back and forth between Evan and the truck. Only confused mutterings escaped his lips until he could form a proper sentence. "Are you...*seriously* wrong in the head right now, Ev?"

For added emphasis, Evan pointed at his chest. "In some strange way, I've never been more serious in my life. We need to get in my car now."

Chief Watson noticed the two men getting animated. "Everything all right over there?"

"Sorry, Chief." Evan pretended to compose himself with

a wave of his hand. "We're all good here."

"*Are* you good?" Flabbergasted by it all, Andrew managed to reduce his volume. "Are you *actually* good here?"

"Do you want to hear what I have to say, or not?" Rigid in his stance, Evan didn't even flinch in his firm facial expression. "That over there..." He pointed at the destroyed truck with bodies inside of it. "...doesn't make sense at all. With what I saw at the gas station before I got here—and I *know* that I *saw* Vivienne—I don't understand it either."

Mr. Lancaster yearned for the chance to hold his daughter alive and well. Nothing made sense, especially Evan's mention of an ominous incident. *And why is he all wet?* "What the heck happened at the gas station?"

"Get everyone in the car." Evan revealed a small grin. "I'll tell you on the way."

"To where?"

"SauraCorps."

TWENTY-THREE

"DON'T."

Something nudged her right hip three times.

"Stop, Arty."

Footsteps around Vivienne preceded more prods against her left hip.

Eyes closed, she realized a pocket of liquid sat inside her cheek which rested on the ground. *What kind of prank is he pulling on me now?* After spitting it out, she rolled her head so the back of it rested on the mud.

More wet footsteps registered in her ears.

With a weary arm, she brought her left hand up to cover her squinting eyes. *Where am....*

Everything came back to her.

Emily-Ann in search of her father.

Men dressed in tactical gear tossing her through the rift.

Killing a giant millipede.

Kamren.

Her fingers letting go of his.

The last two words she managed to call out to him. *"I love—"*

Nostrils flared before a creature nudged her forehead.

Oh God. The most important thing resurfaced. *Dinosaurs.*

Slow blinks revealed a curious crocodilian-like eye staring down at her, inches away from her face. The kind of yellowish, eerie eye that could haunt dreams.

"Whaaaat the *fliiiiiiiiip!*"

Adrenaline coursed through her entire body as she smacked the snouted head away and rolled onto her hands and knees. She removed wet and muddy hair from sticking to her face in a fury. Only then did she recognize the species.

Nundasuchus.

"Wait."

Orange spots around the aquatic dinosaur's eyes seemed familiar.

"Nandy?"

As she stepped closer, she noticed a torn piece of fabric hung from some of its front teeth. To compare, Viv reached behind her to detect a hole in her shirt's left shoulder. Her confused stare morphed into intrigue. "You...*saved* me?"

Annoyed by the tuft of clothing, Nandy raised its blueish webbed fingers and flicked its claws at the area.

Viv noticed that compared to earlier, the nundasuchus hadn't been showing as much animosity toward her. Standing straight, she took a few cautious steps forward. "Did you have a change of heart, huh?"

Nandy didn't budge.

Not even a growl.

"That's a *good* girl…or…boy, whatever you are." Pleased to not have raised a negative reaction from the dinosaur, Viv propped her knees down on the sandy ground. "We gonna be friends now?"

Her fingers closed in on the animal's head.

Nandy opened its jaws wide, drew in a long breath, and exhaled.

It startled Viv at first, until she realized Nandy had only yawned. Still, jaws lined with super sharp teeth were enough to intimidate her.

She managed to snag the torn clothing with her left hand while placing her right hand on Nandy's cheek. She wiggled the tattered bit free from the fangs. "There you go. Not so annoying anymore."

As if to say 'thank you', Nandy's tongue flicked out and tickled the human's cheek. In a way, its growl sounded more like purring.

Viv giggled, stroking the dinosaur's cheek with her thumb. "You're much cuter when you're not hissing at me."

Nandy twitched its head side to side and hissed, but not in a menacing manner.

"Oh, does that tickle?" Viv cooed, enjoying the dinosaur's company for once.

Crack!

Both of them turned their heads, alert to the noise coming from beyond the trees.

Something ran toward their position, snapping branches along the way.

In protection mode, Nandy bared its teeth and growled at the alarming, oncoming presence.

"Holy *mother* of—get *away!*" A dapper man broke through the treeline with his head turned to check behind him. "Damn scorpio-o-o-whoa." As he skidded to a stop, he held defensive hands out to the aquatic dinosaur. "Don't you attack me, too—" Then he finally noticed the young girl behind the creature. The same girl he'd discarded to the prehistoric period the day before. "Oh, jeez."

A loathsome fire lit up Viv's entire body.

Shock and guilt filled Sebastian Sharpe's eyes. "You're… still alive?"

"*You,*" Vivienne spit at him, wishing her words contained actual venom. "Stay the heck *away* from—"

Bone-chilling hisses preceded three small dog-sized scorpions emerging from the forest. Their eerie, beady eyes blended in with the rest of their jet-black bodies. After chasing the businessman for the last while, they'd grown even hungrier.

"Giant scorpions, too?" Viv backed up in fright. *Gonna have nightmares for the rest of my life.*

More animated than ever before, Nandy zipped over to the big bugs, snapping its fangs and swiping its front claws at them. A quick lunge attack enabled Nandy to snatch a pincer of one of them.

The scorpion's stinger jolted forward.

Nandy's webbed foot caught a segment of the tail, pinning it to the ground as it ripped the pincer from its body. The tail also pulled away from the abdomen with a snap.

Ready for the next one, Nandy hissed as it flicked its muscular tail at another. Propelled into a tree, the second scorpion staggered into unconsciousness.

Both Viv and Sebastian observed the battle in wonder.

One scorpion remained.

Nandy faced it with a snarl, swinging its head back and forth, keeping both eyes on it.

Lurching forward, the scorpion snapped its pincers as its tail quivered forward and back. Its aggressiveness intensified with every thrust of its stinger.

After a hiss, Nandy charged with open jaws.

The stinger shot forward at almost lightning speed.

Tough scales on top of the nundasuchus' snout deflected the strike. Teeth sunk into the large bug's exoskeleton with a popping crunch. Like a dog with a toy, Nandy gave it a vigorous shake until the limbs drooped.

Breathing heavily, Nandy turned around and strutted right up to Viv. The dead scorpion dropped from its mouth and landed by her feet.

Nandy angled an eye up at the teenager, proud of its catch.

"Oh, uh, th-th-thank you, Nandy." Viv bent down to pet the dinosaur's head. "You really are a ninja-dog."

Sebastian piped up. "That's a nundasuch—"

"Don't think I haven't forgotten about *you* over there," she shot back at him, enraged with a hint of trepidation weaved through her tone. Sebastian's orders to throw her and her friends through the rift replayed in her mind. "I'd ask what you're even doing here, but at the same time, I don't care."

"Listen, I—"

"Hey, cologne commercial," Viv countered, whipping a pointed finger at the ground. "I'd rather shove this bug carcass *down your throat* than listen to you."

"Right." Rather than try to reason with her, Sebastian sighed. "I deserve that."

"No, you deserve *worse*." Though battered and a bit bruised, a moment of courage pushed her to march toward him a couple steps. "How dare you." By now, she wished her incensed heat emanating from her face would make him burst into flames. "Did you even have a *speck* of guilt when you tossed us through?"

Sebastian simply stood there. "At the time, it was business."

"That's not what I asked, you piece of—"

"And that same business I broke my back for and ruined my family for...." Coming down from the adrenaline rush of being chased, he tried to clear the sore rock from his throat. "They *chucked* me into this time at the first sign of showing a conscience."

About to make a comeback, Viv couldn't form any words. *He was thrown in, too? Or is this a trick to make sure we die out here?*

He couldn't even look her in the eyes. "Because heaven forbid I have something to say about dinosaurs being sold on the black market as food and God knows what else."

She studied his dirty, semi-tattered suit and pants. The man who'd been so sinister just a day before wore a face of remorse and helplessness. *How can this guy be any kind of trustworthy?*

Since the girl didn't make any reply, he continued. "Worst part of it all, voicing my opinions cost me everything."

An ache in his words made her a bit more attentive. "Cost? And you don't think what you did to us made us lose things too?"

"I'm not trying to negate—"

"Now that I'm trapped here, I will *never* see my *family* again." Every emotion she'd tried to reserve came crashing down on her. "Since I so rudely landed in this time, I've had to kill a massive, grotesque millipede, I can't trust anything around me except for my friends, I got separated from the man I…" Only a couple feet away from Sebastian now, she made sure he could see the tears flowing down her cheeks. "The man I *love* probably thinks I'm dead by now." Though spoken in a sentence she never thought she'd have to form, she lingered on the one word in her mind. *Love. I just said that out loud—uninterrupted—for the first time.*

Sebastian nodded, sheepish. "And I may never see my kids again."

Fists clenched, Viv wanted to strike back with a reply but couldn't. *Kids? This jerkwad is…a father?*

With folded arms, he glanced around as if searching for common ground. "To be completely honest, um… Sorry, what's your name, Miss?"

She gauged his apologetic body language. *Do I even give him the courtesy?* At the same time, having another human being around helped keep loneliness at bay. "Vivienne."

"Thank you." He twitched a grin. "I don't expect you to like me. Heck, now that I know how it feels, I'd despise me too."

Viv snorted. "Not quite hitting the mark word-wise."

"All I ask is that we try to work together to stay alive out here." Hope rang true in his tone. "Let me right my wrongs."

Since he'd arrived, Viv had been subconsciously picking at her thumb cuticles. She stared him down, bold and serious. "Fine." Off to her left, Nandy munched on one of the dead scorpions, making a meal of its innards. "But if any more monstrous bugs cross our path, you let me run ahead of you."

"Wait," Sebastian browsed the area. "You got separated from your friends?"

Back to distressing about Kamren, she stepped closer to the river. "Somewhere upstream. Another rift popped up and I tried to swim for it."

"Sorry, *what?*" The notion made him unfold his arms. "Another rift? Was there an explosion of some sort?"

Vivienne searched for the right description of the event. "No, it just…zapped into place, I guess? Its window led to a local gas station back home. Before I could reach it, it zapped back out of existence."

Perplexed as to how it could have occurred, Sebastian quickly scanned his eyes over the river, to the nundasuchus, then to the young woman. "But that—oh, jeez. That changes *everything.*"

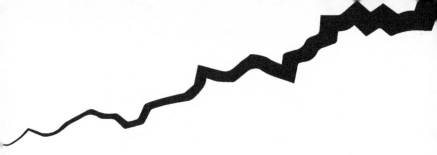

TWENTY-FOUR

HOUSTON, TEXAS – PRESENT DAY

"RIGHT THIS way, please."

The restaurant *Maison Pucha Bistro* brimmed with bustle.

A hostess guided a mid-twenties couple to their table for dinner. Once she seated them, she handed out drink menus and left to give them time to choose.

The unnaturally silver-haired woman skimmed the menu, then laid it down in front of her. "This is quite the high-end restaurant for a first date. Michelin stars and everything."

"You did say you were a fan of French cuisine." Taking in the beauty in a blue and gold dress across from him, the dark-haired man grinned. "So, I thought, why not bring the fan to the best French food in Houston?"

She narrowed her light blue eyes at him. "Question is, are *you* fond of it, Noah?"

"Guess I'll find out after tonight, Abby."

173

"Well, if you aren't, I may have to rethink dating you," For a moment, she picked up the drink menu again. "So, decide wisely."

Noah smirked. "Asking you out on a date felt like the best decision I've ever made."

"Ooooh." Abby chuckled. "Didn't take you long to put that smooth line together."

He laughed along with her as he leaned in. "I have my moments—"

CRRRRACK-ACK-ACK! ZAP! CRACKLE! SNAP!

Both of them tumbled backward as their table blew up into bits.

An electric loop of neon green, surging energy separated the couple.

Noah scrambled away on his back as others screamed and tried to flee.

On the opposite side, Abby couldn't believe what she stared at.

The opening of the rift had startled a herd of golden-skinned chasmosaurus—similar to triceratops but with cavities formed in their frills. In the chaos of it all, two of the chasmosaurus bumped into each other, knocking one of them through the time anomaly's window.

Abby rushed out of the way before large flat feet trampled down tables and chairs. "Oh my God! How…. *What?*"

Another chasmosaurus—nearly as long as a school bus—stumbled into the restaurant with a frightened bellow. It tossed a table into a wall with its beaked mouth as if it weighed nothing.

One of the waitresses shrieked when she came out from the kitchen.

The noise startled the dinosaurs, causing them to charge and trample everything in their path on their way out of the restaurant. Their tall boney frills tore through the ceiling.

Now out on the street, both chasmosaurus glanced around at the unfamiliar environment. A hard, gravelly surface had replaced the soft, grassy ground they had been used to. Walled structures stopped them from running as free as they once had. Strange metal creatures with rubber circles for legs met them with obnoxious honks.

Once the anxious dinosaurs chose a path to run, their tough hides protected them from the vehicles around them.

Back inside the restaurant, Noah rushed over to his date. "Abby! Abby, are you okay?"

She couldn't pull her eyes away from the bizarre rift.

"Abigail?" Noah placed his hands on her arms. "Are you hurt?"

All she did was raise a shaky, pointed finger at the crackling electric ring. "Is…that—"

A thunderous roar carried through the rift into the nearly demolished bistro.

Slow and careful, Noah turned only to freeze in place. "But…*how?*"

A burnt-red-scaled tyrannosaurus rex with black stripes gazed through the window into the present time. Its orange eye with a black iris seemed to stare deep into the human's souls.

Abby's voice tremored. "We n-n-need…to get out of—"

Z-Z-ZAP-CRACK! SNAP!

The green energy of the rift glitched for a moment.

Caught by surprise, the rex backed its head away with another room-shaking wail.

ZZZZEEEEUUUU-POP!

The rift shrunk into itself and fizzled into nothingness.

Its disappearance cut off the large reptile's roar.

Noah finally stood up and helped his date onto her feet. "Did *that* just happen?"

Just as confused as him, Abby placed her hands on her cheeks. "Those were all...*dinosaurs,* right?"

"Yeah," Noah confirmed. "This date's gonna go in the record books."

TWENTY-FIVE

KAMREN MARCHED on with undying energy in his legs. No change in the terrain and no hidden screeches or growls would stop him from pursuing Vivienne.

As they trekked, they'd come across a blackberry bush—a new, welcome snack for a quick break.

Taking his hurried countenance into consideration, Emily-Ann suggested that they eat most of them along the way.

Holding a handful of the sweet-tart berries in his left hand, he wiped humidity and sweat from his brow with the opposite. *I will find you, just please still be alive.* Though he worried for his best friend's safety, conversation with Emily-Ann helped keep his mind on other things.

"I still think you're wrong." E-A finished off her bunch of berries. "Smith was the best Doctor Who, hands down."

"Meh, he was okay," Kam countered, keeping an eye on the overgrown riverbank for tripping hazards. "Tennant was born for the role. Or, did you not watch all three of his seasons and all the specials?"

"Oh, I've seen them."

"He even married another Doctor actor's daughter, who actually played the role of the Doctor's daughter in the show." Riled up, Kam laughed at the fun topic. "If that's not sheer awesomeness, I don't know what is."

"That's all circumstantial." E-A dipped her hand in the river to wash off berry juice. "Smith had a quirky charm and really came into his own."

"Are you kidding—and Tennant *didn't?*" For the first time in a little while, Kam glanced up to give her an almost offended glare. "Besides precarious tree roots, you're stepping onto thin ice now."

E-A laughed at the direction their opinions took them. "Agree to disagree then."

"And if you want to get into companions, other than the perfect romance of Amy and Rory, Martha was *the* best, hands down."

A grin formed on E-A's face. "Now *that* I *will* agree with, she was one of the smartest written characters and didn't do dumb things just to further the plot."

Kam quieted down, taking Viv's cellphone out of his back pocket as he strolled. Since they'd used each other's phones the odd time, he unlocked it with no problems. The first thing to pop up was the picture they'd taken together.

Viv had set it as her background.

A silly grin snuck onto his face. *Wonder how long she's liked me for.*

"Are you more open to talking about what's going on

between you two?" E-A matched his stride, sneaking a peep at the phone screen. "Cute pic, by the way."

Immediately, his cheeks flushed. "Um, thanks."

"She's something special."

About to make a reply, he closed his mouth and nodded.

"In my humble opinion, if you can find a girl that can take down a giant millipede…" As E-A spoke, she raised an eyebrow while smirking. "…you need to lock that down."

"She was pretty amazing, wasn't she?" Still nodding, Kam came to a complete stop. "She…*is* amazing."

"Saying it out loud for the first time, huh?" Seeing the teen going through a romantic discovery kept her grinning. "As annoying as you are, you're *almost* adorable when you're lovestruck."

He let out a nervous laugh. "Yeah? Well, you're proficient at backhanded compliments."

"Oooh, deflection." By now, E-A started to enjoy getting him going. "Guess you're not entirely ready to talk about your *princess.*"

Her word choice caught him off guard. "What did you just say?"

She lifted a finger and bobbed her head back and forth. "Don't think just because I've been up ahead of you two that I can't hear what you say or call each other."

Having someone else notice the signs and everything more than he did made Kam more insecure. After all the years he and Viv had grown up together, now he finally clued in. Once he pocketed the phone, he ventured on. "Should probably save the battery."

Taking his cue, E-A decided not to push things and followed.

As they continued in silence, the wind kicked up around them. Leaves flittered on the trees. Thinner branches swayed against their will.

E-A glanced to the sky behind her. "Might be a storm blowing in."

The thought of having to stop for cover and wait it out concerned him. "No storm's gonna keep me from getting to Viv."

Admiring his will, she patted him on the back. "Not even a lightning strike—"

REEEEAAAAOOOOW!

A piercing shrill assaulted their ears.

Kam almost tripped over a root. "What in the name of Falcor was that?"

As gusts came at them even harder, E-A noticed something odd. "There's a pattern to the wind. It isn't constant. Every couple of seconds it stops, then picks up again…." She gazed skyward.

The size of a small plane, a large pterosaur hovered almost directly above them. If it had been nighttime, its mostly black body would have blended right in. Yellowish spots on its wings mimicked modern-day moths, and the irregular spots on its underbelly were reminiscent of a giraffe's. The yellowish beak opened to let out another impressive cry.

Every flap of its large, strong wings kicked up loose dust and grass bits around the humans. Its power rivaled modern-day helicopters.

"That thing's massive." Kamren arched his neck to take in the superb creature. "Bet you it's the size of a fighter jet."

"Kinda weird how it's just staying in one spot like that, like it's watching us." E-A became more uneasy as she finished the sentence. "My dad didn't mention much about flying dinosaurs. Hopefully it's just curious and not predatorial."

Another screech erupted from the giant pterosaur as it ascended and carried on.

The atmosphere around them returned to normal.

"Well, that was odd and slightly unsettling." Kam realized the dinosaur had taken off in the direction they were also heading. "Wonder if we'll come across it again up ahead."

"Maybe." E-A worked a berry seed from her teeth with her tongue and spit it out. "When it comes to flying dinosaurs, I'd say be prepared to run for cover."

TWENTY-SIX

"WAIT, WHAT are you saying?" Vivienne struggled to follow along with the SauraCorps ex-employee's explanation.

"I'm saying that isn't the first instance rift energy has popped up out of nothing before." Concerned by what she'd told him, Sebastian slipped his soiled and tattered suit jacket off to relieve him of built-up body heat. "Everyone thought I simply worked the business side of things, but I had some good friends in the T.S.—time-space—science department."

Nandy trotted up and leaned against the teenager's side with a purring growl.

Viv chuckled at the awesome ridiculousness of it all. "Weird to think a group of people can have that designation, but here I am with a dinosaur rubbing against my leg like a big cat."

Sebastian let a flicker of a smile slip out. "About two years ago, a couple of our scientists reported a blip on the worldwide radar in Barcelona, Spain. We keep track of the

T.S. energy."

"Another rift opened up?"

"More like a ball of the energy popping to life for ten seconds then disappearing." Casual about the topic, he swung his jacket over his back.

As she ran her fingers down Nandy's deep blue, crocodilian-style plated back, Viv cocked her head. "And the world didn't report on it?"

Bobbing his head side to side, Sebastian figured he'd lay everything out on the table. "SauraCorps is a multi-*trillion*-dollar company."

The figure put things into perspective for her. "Right. You guys had it buried."

"Not quite hitting the mark word-wise, but that's putting it politely," he quipped with a slight touché to his tone. Since scorpions were no longer an imminent threat, he checked himself over and pulled a small twig out of the waistline of his pants. "A month later, another materialized in Northern Australia. Then Peru shortly after."

One of the scorpion's abdomen legs hung from Nandy's row of teeth on the right side of its head. To be kind, Viv flicked it away with her fingers. "Sounds like things started getting out of hand."

"We found ways to…*control*…the situations." Sebastian stared at the ground as more guilt presented itself. "While we used money to fix things in ways I'm no longer proud of, we tasked our scientists with figuring out why they'd been occurring more and more."

"Any answers?"

He gazed at the treetops. "That's still the multi-trillion-dollar question."

At a loss for any kind of scientific reasoning, she huffed. "It's like I'm trapped in some crazy sci-fi story."

Having made his way over to a fruit-bearing tree, he pulled a pear off a branch. "At least the food here's good."

Viv shook her head as two different things took place.

Sebastian sunk his teeth into the perfect pear's juicy flesh.

Still at her side, Nandy enjoyed being petted.

Out of nowhere, she began glancing all over. "Wait, maybe….?"

Chewing on a morsel, he asked, "You have a theory?"

"Sci-fi story." Vivienne realized her thought process would most likely sound foolish to someone else. "What's the one thing that most time travel books and movies have in common with their laws of time?"

Somewhat amused, Sebastian played along. "You talking like, Back to the Future and Terminator type stuff?"

"Sort of."

"I guess, they always focus on what you do in the past affects the future," he reasoned, curious as to her thought process. "Which never made sense to me, because if you alter the past to fix the future, then in that future you wouldn't exist or have the same life and the universe should implode with how crazy it would become. Butterfly effect and all that."

"The other thing usually mentioned is that the *present you* should never come in contact with the *past* or even *future you*," Viv pointed out, letting her nerd brain work things out. "If you come at it from an energy perspective... ow, my head."

"Keep going." Sebastian appreciated hearing her ideas. "Nothing's out of the question at this point."

After taking a moment to collect all of her thoughts, Viv focused. "You and I, we came into the world at certain points in time. We exist with our own kind of time energy, like a vibration of sorts."

"I can agree with that."

A question she'd never fathomed to ask came out. "So, what happens if people or things of *our present* spend too much time in *the past?*"

On the same track, Sebastian added, "Likewise, if dinosaurs spend too much time in our present?" The reasoning seemed to make some kind of bizarre sense. "Two completely different time energies would be warring with each other, it's an unnatural balance."

A line she'd heard in so many movies and read in books finally clicked on a whole new level. "The fabric of space and time could theoretically be ripped apart."

Sebastian nodded. "Rift by rift."

"Hold on a sec, *dinosaurs* in our time? *Plural?*" Viv's gaze went from Nandy to the dark-haired man. "How many dinosaurs are we talking?"

"Since we started, I'd say probably a few thousand." Sebastian shook his head. "Damn hindsight." Before taking another nibble, he turned the yellowish-green fruit in his hand. "And I'm eating a pear from the *past.*" Sebastian closed his eyes as he recalled what had been happening in their present time. *Stegosaurus steaks in Asia.* "Bartelloni doesn't know how much damage he's causing."

"Who and what now?"

After taking one last generous bite, Sebastian dropped the fruit and slipped his jacket back on. "Have you come across any other humans out here? Army-like?"

Viv remembered hearing about what Kam and E-A had witnessed. "Yesterday. Aren't they your people?"

"Not my people anymore," Sebastian countered, callous toward the company. It took him a moment to somewhat recognize where he was. "If we head…East, I think…there's an outpost where some of them bunk and keep dinosaurs before they're transported to our facilities."

Arms crossed, Viv glared. "I'd rather keep my distance from them."

"You don't understand, they have special communication devices that connect through to the present." Getting anxious, the excitement in his voice met a wall of hesitancy. Not being part of the company anymore also meant he'd become an enemy. *What would happen if I show up there unannounced? Getting shot would add insult to injury, and injury.* "If we can sneak in—"

"We need to stay here," Viv rebutted, firm in her stance.

Ready to leave, Sebastian stared at her in disbelief. "Seriously?"

"My friends could be minutes away from finding me." She glanced upstream with hope in her eyes. Resolved to stand there until they arrived, she shook her head at Sharpe. "Leave if you want to."

About to laugh at her, he refrained. "You've got to be joking, Vivienne. For all you know, they could be another hour or—"

"Then I'll *wait* an hour," she shot back. "And I may have given you my name, but don't you dare say it out loud."

Exasperated, he threw his arms in the air. "Is this some kind of teen drama thing you're pulling, or what?"

"You want teen drama?" Viv dropped to the ground and sat cross-legged, making sure to get the point across. "I'm not moving from this spot. Nandy will keep me company and protect me."

The nundasuchus plopped its backside on the ground beside her like a dog and nudged its crocodilian head into her shoulder.

Sebastian's temper reached a dangerous teetering point. "Listen, *blondie*. If we don't go and try to reach the other side, then we might actually *die* out here."

She snorted. "Should've thought of that before you threw me through the rift."

Her retort made him clench his fists and narrow his gaze. Without warning, he marched over with a fire in his eyes.

Sitting her ground, Viv threw her arms around Nandy's neck and brought its scaley head closer for defense.

Sebastian brought his face two feet away from hers. "Aiden and Olivia are *counting* on me to get back."

"And they are?"

"My *children*," he spat out through clenched teeth.

Viv rolled her eyes. "At least they still have their mom."

Sebastian raised his voice. "Their *mother...cheated* on me

with her boss and is trying to *drain* me of *everything* she can." Unprepared to have divulged so much to the girl, he proceeded to tear up as it all came rushing to mind.

As much as she still held some hatred for him, Viv had never been able to handle crying men. Being face to face with someone dealing with so much turmoil made her eyes brim with tears. "I… I'm sorry."

Once he realized he'd invaded her personal space, Sebastian stood up and backed away. "We've all got our own crap to deal with." Running tense fingers through his hair, he turned his back on her in shame. "Work consumed me and I…stopped paying attention to her. Every mistake keeps haunting me."

Viv kept silent.

Sebastian pointed in the direction of the SauraCorps base. "That outpost is our best shot. I get that you hate me. But if I leave you here alone and something bad happens… I wouldn't be able to live with myself."

A few seconds dragged by until Vivienne spoke up. "Half an hour. Then we'll go."

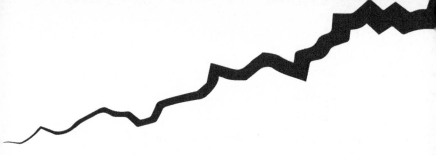

TWENTY-SEVEN

"**HOW IS** that even possible?" Andrew Lancaster simply stared at his friend.

Once he'd parked, Evan Eckhardt whipped his seatbelt off. "I'm telling you, I saw Vivienne on the other side of… whatever that thing was."

In the back seat, Cassie Eckhardt showed Denise Lancaster the bit of footage she took from her cellphone of the event at the gas station.

Denise had watched the video a few times. "How does that even happen?"

"Maybe we'll get some answers here." Evan hopped out of the SUV.

"At a dinosaur museum?" Cassie hesitated to join her husband.

Already outside the vehicle, Andrew popped his head back in. "As weird as all of this is, most of the time 'weird' can usually be explained by something simple."

Andrew jogged up beside Evan just as he'd reached the glass front doors of SauraCorps. "You really think you'll get answers here?"

Whipping one of the doors open, Evan marched with purpose. "First, I see Viv alive, then I'm told she's died in a freak truck fire. Whoever it was from here that called it in makes all of this seem a little *fishy* to me."

"Hopefully you're right." More than anything, Andrew held onto a sliver of optimism. *Please be right.*

The young redhead at the ticket desk smiled as the two men approached. "Good afternoon, welcome to SauraCorps. For how many?"

Evan went into serious mode. "We're not here to look around."

"Oh, um, what can I help you wi—"

"We'd like to speak with the manager or owner, or whoever's at the top of the chain here," Evan requested, eager to get down to business with no nonsense.

Across the lobby, Felicia Voorhees paused in conversation with one of the guards.

The redhead tried to keep her customer service voice secure. "I'm sorry, sir. But to see a board member, you'll need to make an appointment."

As he gripped the edge of the counter, Evan leaned in. "Listen, someone who works here called in an accident which had led to our children's *supposed* deaths." He pointed at himself and Andrew, then realized he needed to rein himself in a bit. "Please. We just want to speak to whoever it was—"

"You must be looking for me, then." Felicia's heels clicked against the sandy-colored tile as she made her way over. "I'm Miss Voorhees. You're the fathers of the deceased?"

"We are," Andrew answered in a less intimidating manner than he figured his friend would've used.

"Such a horrible thing," she responded, making sure to make eye contact with both of them. *Gotta sell this.* Able to think of something unrelated but sad to her, she willed her eyes to convey compassion. "There's no way for me to comprehend what you're going through."

"Confused more than anything," Evan countered.

Felicia hadn't expected that kind of answer. "I'm... Is, um... Can we help either of you in any way?"

More determined than ever, Evan stepped forward. "Yeah, you can—"

Andrew stepped in front of him. "Obviously, some of us aren't taking what's happened very well."

"Of course, this must be an emotional time for you." She wiped the bottom of her eyelids of the faked speck of tears. In her purse, her cellphone rang a jingle. "Excuse me for one moment." She pulled the phone out and identified the sender as one of the SauraCorps scientists.

Science wing, now. Another rift popped open.

After trying to hide an alarmed stare at the message, she turned back to the pair of fathers. "I apologize, but I have a meeting in five minutes." Felicia shook their hands as she gave her farewell. "Again, I'm sorry for your loss."

Evan tensed his jaw. "Interesting choice of *word*."

Having only taken a few steps away from them, she turned around. "Excuse me?"

Worried that his friend may be getting too extreme, Andrew grabbed his arm. "Ev, be careful."

Resolved to not leave without answers, Evan ripped his arm away from Andrew. "This may be totally out there, but something tells me that our kids are *lost*. Not dead."

Felicia gave him a doubtful glance. "What makes you—"

"Some massive ring of electric-something appeared at the gas station in town, where I was filling up before coming out to the so-called *accident*." Evan only took one last step toward her and pointed a finger back at Andrew. "It sent water pouring into the building, and on the other side of whatever it was, I saw *his daughter* swimming toward me."

Felicia mustered all she had to keep her countenance in check. "You must be mistak—"

"Then I'm told that you were the one who called, finding our kids burnt to a crisp on the side of the road." At this point, Evan's entire body burned with intensity, making him unzip his jacket and reach inside. "Is *coincidental* the right word here?"

Felicia came up with a quick excuse. "Th-that's entirely circumstantial."

"Then explain *this*."

The security guards in the room had no chance to unholster their guns in time.

Evan revealed a wiggling creature to the whole room. "Once the electric thing closed and the water dispersed, this little guy had landed at my feet." After holding the pill bug-like arthropod up in the air for a few seconds, he set the shelled animal on the tile floor. "I believe you SauraCorps people would recognize it as—"

"Trilobite." Felicia stared at the curious, brownish-grey marine creature. *Damn, he's onto us.*

Shocked, Andrew gave him a quizzical look. "You had *that* in your jacket this whole time?"

Now that he had her attention, Evan folded his arms. "Would you like to give a *new statement* to the police?"

In a split-second decision, she swirled around calling out, "Guards, remove them from the premises. With force, if required."

As soon as the command left her mouth, Evan bent down and scooped up the flattish, squirming trilobite into his jacket. "What did you do with my *son? Where* is he?"

Finally, Andrew clued in to his buddy's insinuation as two guards swarmed him. "Hey, lady!" About to charge at her, the two security men seized him by the arms. "Let go of me, dammit!"

Back outside, the wives had been keeping an eye on the front entrance.

The doors flew open as their husbands got tossed out of the building by SauraCorps security. Both men stumbled back and regained their footing.

"Hey." Andrew managed to snag Evan's arm before he could attempt to march back inside. "*Hey*, let's go, Ev. Don't chance it."

The four guards kept watch, prepared to act as a barrier

to keep them out.

About to leave for the SUV, Evan turned back. "You tell your higher-ups I'll be bringing the police with me next time."

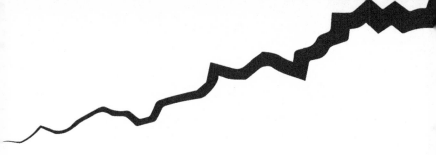

TWENTY-EIGHT

GROWLS EMANATED from Kamren's stomach.

"Sounds like it's supper time." Slowing down, Emily-Ann knelt to unzip her backpack. "Would you like the usual apple, or maybe try to scrounge around for something else?"

"Apple's fine."

E-A picked up on the weariness behind his short reply. "We're going to find her, Ka—"

"We've been going for almost a couple hours now." Hunger became the last peg pulled out from under him. The amount of anxious time away from Vivienne had eaten away at his mental state. "I'm trying hard to hope for the best, but… She…." Unable to voice his growing concerns, he chewed on his bottom lip.

"She might be around that next corner." She hoped to keep his morale up. By now the sun had passed its noon position in the sky. "Hopefully we can make it to her before nightfall. We'll have to set up camp again."

Anxiety took over, making his feet fail to respond and come to a full stop. "I never got to say it back."

"Say what?" Since E-A had been up on the riverbank when they lost Viv, she hadn't heard their exchange of words in the water.

"Before she slipped away from me, she started to say...." All feeling seemed to drain out of his body. Like a mountain crashing down on him, Kam buckled at the knees, unable to bear the weight of it anymore. "She was about to tell me...that she *loved* me."

"Oh, Kamren." In moments of loss, E-A had never been confident in her ability to be comforting to a griever.

The loss of a loved one is never easy, no matter what circumstance.

In Kamren's case, he'd only just comprehended that his love for her had grown over the years to a much deeper level. The term 'best friend' encompassed a whole new meaning to him, which he now accepted within himself.

Love.

Such a simple, little word can also be big and sometimes terrifying to say.

Then it had floated out of her mouth.

Cut off by the obnoxious, rushing water, she'd still managed to reveal what her heart had yearned to say.

"All this time." Kam finally spoke after wading through his emotions. "All those times when she'd cancel her plans to spend an afternoon with me. Even if it was to just go somewhere and not even end up doing much of anything at a park or something."

E-A smiled. "Doing nothing with someone you love can mean everything."

"Every time she nudged or even punched my shoulder...." Even thinking about it made him rub his left shoulder with a new appreciation. "Always figured it had been a subtle way of showing her affection. Never knew how deeply." An exasperated sigh left his mouth as he kicked some grass. *You're an idiot, Kam.* "I've been so brainless and *blind.*"

If he'd said that when they'd first met, E-A would've agreed with him. "You're not stupid."

To let off some steam, Kam strode over to what he discovered to be a large and lush raspberry bush. "Then why did it have to take a dangerous situation like this for me to finally see that I..." He picked some more berries and held them in the palm of his hand. "...*love* her, too?"

Coming up beside him to pick some raspberries for herself, she still had no idea of how to even begin to console him. "At least you've got someone who cares for you that way."

After popping some of the larger-than-modern-day fruit in his mouth, he got little comfort from the tartness and burst of juice. "No one's missing you back home?"

"Nah, and I don't need anyone to miss me either," she answered with a proud grin. "Spent most of my life working on how to make myself happy first. Gotta learn to love yourself before you're ready to love someone else, and all that jazz."

Grrrr.

E-A gave him an odd stare. "Was...that your stomach again or did I upset you?"

Kam gave her a side-glance. "That definitely wasn't me—"

Grrrrooooowl!

A creature with a head the size of a shopping cart flopped onto the raspberry bush with a threatening roar.

As Kam fell backward from the surprise, he noticed it had two rows of teeth on both its upper and lower jaws. "Holy baby Yoda!" He flung the remaining berries into the air as he staggered backward. "How did we *not* see that thing?"

E-A also tumbled back and winced as her duffle bag broke the fall. Residual pain emanated from her possibly cracked rib. *"Dammit...* This guy doesn't look too friendly. Keep your distance, Kam." Once the animal's prominent, violet sail could be seen from behind the brush, she identified the species. "Dimetrodon."

Thankfully, the massive creature didn't come any closer.

"A *carnivore?*" Kamren hopped back onto his feet.

Once the initial scare had worn off, E-A stepped toward the thrashing lizard. "Only one way to find out."

Kam couldn't take his eyes off the steak-knife-like fangs snapping at the air. "You freaking *serious*, Em?"

"It's not coming at us," she countered, inching her way around the bush. "Almost like it can't move."

"That's supposed to be a *good* thing, right?"

On the other side, E-A gained a better vantage point of the creature. Rays of sun turned parts of its purplish sail to a pinkish hue. The purple blended into the main body almost to where it looked black to onlookers. Streaks of golden stripes flowed down from its shoulders to the tip of its tail.

The dimetrodon wailed like a lion mixed with a snake's hiss.

"Whoa, big guy." Since they hadn't encountered any meat-eaters yet, E-A remained guarded as she approached it even closer. "I'm not gonna hurt you."

Every muscle flexed as the dimetrodon whipped its girthy, strong tail to-and-fro in panic.

A few feet away from its head, she noticed moisture running down under its right eye.

Tears.

"It's in pain," she called over.

Kam remained by the river. "As long as it stays over there and doesn't cause me any, that's fine."

The dimetrodon yanked on its front left foot but couldn't budge. Its growls morphed into sad whines.

E-A crouched down as her fear lessened. "What's got you, huh?" Reaching out, she pulled back some tall grass. "Oh man, you poor thing."

About to take a step forward, Kamren's curiosity grew.

"Is it…okay?"

"Gonna need your help with this, Kam."

"Uh…." The reptile's squirming and flailing kept him skeptical. "You want *me* over there beside *it?*"

"If we don't get this trap off its foot it might lose the appendage," she fired back, almost annoyed with him like their earlier time together. "It's like a bigger bear trap. Freaking SauraCorps. The anchor spike's way too deep in the ground to pull out."

Halfway to them, Kam noticed the dimetrodon close its eyes in agony. The groans of suffering moved him to stride even faster to join E-A. "So, how do you propose—jeez this guy looks *deadly*—we um, free this poor thing?"

"Get your hands on the other side of the clamp and pull."

Kam glanced at the animal's head, then back to her. "On the side where the *teeth* are?"

"Dammit, Kam, do you want to free it or not?"

Seconds went by before he thrust his apprehension aside. Once he'd squeezed between the dimetrodon's head and the berry bush, he gained a clearer view of the creature's eyes, which leaked defeat.

With the bulky reptile in front of him, Kamren truly came to understand that essentially, SauraCorps was a corporation of poachers. Dangerous or not, no creature deserved to be unethically trapped. Especially by a company that doesn't care about the well-being of the animals it captures.

Kam positioned his hands on the clamp's other jaw. "Okay, we doing this on three?"

Though her hands still stung, E-A held on as best she

could. "Three."

"Two."

"One."

"*Now!*"

Between the two of them, the trap opened only by a smidge. Metal teeth still dug into the dimetrodon's wrist. By now the foot had become drenched in blood. The jostle of the humans trying to free it only caused more red fluid to seep out.

"It's too…" Kam grunted as he fought to apply more oomph. "…strong. It won't…budge."

"Just…keep…going." Determined to save the helpless creature, E-A let out a roar of exertion. "We *can* do this!"

For a moment, Kam became fully aware of fearsome teeth only inches away as the dimetrodon let out another whine. Yellow spots along its lips and eyes added a vibrant beauty to the animal he hadn't seen yet. As his abs and arms began to shudder from exertion, Kam had the dimetrodon rest its heavy head against his chest. Its tough scales grazed his chin. *Aw, it's not scary at all.*

"Come…*on!*" E-A screamed through clenched teeth.

Both humans closed their eyes, giving it all they could.

Overhead, a large shadow swept by.

A residual breeze swayed the surrounding grass and met their skin.

Kam picked up on the momentary blockage of sunlight. "Uh, Em, should we…be worried by that?"

Unwilling to let go, she yelled out, "Can't stop now. *Puuuull!*"

"I'm…pulling as hard as I can." Seeing no way of freeing the beast, his confidence quaked just as much as his entire body. "It's not…budging."

Opening her eyes, she locked her gaze into his. "Don't give up on me, Ka—"

To her left, a foot slammed down on one of the trap's spring levers. The person arched their body over the dimetrodon's foot, their hands pressing down on the other lever.

The unexpected assistance eased the snare open enough for the animal to finally slip its wrist free.

Once the creature limped back a bit, Kamren and E-A released their grips.

The trap's teeth snapped back together.

Whimpering, the dimetrodon rubbed its head against the teenager's torso.

Kamren patted the side of its head as he sat back to rest. Then he stared up at the man who'd come to their aid. "Thanks, uh… Who are you, exactly?"

Back on her feet, E-A noticed the man's bushy red beard. Freckles under his smiling eyes made her stare in utter disbelief. "*Dad?*"

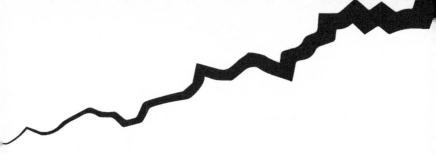

TWENTY-NINE

SPACE AND time.

Two of the most essential things in the universe. As well as being the hardest to fathom when it came to things like time travel and rifts.

As Vivienne tried to wrap her head around it all, she kept having a nundasuchus dinosaur bump into her leg every few feet as they followed an ex-businessman through a prehistoric forest. More times than not, she kept asking herself, *Am I losing my mind?*

"Come on, keep up." Up ahead, Sebastian checked the map on his cellphone and shoved it back into his pant pocket. "We might be able to make it there before nightfall."

Pulled out of her thoughts, she crossed her arms as she strolled. "Forgive me for being a bit frightened over where I am right now."

In a quick spin as he walked, Sebastian glanced at her. "If you speed it up a bit, we may not have to worry about being here for much longer."

Viv went silent.

To her left, Nandy sauntered along like a trained pet. It snapped its gaze to anything and everything that made a noise, adding more quirky charm to the primordial reptile.

Under her breath, Viv whispered, "*Sick 'em, Nandy.*"

The dinosaur careened off to the right to stick its snout into a small bed of tall flowers with bulbous ends, picked a few out with its mouth, and returned to its human friend.

"Not quite what I had in mind, dummy." She shook her head while chuckling. Taking a note from the creature, she went over and ripped some of the plants out for herself. After taking a nibble of the stem, she recognized the subtle bite. "Hey, these are…chives, I think." She plucked one of the purple buds off the top and began chewing. *The things you don't think about.*

"Did you say *chives?*" Sebastian ended up turning around to see for himself. "I'm starving."

"Find your own grub," she countered with a cheek full of chive flowers.

Sebastian bit his tongue. A quick survey of the area helped him figure out where they'd plucked them from. He passed the teenager and dinosaur on his way over to the edible vegetation. "You'd be surprised how much food there actually is out here." Once he scooped up a handful for himself, he lagged behind a few feet. "Some of the guys back…." Sebastian winced. "They, uh, even tried some dragonfly. Said it wasn't horrib—"

"Yeah-no." She swallowed another bite of the stems. "I've

already decided I'm not eating any bug meat, under no circumstances whatsoever. I'm on a bug-free diet."

He cleaned off one of the wild chive bulbs and picked off the roots. "Sounds like you had a rather unpleasant run-in."

"I had to kill a giant millipede to save my friend."

"You?" He stopped chewing. "*You* killed an arthropleura?"

"Knife to the head." Viv kept trudging along. "Let that be a warning to you."

"Okay then." Once he swallowed down the morsel, he caught up to a few feet away from her. Not a fan of awkward silences, he cleared his throat. "So, you and your boyfriend thought you could actually break into our museum?"

Mention of the word 'boyfriend' made her slow down a little. "We just wanted to do some crazy teen stuff, that's all." The more her mind combined 'Kamren' and 'boyfriend' together, it made her want to turn back and head for the river.

"This turned into quite the backfire, then."

She snorted. "Understatement."

Her abrupt reply led to another uncomfortable quiet.

Both of the humans ended up watching the nundasuchus trot along, checking things out as they moved forward.

"So…." Sebastian picked a fleck of vegetable out of his teeth. "You're from Utah then?"

She sighed. "Seriously? Petty small talk?"

Hands up in defeat, he responded, "Man, you're just full of sass, huh?"

"Oh, believe me…" Viv shot back a confident smirk. "…I haven't even fully opened my can of sass on you yet."

THIRTY

"SWEETIE, I can't believe you're *actually* here!"

Sniffles worked their way between Emily-Ann uttering, "It's you… It's really *you*." Bear-hugging her father, she refused to let go. The longer she held onto him, the more she squeezed. To have him in her arms again gave her the strength and faith she'd almost given up on. "And you're still alive."

Theodore chuckled. "There's been some close calls."

Off to the side letting the family members reconnect, Kamren called over, "Of the dinosaur kind?"

Pulled out of the glee Theo had wrapped himself up in, he gave the teen a slightly perplexed stare. "If that were the case, I would've been dead four days after I was thrown through." Once he broke away from his daughter, he stepped closer and held an open hand out. "I'm Theo, by the way."

"Kamren Eckhardt." His hand met the scientist's weathered palm. "Feel like I've learned a fair bit about you already."

"That so?" Theo smirked, curious about the kid's link to E-A. "Have you two known each other long?"

A laugh erupted from E-A. "He blackmailed me into sneaking him and a friend into SauraCorps because they wanted a night tour." While she'd been talking, she fished a hand into her duffle bag. "Long story short, they were thrown through the rift with me."

Contentment on Theo's face altered to disdain at the mention of the company's name. Even after five years, it left a horrible taste in his mouth. "Those *wretched* monsters are still disposing of their problems that way, huh?"

"Unfortunately." E-A pulled out her father's journal and presented it to him as if it were a sacred item. "We used this as our guide."

His disdain waned back into pleasure in a mere second. Mouth open and excitement in his eyes, he flipped through the pages. "My notes. All of my early notes." As he held it open with one hand, he ran the other hand through his copper-red hair. "I can't believe you still have it after all of this time."

Delighted to simply search his sky-blue eyes again, she couldn't stop smiling. "Of course. It's all I had left of you, *Dad.*"

As soon as she'd uttered the last word, his eyes brimmed with tears. He managed a chuckle while pulling her in close with his left arm, and kissed her on the forehead. His chin tremored, making his beard tickle her as he shook his head a little. "This is...something else."

Upon turning around, Kam noticed the dimetrodon

hadn't made it far from where it had been trapped. More than likely, it'd needed a moment to rest. The whole situation replayed in his mind, which brought him to an inquiry. "All this time we'd been looking for you, how'd you end up finding us, Theo?"

"I had a little help." After taking a moment to compose himself, the scientist raised an eyebrow. "Allow me to introduce a friend of mine." Pinky fingers to the corners of his mouth, he positioned his tongue and blew a shrilling whistle.

What started as a gentle breeze increased to enough wind to rustle the hair on everyone's head. Even the surrounding trees swayed like lapping waves of an ocean.

RREEEEAAAAAAAAOOUU!

High above the clearing, a massive, winged dinosaur revealed itself.

E-A and Kam gazed in absolute awe.

Theo wore a big grin.

Leaves kicked up. Grass looked as if it would rip right out from the dirt due to the sheer force the creature produced.

Each flap of its wings lessened in strength as it lowered itself to the humans.

Backing away, Kam's wonder morphed into a respectful fear. "Holy mother of—"

SLAM!

The birdlike reptile's back feet hit the ground, followed by its three-toed claws attached to its wing. Almost completely black, the creature had the same yellowish spots like the one that had been seen earlier. A closer look revealed streaks of tiger-orange from its shoulders to the wingtips. Black continued up its slender neck until the same shade of orange began under its chin until the dangerous, lethal beak took over.

"This thing is…" Kam ended up falling backward as he took in the immense stature of the animal. "…*freaking* huge!"

Dumbfounded, E-A remembered the large shadow moments before her dad had shown up. "Were you…*flying* that thing?"

The other's reactions made Theo laugh. "Meet Quinley, the quetzalcoatlus."

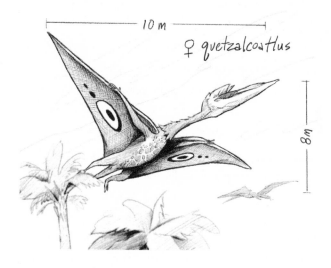

A blend of confusion and intimidation formed on Kam's face. "What? Quest-coat… huh?"

"Say it this way." Theo strolled right up and rubbed the dinosaur's muscular back. "Ket-zull-coat-lus. Once thought to be from the late cretaceous period. Found in North America, interestingly enough."

E-A kept her distance. "Apparently everyone likes using alliteration names."

"It's…" Back on his feet, Kam gulped as the tip of the animal's beak came within a foot from his face. "…as tall as a giraffe?"

Like a cowboy with his horse, Theo patted Quinley at the base of its neck. "That's the average height of their species. Some are even taller and have the wingspan of a small plane or jet."

"Which brings me back to my question." Since her dad didn't show any trepidation, E-A approached it a little closer. "Did you fly it here?"

Once he'd cleared his throat, Theo clicked his tongue against the inside of his teeth twice.

In response, Quinley brought its right shoulder lower to the ground.

Kam snorted in disbelief. "You've *trained* it?"

Grunting as he pulled himself up onto the front of the quetzalcoatlus' back, Theo locked his legs around its neck. "Wasn't easy." With his hands on its scaley hide, he began scratching. "Took me over half a year to get her to trust me, ain't that right, girl?"

The scientist's scratching made the dinosaur squeal with joy, and it began swaying its large head from side to side.

"And to better answer your question of how I initially found you, I keep tabs on SauraCorps' operations." Glancing back and forth between her and Kam, he grinned.

"When I saw your campfire from above, I had to check it out with some other *friends* of mine first."

From where she stood, E-A gave her father an odd stare. Ecstatic to finally see him after five years, to be in his parental presence once again gave her the greatest sense of comfort she'd experienced in a long time.

Being in his arms again stirred up her heart.

Yet, something seemed lacking in his eyes.

E-A gazed up at him. "Dad, can we ta—"

"Do you think you could help us find someone else?" Kam grew excited as he hoped using a flying dinosaur could aid in their search for Vivienne. "We got split up from farther up the river."

Theo furrowed his brow. "There's another person?"

Instead of chatting further about what she wanted, E-A gave in to Kam's beseeching. "Her name's Vivienne, blonde-ish hair. She saved me from a giant millipede earlier."

Theo's creased brows arched up to attention. "Gotta watch out for those arthropleuras. Nasty things."

"Yeah yeah, we know all about that." Impatience made its way into Kam's tone. "Can you help us find her? She... means a lot to me."

The teen's plea made Theo nod. "Hop on."

E-A and Kam exchanged shocked glances.

"It's perfectly safe," Theo reasoned in full confidence. "There's no way you'll be able to keep up with us, and I can't just leave you here." He scanned the clearing with alert eyes. "Plus, SauraCorps' team of brutes might find you out here. Wouldn't want to be around when they don't find their dimetrodon meal ticket."

"Gimme a boost, Kam." E-A lifted a foot, which the teen cradled with his interlocked hands. "Got any barf bags on board, just in case?" Up on the quetzalcoatlus' back, she reached down to grab Kam's hand.

"For the record…" Kam's right hand clasped into hers. "…this might just be the most insane thing I've ever done."

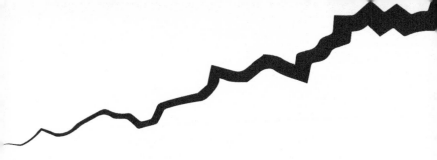

THIRTY-ONE

THE SCIENCE wing of SauraCorps.

In a laboratory within the science wing of SauraCorps, Felicia had met with a group of scientists. She kept rubbing her neck, trying to keep tension at bay. "Dr. Winters, are you saying this rift popped open on its own?"

The head scientist, a bob-cut brunette nodded. "Essentially, yes."

"There's no way of predicting anything like it," another expert added.

"Reports indicate a pair of chasmosaurus came through."

A huff left Felicia's chest, which turned into an exasperated sigh. "I'll let our friends in Houston know. They'll dispatch a retrieval team. It's going to be one heck of a story to twist for the media, though."

"First time for everything."

What the scientist said made Felicia shake her head. "Elasmosauruses fueling Ness reports in Scotland was one thing. Now Houston, and another rift in town earlier today, where do we even begin?"

Frazzled, Dr. Winters left the group and hurried over to a computer. Furious typing from her fingers brought up a program with an indicator screen. "Residual rift energy. My God."

"It probably happened less than an hour ago," Felicia brought out, wondering if it would help in any way. "Had an angry father bring a live trilobite into our facility for proof."

"What?" Dr. Speer—the other head scientist—gave her an agitated look. "Who did that?"

"We have bigger issues than that." Felicia went back to rubbing her taut neck muscles. "Keep me in the loop if anything else transpires." Heading for the door, she heard the people behind her squabbling and throwing scientific terms around.

As she walked out into the hallway, her phone made a little ding.

Due to the time she'd spent in the lab, she now realized how preoccupied she'd been as she scrolled through texts she'd missed from her assistant.

L. Cook wants a three-for deal.
Velociraptors for $825K each.

She answered:

Need to get rid of them.
Tell him $950K and throw in a triceratops juvie.

Then she came to the latest message:

Bartelloni called. Will be arriving @ 4 PM.

Later that evening she would be holding a conference call with the rest of the SauraCorps higher-ups to welcome Bartelloni into their circle. With everything else going on with the rifts, she found it difficult to pull herself away from worrying about them. *Maybe there are other rift issues happening elsewhere. Should I bring it up?*

THIRTY-TWO

SINGAPORE, MALAYSIA – PRESENT DAY

"STOP FIDDLING with your seatbelt, honey."

Sitting next to her son, the woman fidgeted with his seatbelt to make sure it was secure.

"Excuse me, please make sure your tray is in the upright position." The airline steward got the mother's attention before moving on to others. "Sorry, sir, you need to remain seated at this time."

"Mom, I'm scared." Recalling the first take-off he'd experienced to head to Singapore, Malaysia, the little boy disliked the thought of even looking out the window to his right. "I don't wanna do this."

"It's going to be fine, Will," his mother cooed. "Just like last time was fine."

Out on the tarmac, the plane came to the end of its taxi drive to the main runway. A few seconds passed by until the engines fired up into their fury of propulsion.

"*Moooooom.*"

"Honey, it's fine."

Little by little, the airplane pulled itself forward.

Will cried out, "I don't want to be here!"

"This is the only way for us to get home, sweetie."

Up in the cockpit, the pilots flicked switches and increased the speed for take-off. In a matter of seconds, they would soon engage the wing flaps.

Co-pilot Buchanan looked over to his co-worker. "Should be good."

"All clear," responded Captain Donegan.

Ahead, a blue sky with few clouds welcomed them.

Grinning, Buchanan remarked, "See you later, Singapore."

Donegan glanced to his flying partner. "Should be smooth sail—"

CRRRRACK-ACK-ACK! ZAP! CRACKLE! SNAP!

Smack-dab in the middle of the runway, a blueish rift materialized.

Scrambling to halt the air vessel, Donegan spit out, "The heck is *that?*"

"Are those…trees?"

Already three-quarters of the way to hitting one-hundred-sixty miles-per-hour, they struggled to slow down the careening plane. Buchanan engaged the reverse thrusters and yanked on the brake.

Frantic, Donegan barely blinked. "No, it's too soon for tha—"

SCREEEEEE-CRUNCH!

Below the aircraft, the wheels snapped off.

Asphalt scraped against the metal hull.

The nose of the plane veered to the left.

Crackling, the rift still stood open, threatening the oncoming vessel.

Inside, among the screams and panicking travelers, Will's mother threw her arm across his seat for protection.

Centripetal force sent the backend of the airplane swerving into the electric anomaly, slicing the tail just behind the last passengers right off. The hunk of aircraft crashed into a bunch of trees on the other side of the rift.

Coming to a complete stop, the right-hand side of the plane faced the strange opening.

Stunned by the events, the co-pilot's hands shook. "W-w-what is… What do we do?"

Eyes on the rift, Donegan subconsciously reached for the com. After taking a moment to gather whatever thoughts he had, he began. "Folks, um…this is your captain. These are circumstances we've… Well, we've never experienced something like this before."

Once he'd unbuckled his seatbelt, Buchanan stepped over to the window to get a better look. "What do we even classify that as?"

The door to the cockpit opened, and a steward hurried in. "Passengers are freaking out back there."

Mayhem.

Up and down the aircraft, people scrambled and shouted at each other to try and comprehend what had just occurred.

Will's mother kissed him on the forehead. "Honey, I'm going to get your father and make sure we're together, okay?"

From his angle, Will caught a glance of feet undulating past the top of the window. "Mom. Mom *something's* out there!"

At the rear of the plane, confused passengers bickered with their backs turned to the opening.

"Does anyone know what that thing is?"

"Maybe if we all sat down and calmed ourselves, we could get some—*aaaaaah!*"

Pulled out of the vessel, the man's scream got cut short as mandibles dragged him out of view to the top of the plane.

Eyes wide open, the younger man staggered back. "Holy jeez—*aack!*"

A ravenous, giant millipede snagged his left foot, making him stumble to the floor.

Others near the back yelled in fear as they backed away.

Throwing his arms behind him, the blond became paralyzed with fear as the massive bug's legs struck him in the sides as it went for his head.

"No, please! Someone help—"

THIRTY-THREE

"HOW MUCH farther do we have to go?" Vivienne fought to keep her leg muscles engaged, considering she'd swam for her life earlier, and now trekked with the ex-SauraCorps bigwig. Exhaustion became harder to ignore.

Sebastian leaned his head side to side. "Ten, maybe fifteen minutes."

Up ahead of them, Nandy still trotted and sniffed different areas of the forest.

Stuck with the man, a somewhat reluctant Viv tried some conversation. "So, what makes someone decide to get into, the uh...dinosaur business?"

Without looking at her, he coughed before answering. "Um...money."

She snorted. "Oh yeah? How much would it cost me to buy a T-rex?"

Giving her a half-amused grin, he raised an eyebrow. "With the discovery of their population being in what we call a 'common' category, highest they'll go for is just under two million."

The number made her whistle. "Only two? Unfortunately, that's out of my bank account's range."

He shook his head. "SauraCorps does take payment plans."

"Hard pass." Something he'd mentioned earlier nagged her to expand on it. "Common category, huh? What would a super rare dino be?"

By this point, Sebastian came to a stop and rubbed his calves. "Based on notes from the archaeological society, and what's discovered thanks to the rift...." With his left hand, he stuck his fingers out in succession. "Giganotosaurus, bigger than a rex. Abelisaurus, also a cousin of the rex. Psittacosaurus, an herbivore with a weird turtle-ish head and side tusks, and a frill coming out of its tail. I'd say those are the top three."

"And the cost of just one?"

He counted in his head. "Unless we find more, pretty close to a hard billion."

Vivienne's jaw dropped wide open. The sheer amount of casualness in his tone made her almost livid. "If that isn't *repulsive* trafficking, I don't know what is."

"Yeah." Sebastian closed his eyes, letting guilt trickle in. "Other than making things comfortable, it paid my lawyer bills." A callous exterior overtook him. "But since my ex-wife knew how much I was worth, she became an extortionist when it came to joint custody of the kids."

Sorrow seeped from his voice, tugging on Vivienne's empathetic strings. It reminded her of how Kamren would talk about writing his books and how he would write his villains.

He would always say: When a villain has the right backstory, even they have the chance of winning your heart.

"But I won't bore you with all that." The more Sebastian spoke about it, the more he didn't want to. To be stuck with a teen girl in the time where he'd made his livelihood was the last thing he'd anticipated. "So…you and the guy, how long have you two been going out?"

"Haven't started." She wanted to keep things on that front brief. "And I'm not about to talk to you about my love life, either."

Near exasperation, he caught sight of Nandy picking up speed as it neared a small clearing. "There's no sign of the base. Wonder what it found."

The humans left the cover of trees.

Nandy had started making new friends.

"Therizinosaurus," Sebastian recalled, impressed with the number of them in the pack, also known as a 'lounge'.

The first thing Viv noticed was the three-foot-long, scythe-like claws protruding from each of the therapod dinosaurs' hands. "Charlize-Theron-what-a-saurus?"

Sebastian snort-laughed. "Ther-eh-zee-know-saurus. Also known as the 'scythe lizard'." He took note of one of them in the distance raking its sword-length claws through the ground to loosen vegetation.

Then it lifted a sapling to its petite-beaked mouth to rip a stringy branch off and mow down.

"Guess that answers my question if they're herbivores or

not." Viv took a trepidatious step forward while keeping her gaze locked on the creatures. "Still wouldn't want to meet one of those in a dark alley though—"

therizinosaurus
♀
6 m
10 m

Crackle.

Viv looked down at her foot.

Shards of egg mingled with albumen and liquid embryo.

One of the female therizinosauruses cocked its head, making the bristly feathers running down its neck twitch as it honked.

"Oh no." Viv scraped the bottom of her shoe against the grass as she backed away.

Sebastian followed her lead. "I think you made her angry."

Other therizinosauruses joined in, creating a chorus of agitated bellows as they massed toward the humans.

"Yeah, I kinda got that…" Viv's voice grew louder as she retreated to the forest. "…from their *rage-filled* cries!"

One of the dinosaurs swiftly broke away from the group, whipping its lethal talons through the air at her.

Viv darted behind a tree. She glanced right as a trio of claws flung at her, but only one of them tore into the bark. Before the therapod could land another swipe, she pushed forward and didn't look back.

Sebastian had also been running from the creatures and had Nandy zoom past him. "Thought you were supposed to be her protector."

Behind them, Viv failed to summon more energy to keep pressing on.

A few therizinosauruses gained on her.

One of the scythe-like claws clipped the back of her shirt, creating a tear as she lunged through two young saplings. Two steps after—

Ka-thunk!

Tread of her shoe lost traction on a nefarious tree root sticking out of the ground.

Leaves and dirt met Viv's left cheek.

Wincing, she dug her fingers into the ground before flipping onto her back.

Three of the dinosaurs circled her, their distressed honks and screeches filling the air. The mother who'd lost her unborn young stepped forward, twitching the talons on both of its hands. It shrieked at the small human.

Smack!

A softball-sized rock connected with the side of the

Therizinosaurus' head, making it rear back and screech at the source.

"Hey!" Sebastian yelled out before swinging a thick tree branch at one of the dinosaurs to the right. "Get *back!*"

Viv looked over only to see the club getting knocked out of Sebastian's hands by the other therizinosaurus. Her lips trembled faster than ever before. Though the animals in front of her weren't carnivores, she recognized a simple truth. *Even if a creature won't eat you, it can still be dangerous.*

All of her strength drained from her muscles.

Only one thing kept her will alive.

Kamren's face remained a constant in her mind.

As the therizinosaurus approached, raising its deadly claws for a strike, it turned its head enough to lock its gaze with the teenager. One last reminder of its superiority.

And of its primeval, unforgiving world.

Vivienne closed her eyes. *Goodbye, Ka—*

"Fire!"

KA-BLAM!

Nets entangled the first therizinosaurus, sending it into disorientation as it jumbled itself within the strong webbing.

Some of the dinosaurs behind the scorned mother turned back.

As for Viv, she rolled onto her side to look behind her.

What looked like army men held bazooka-type weapons. They'd fired the heavy-duty nets at the herbivores, while others formed a perimeter with modified rifles.

At the rear of the group, Sebastian watched as they took

control of the dinosaurs.

One of the men, a superior, stepped out from the squad. "We only need a pair of the therizino's. Let the rest retreat." As he stepped toward the girl, he wore an intrigued grin. "Got ourselves quite the catch today, gentlemen."

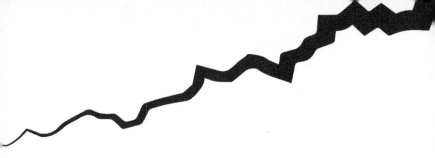

THIRTY-FOUR

"I CAN'T believe I'm doing *this!*"

Wind whipped past the sides of Kamren's head. His face had been protected by Emily-Ann's back, who was holding on tight to her long-lost father.

Flying on the back of a toothless species of pterosaur terrified Kam. There were no seatbelts, no complimentary drinks and snacks, and especially no on-flight bathrooms. *Might need one of those soon.*

"Hold on, kids," Theodore called back. "We'll be descending soon."

Though excited to be experiencing a once-in-a-lifetime flight, E-A breathed a sigh of relief. "Oh, thank God."

For most of the ride, Kam had kept his eyelids shut. By now, he'd gathered enough courage to finally open them.

A large lake could be seen off to the right, just past a wooded area of mingling coniferous and deciduous plantlife.

His inner child squealed as a remarkable sight graced

his gaze.

Long necks extended past the treetops, making the trees seem tiny in comparison.

"Small herd of Giraffatitan," Theo remarked, almost like the captain from a plane's cockpit. "On average, they can grow to about eighty feet long from head to tail."

Herds of Kam's favorite dinosaurs currently drank from the edge of the lake. "Are those Triceratops? And ankylosaurus!"

E-A noticed the most startling of creatures not too far from the well-known herbivores. "Dad, is that a—"

"Tyrannosaurus rex." Theo grinned, giving the side of Quinley the quetzalcoatlus's neck three pats. The creature recognized the signal to decrease altitude. "From what I've witnessed, assumptions of watering hole behavior being neutral grounds doesn't apply anymore."

The lake passed by as Quinley came closer to the treetops.

Another fifty feet down, and Kam figured he could've brushed his hand along the leafy tips. *I wish Viv could be here for this.*

The trees came to an abrupt end.

Gazing downward, Kam's stomach leaped up to his throat.

A dead drop into a valley with cliffs intimidated the newcomers.

As for Theo and Quinley, they didn't even flinch as they made a wide turn and headed back to the cliff face.

"Are we flying right at it?" Kam grew fidgety.

E-A grimaced as his arms clenched her torso—including her wounded rib—tighter. "Kam, lessen the grip, dude."

"But we're *flying right at* the mountain of rock!"

Theo leaned into Quinley's neck for a better grip. "Easy there, everyone, just a little more, and...."

The quetzalcoatlus floated upward, making itself almost vertical before it touched its feet down in the opening of a cave formation. Tucking its wings in, Quinley squawked into the rocky void, which reverberated it back at everyone.

"We're home," Theo announced as he disembarked the saurian and began helping the others off Quinley. "Well, my makeshift home, that is."

Kam hit the stony floor and hunched over. "Jeez, that... I need more warning next time, or..." Something churned in his stomach. "...a bottle of Pepto right now."

Once E-A's feet were on solid ground, she took in the hewn-out space. "You've been living here?" She noted the smattering of military-style lamps and a pair of large, heavy-duty cases. "And I approve of your pilfering."

Theo went to rest on the edge of a man-sized bed made out of random man-made and natural materials. "Yeah, I've been able to sneak some equipment from the SauraCorps goons here and there." He slid his hand under some of the large leaves and soft materials he'd scrounged up. "It's the furthest thing from a motel, but it does the trick." By the end of his sentence, he'd unearthed a handgun.

E-A's internal picture of her father seemed to shatter in that moment. "Whoa, *Dad,* what are you doing with *that?*"

Theo glanced at the weapon before holstering it into his jacket. "You mean my protection in case SauraCorps ever finds me?" Chuckles came out of his mouth as he casually strolled over to one of the greyish cases. "They figured I was as good as dead when they threw me through the rift. Since that hasn't happened, I've had the odd run-ins with them." After unclipping the rectangular chest, he pulled out a rifle. "Five years in a prehistoric world with people who still want you dead can change a person."

Some of what he'd said computed in her brain, while other parts still had a rough time breaking through barriers. "Guess I hadn't expected to find a different version of you."

Theo took a good look at his daughter, left the rifle leaning against the case, and came over to place his hands on her shoulders. "And you're still my beautiful, tenacious Emily-Ann. I still can't believe you're here."

E-A looked up at him with adoring eyes. "Nothing was going to stop me from finding you." A flicker of her eyelids pushed a pair of tears down her cheeks. SauraCorps' disposal of her into the past and the partly daunting trek intertwined with the relief of being in her long-lost father's company. "Not even a rift in time and space."

Over by the cave opening, Quinley the giant quetzalcoatlus had folded its wings in and tucked its pointed beak beside its core to take a nap.

Meanwhile, Kam finally felt his stomach settling as he sat down and leaned against the rock wall opposite from the pterosaur. He figured E-A needed this moment, so he kept to himself.

Thoughts of Vivienne still revolved in his mind. *Is she okay? She* needs *to be okay. What if something got her?* Before his thoughts could turn more disheartening, he remembered he had her cellphone in his right pant pocket. He pulled it out, saw it still had about twenty-three percent battery left.

The first thing he did after unlocking it was snap a picture of the sleeping pterosaur. Then he took one of the glorious views from the cave's entrance. He found a measure of comfort in a shimmering river cutting between glowing greens of forest. It all stretched on until it reached the base of a short mountain range. Other flying dinosaurs congregated in the sky off in the distance.

Kam's thumb pressed a button on the lower left of the screen. The camera display swiveled over to reveal her music app. It had been paused on the song she'd played while journeying along the river.

He stared at the playlist title for a good few seconds.

♪ ♥ Kamren ♥ ♪

He recognized some of the songs, which now had a whole new meaning to him.

Kiss Me Slowly **by Parachute.**
Kaleidoscope **by A Great Big World.**
Love Like This **by Ben Rector.**
Scarecrow **by Alex & Sierra.**
I Hear a Symphony **by Cody Fry.**
What You Do to My Soul **by Air Traffic Controller.**
Radiate (Like You Do) **by HARBOUR.**
In Your Arms **by Kina Grannis.**

The last one hit him harder than the rest.

Tell Me That You Love Me by James Smith.

Before now, the romantic sense of those words had seemed unfamiliar to him. With them being separated and her whereabouts unknown, he wished he could blurt them out to her. Instead, he brought the pressing matters back up. "When are we leaving to find my friend?"

Theo heard the boy's inquiry. "Give me a couple more minutes to gather some things, then we'll be on our way."

Impatient, Kam stood up as he shoved Viv's phone back in his pocket. "Every second we wait is a second wasted. We need to go—"

"Now, hold on, son," Theo responded, more level-headed than the teen. "Unless she falls into an arthropleura burrow, she'll be fine among the dinosaurs. Even then, the bugs only eat what they think is dead." By the time he finished his sentence, he'd picked up the rifle. "If only you've seen what I've seen in these last few years."

Something clicked in E-A's brain. "You mean the bug that attacked me was just being a scavenger?"

"Most likely." Theo caught sight of his daughter's hands, then recalled that he had some bandage wrap in his side pouch. "I've walked side by side with one, never bothered me." He pulled the wrap out and handed it to her. "But laying down on the ground? That's a big mistake."

All the information gave Kam a slight headache. "Are you saying that absolutely nothing has carnivorous tendencies?

What about recorded findings and—"

"Let me tell you something, Kam." Theo used the rifle as a sort of cane as he stepped forward. "Paleontologists have been guessing and assuming since day one. An educated guess is still a guess. When it comes to things like ancient cities, sure, you can record a lot more details because *humans were there* back in the day. But the dinosaur era? You can guess all you want because there's *no one here* to tell you that you're wrong."

E-A piped up. "Not even early man?"

Theo chuckled. "When it comes to them, they're not here yet. Or at least I haven't found any trace of them." He leaned against the rock wall. "What I have seen, and this was perception-*shattering,* is a brachiosaurus herd mingling with a giraffe herd over where Africa will one day be. Quinley and I took a flight over there. I've seen a tiger up close and personal with juvenile dinosaurs, and it never even took a bite to see what they tasted like."

Mention of the animal's name got Kam excited. "Like a *saber-toothed* tiger?"

Theo shook his head. "Modern. Orange, black stripes." He strolled up to the mouth of the cave and gazed out over the prehistoric view. "There have been so many species of birds in this time that have been living side by side with what everyone thinks dinosaurs had turned into." He sighed over the modern world's views. "People have been taught the wrong things for so long."

Kam began pacing back and forth, which caught Quinley's attention as she woke up from her nap. "But how can… That doesn't… This is hurting my brain."

Even E-A had been having a tough time processing her father's words. "If the present even had a clue about what you're saying…." It hit her. "*SauraCorps* doesn't want people to know."

"Exactly." Theo slung the rifle strap over his shoulder. "The only truly dangerous thing in this time is SauraCorps."

THIRTY-FIVE

"HAVEN'T SEEN you out here in a while, Sharpe."
Keith Archer's voice was as rough as his skin. The head of the
Asset Retrieval Units, he'd seen a lot since he'd been hired
by SauraCorps in their infancy. "But what are you doing
out here in this God-forsaken time with a teenybopper?"

Viv scoffed. "I'm eighteen, Sergeant Boomer—"

"There's been, um…." Inside one of the A.R.U.'s
meeting tents, Sebastian had to think fast. "Somehow,
rifts are popping up more randomly and frequently in the
present. This young woman and I were victims of this,
unfortunately."

"That so." Archer stood up from his foldable chair and
stared Sebastian down as he paced on the tent floor.

Viv and Sebastian traded subtle, apprehensive glances.

"That would explain why our radio connection to the
present has been fairly glitchy lately." Sighing, Archer
stopped right in front of a dining-sized table with a high-

tech radio, maps, and dinosaur order forms on it. "Ever since we sent the scuto's through the main rift, the connection's been shotty."

Sebastian tried to work out a timeline in his head. "You haven't talked to anyone from HQ *today?*"

Archer tapped a finger on the radio. "Affirmative."

Internally, Sebastian sighed with relief.

"There's absolutely no way to contact the present then?" Viv leaned into the 'accidentally lost' act, though it mostly wasn't an act to begin with. "But I need to get home."

As the information sunk in, Archer crossed his muscular arms near the tent opening. "If the rifts are misbehaving like you say, maybe we all should be trying to head home." He looked out over his men tending to vehicles and checking on captive dinosaurs. "It's about time we all got to see our families again. I'll be back, gonna update the team."

As soon as Archer left the large tent, Sebastian and Viv looked at each other and noticed tension draining from their clenched shoulders.

"Hate to say it, but it's a good thing the radio's down." Sebastian glared at the piece of tech. "If they try to contact SauraCorps and mention me, they'll kill me."

The severity of what he'd said made Viv's shoulders return to their edgy position. "Does that mean the same for me?"

A gutted Sebastian only managed a small glance into her eyes. "I'm...sorry."

Two thought processes clashed within Viv. One side told her to curl up into the fetal position and give in. The other told her she'd come this far, and there was still a chance she could get home.

With Kamren.

After rolling her shoulders to loosen them, she stood up from her chair and took timid steps toward the command table.

Off to the left, Sebastian rubbed his face with both hands, obscuring his view of her.

She picked up the chair Archer had been using and sat down right in front of the radio. A quick study made her assume to flip the switch on the left-hand side of the sleek black box. Whirs and hums notified her that the radio was now operational.

The odd sounds broke Sebastian from his anxiety-induced face massage. "Vi—" He dampened his shout as he glanced to the tent's front flaps. "*Viv!* What do you think you're doing?"

She placed her fingers on dials as tremors infiltrated her reply, "If there's a chance we can get home, I'm gonna take it."

Her sudden choice made him rush over. "Do you even know how to operate this thing?"

As one of her hands fiddled with dials, the other pulled a microphone closer to her mouth. "Give me five minutes and I can probably get the hang of it."

Another fast glance to where Archer had left showed Sebastian no one was there. "No. Leave it alone."

"But we *need* to—"

"I want to get home to my family just as much as you do."

"I'm not just going to sit back—"

"But if we get caught—"

Crackles came from the radio.

"Alpha team, can you read us?" A feminine voice from the present came through. "Alpha team?"

Sebastian and Viv looked at each other with a collective 'what next?'.

The voice spoke again. "Alpha team, are you there?"

Taking the microphone, Sebastian pressed a button at the base to patch through. "Yes. Yeah, we're here."

Viv kept quiet, allowing him to take over.

"Sorry we haven't been able to get clear communication lately, there's been interference due to unpredictable rift activity," the woman reported. "New asset orders are coming through—"

"Is that them?" Another woman's voice could be heard in the background. Some shuffling preceded the other continuing. "Archer, is that you?"

Sebastian tightened his throat to add some rasp. "Yeah, it's me."

Viv nearly snort-laughed before whispering, "That impression sucked."

"This is Felicia."

As soon as she had uttered her name, Sebastian winced.

"We have some updates for you of a different nature," Felicia carried on, business-like in her delivery. "Recently, we've had four inconveniences that we've had to rectify. They've been disposed of through the rift. Two of them are teenagers, another is the daughter of Theo. If they've survived so far and you come across the teens, bring them back through, as it will help put out some potential fires on our end."

Flabbergasted, Viv's jaw dropped wide open.

"Should you find Miss Lewis, take her out." Felicia cleared her throat. "As for the fourth individual…. Unfortunately, we had to dispose of one of our own." She paused again, taking a deep breath. "If you come into contact with *Sebastian Sharpe*…you have orders to *execute* him."

All Sebastian could do was sit there in silence.

SauraCorps had left him to die in the prehistoric wilderness. Now they had just put a hit on his head for added insurance.

Viv didn't say a word either. She'd learned so much about him in the last half a day. He'd displayed remorse for what he'd done to them. He had kids which he yearned to return to. Earlier, he'd shown courage when trying to fend off the deadly herbivores.

Her silent, caring look told him 'you're coming with us.'

"Archer?" Felicia's voice pulled them out of their thoughts. "Archer, do you comply?"

Sebastian opened his mouth. A response failed to materialize.

"Archer?"

"Loud and clear, Miss Voorhees." Sergeant Archer strolled through the front flaps with a wry grin. "And I've got Mr. Sharpe right in my sights."

THIRTY-SIX

ARCHER HAD two of his men accompany him as he dragged Sebastian out of the command tent. "Thought your story seemed a little odd." He kept a hand on his captive's arm while carrying a rifle in the other hand. "We'll spare the girl from seeing your death."

"Leave him *alone!*" Vivienne, although restrained at her wrists by zip-ties, hopped up from her chair.

Archer barked at one of his men, "Harris, keep her quiet."

"He tried to save my—" Viv managed to get out before one of the SauraCorps operatives zipped the tent flaps shut. "—life."

Sebastian stared at the ground as they led him through the center of the campsite. "You don't understand, sporadic rifts are popping up and creating mayhem."

"That so," Archer stated, unconcerned as he kept walking.

Frustrated, Sebastian tried to wrestle his arm free. "The more SauraCorps keep bringing dinosaurs to the present, the more they're messing with time-space energy."

Still nonchalant, Archer kept staring straight ahead. "Of course they are. Now how 'bout you shut—"

Sebastian got yanked back a step. His arm had still been in Archer's grasp, who had stopped in their boot tracks.

One of the accompanying men spoke up. "Something out there, Sir?"

Pointing his rifle at a portion of the brush, Archer took wary steps. "Keep your heads up, we've got comp—"

SWISH-THWAK!

A sleek beast exploded out from the bushes, knocked into Archer, and kept careening through the campsite.

One of the men cursed under his breath as he helped his superior up from the ground. "You all right, Sir?"

"Was that a damn Utahraptor?" Archer brought his weapon back up and spun around to check everything. "They're back *again?*"

REEAAOOW-HISSSS!

The chilling cry came from the left. A different angle from where the first dinosaur spooked them from.

KAOW-KAOW-KAOW!

Everyone turned right.

Another hidden cry.

Wind picked up from an unseeable force, making every tree in the vicinity sway and add more ambiguous tensity to the situation.

On full alert, Archer shouted, "Centralize!"

Most of the SauraCorps A.R.U. team convened in the middle of the site. Rifles up and ready for anything, they all kept tight formation like elephants protecting their young.

Off on the west side of camp, one of Archer's men exited a tent with a handgun and looked to the left. He glanced to the right.

A lethal, reptilian face hissed through its sneer.

His back hit the ground as he let out a scream.

Archer tensed even more as the cry sent shivers down his body. "Dear God."

Terrified yells came from another direction.

Gunshots erupted from behind him.

"What?" Archer realized one of his close men had fired. "What'd you see?"

"Some *raptor* of some sort."

Archer's eyes flared open. "We're under attack."

Stuck in the tent, Viv heard the stationed guard leave his post. *Now's my chance.* Recalling a video she'd watched, she raised her zip-tied wrists in the air, then whipped them downward as hard as she could.

Snap!

"Ow, jeez." Pain aside, she'd freed herself. She shot across the tent and came to the front zipper. Tentative, she considered her options while reaching down for the heavy-duty slider tab. *Do I make a run for it? Do they still have Sebastian?*

Something whooshed past the tent's entrance.

Viv pulled her hand back as a rushing creature's shadow

cast onto the left side of the structure. It bared sharp teeth and large, curled talons on its feet.

"Oh God." She gulped. "Raptor."

Rustling came from the front.

The zipper ascended at a slow and ominous pace.

Viv backed up as her nervous breaths raced.

The chair she'd been sitting in impeded her backtrack, tripping her to the floor.

Ziiiiiiiip.

She threw her arms over her head.

Footsteps entered the space.

"Vivienne?"

It took her a moment to recognize the voice before she uncurled her body and looked back. "Kamren!"

Both of them ran toward each other and collided into an embrace. Tension flowed in and out of them as they hugged tighter than they'd ever done before. In that moment, the prehistoric world and everything SauraCorps melted away into nothingness.

Kam loosened his arms a tad. "I thought I'd...." He repositioned his hands to cradle her face in his palms. Subconsciously, he brushed his thumbs against her temples. It helped solidify that he wasn't imagining anything. "I'm sorry I couldn't hold—"

"Kam, it's okay," she countered as tears dribbled down her cheeks. All the worries she'd had since they'd lost each other didn't matter anymore. "You found me."

Her tears made him well up in response. "I would've searched all of Pangea to find you."

Their eyes locked.

It was as if they had entered a rift where time stopped completely.

Kam angled his head slightly to the right as he grasped at her back.

Viv lost control of her feet, as her toes pushed her face closer to his.

Both of them had closed their eyes, but when their noses grazed each other's, they opened their smiling eyes for a mere second.

Her cheeks were tickled by the heat in his breath as if it had hands of its own pulling her in even closer.

His upper lip connected with the soft skin just above hers. *This is it.* He leaned in more as she clasped onto his biceps. *I love her—*

"What the heck's going on in here?"

A strong grip hauled Kam away.

"No!" Viv tried to cling to him before a SauraCorps employee restrained her arms. "No, stop it! *Let…us…go!"*

Archer turned the teenage boy around to get a better look at him. "Trying to be some knight in shining armor, kid?"

"Maybe." Kam went into defensive mode. "Are you trying to be idiots? Spineless dinosaur traffickers definitely fits the bill."

A cynical chuckle left Archer's mouth. "Idiots, maybe. But spineless?" He opened the front tent flaps. "Tell that to your friends that we just caught."

An unconscious Quinley laid flat on the ground as SauraCorps' men restrained her the best they could.

Off to the side, E-A and Theo had been apprehended with security keeping close tabs on them.

"Sorry, Kam," E-A called over, disheartened. "We tried."

THIRTY-SEVEN

"NOW THIS is what I call an interesting situation."
Archer smirked. In a secure circle of sorts, he had the
teenagers under the watch of his men to the right of him.
Theo and Emily-Ann were in front of him, and Sebastian
stood off to the left with more SauraCorps personnel. "All
this time we thought curious dinos were picking stuff off
from our sites, and it was you all along, Mr. Lewis."

Theo flexed his cheek muscles. "Do whatever you want
with me, just let my daughter go."

"No can do, Doc." Archer shook his head. "I've got
orders to eliminate everyone except the kids."

Kamren piped up and nodded at Sebastian. "Even Mr.
GQ over there?"

Head down, Sebastian said nothing.

"No, you're not," Viv called out as she stepped into
the open space between everyone. "You're not touching
Sebastian."

Everyone who wasn't associated with SauraCorps glared at her.

Emily-Ann gave Sebastian a disgusted glance. "Viv, why are you defending that human trash?"

Kam joined in, "He tossed us into this mess—"

"And he also tried to *save my life* earlier," Viv answered without waver. Having an audience gave her a bit of anxiety, but her gut told her to continue. "Mistakes can define someone, but definitions can change."

Archer coughed to break things up. "That's enough kumbaya for one day." He began walking towards the ex-businessman. "If y'all want to stand around and watch, that's your choice—"

Viv situated herself between the two men. "By the sounds of the radio-lady, you need me and my friend alive." Arms folded, she mustered all she had to stare back into rugged Archer's eyes. "If you kill Sebastian, I guarantee you we will *never* be compliant."

Kam's ears burned as he listened to every word coming out of her mouth. "They *what?*"

Putting pieces together on the sidelines, E-A knotted her eyebrows together. "SauraCorps wants you back in the present?"

Viv nodded, remaining in place as she kept addressing Archer. "That won't happen unless you let Sebastian go free."

After rubbing his lips back and forth along his teeth, Archer broke into a menacing chuckle. "How's about I just kill all of you and tell my boss the bugs got ya?"

Sebastian pushed past Viv, having had enough of the

bickering. "Just get it over with." He slipped a thankful glance at the young girl. "If it wasn't for me and what I did with SauraCorps, none of us would be here right now."

Archer shrugged and readjusted his rifle's strap. "Fine by me."

"I know where giganotosaurus' can be located."

All gazes turned to Theo.

The scientist surprised himself that he'd silenced and caught the collective attention of everyone.

Whether some didn't understand the importance or comprehended completely, everyone anticipated the next words out of Dr. Lewis's mouth.

"If I'm not mistaken, that's a rather large payday for you," Theo remarked with a bad taste in his mouth. "I've heard the chatter. They're considered rare, correct?"

Even Sebastian perked up. "That's the dinosaur *mother lode.*"

E-A looked to her father with bafflement. "Dad, what are you doing?"

"The way I see it, they now have the most valuable prehistoric asset in their custody." Confidence and regret mixed within Theo's voice. "Me."

E-A immediately thought of the journal he'd given her. "You're offering them your knowledge so they can keep doing what they're doing?"

Theo gave his daughter an endearing stare. "If it means saving you and everyone else here, then yes."

"Interesting proposition." Archer stroked his chin as the temptation of a big payday held on to him. "I'll have to run this intel past my higher-ups, of course." He began walking back to the command tent. "Sharpe and you kids, you're with me."

Without any snippy remarks, Kam followed beside Viv. After what she'd said earlier, he needed to understand. "You seriously trust that Sharpe guy now?"

"I've learned a lot about him in the last few hours," Viv responded with a shrug, which was all she could do with her wrists bound once more. "And it's true, he tried to save me from dinos with wicked talons."

What she'd said silenced him. Earlier that day, he thought there had been a chance that she'd perished by the torrent river. To discover that she almost could've died twice sent his insides into a tizzy—which reminded him of the other unrelated tizzy she'd given him just a couple of minutes ago in the command tent. "Also…are we gonna talk about what *almost happened* in there?"

Seriousness in Viv's face waned into bashfulness as they entered the tent. "Later, but definitely."

On their own in a different tent, E-A sat across from her father. "I'm supposed to be saving you from all of this." She rubbed the back of her calf with her sneakered foot. "Not get you deeper into it."

Theo looked her in the eyes before switching his gaze to a distant corner where a SauraCorps operative stood watch.

His uneasy reserve made her pull her head back in

puzzlement. "Dad, what aren't you telling—"

"Em, you shouldn't...." He closed his eyes as he hung his shaking head. "I love that you came for me, honey, but... you shouldn't have come for me."

Within seconds, E-A's heart seemed to swell and shatter at the same time. Wanting to reply, all she could respond with at first was an audible exhale from her open mouth. Unexpected ache coated the one word that finally came out. "*Dad....*"

"Sweetie, when I first ended up here not on my own terms, believe me, it was stressful." He lifted his fettered hands to awkwardly rub the back of his neck, as recounting his time in the era made him rethink everything he'd faced. "But over time, I went from surviving to *thriving.*"

E-A struggled to accept his perspective. "Are you saying you want to...*stay* and live out the rest of your life here?"

Theo gave her the most loving stare a father could give his child. "Emily-Anne, most of my life has been studying dinosaurs in the bone. Now, I get to do it in the flesh." He leaned forward and took one of her hands. "I know you were hoping for me to come back home with you, but—"

"This has become your home now," she finished off for him, though it sent her body into a worse ache than what her hands had experienced earlier.

With her hand in both of his, he rubbed hers with both thumbs. "Of course, you always have the option of staying here with me."

The complete opposite of what she'd hoped for. She stared at their joined hands as his alternative slowly seeped into her mind. "I don't…" She recoiled her hand back with a small jerk. "I don't know."

Inside the command tent, Keith Archer sat in front of the radio while Sebastian and the teens were being guarded behind him.

A tiny bit of static popped from the radio before a voice came through. "This is Voorhees, what's going on Archer?"

"Certain variables have been brought to my attention, which I wanted to bring to yours as well," Archer began with an ominous tone. "Seems we now have quite the useful resource who's offering their intel."

"Offering their…." Felicia finally understood. "You found *Theo?*"

Archer chuckled. "More like he tried to organize an attack on our base, but we handled the situation."

"So he's dead?"

Grinning, Archer leaned back in the chair and folded his hands behind his head to stretch his bent arms. "Even better."

"Better than being dead?"

"He knows where to find giganotosaurus'."

Nothing came from Felicia's end.

Five seconds turned into ten.

Archer turned to look at his captives.

Kam, Viv, and Sebastian didn't say a word.

"Uh, Felicia?" Archer grew uncomfortable with every

passing moment. "Are you still th—"

"Sorry, something else came in." Felicia held a serious tone, followed by clearing her throat. "So we're using Theo for his knowledge of the dinosaurs and terrain? What if he's lying?"

"He knows the stakes, considering we also have his daughter," Archer responded without an ounce of bother. That changed when he added, "And these kids you want us to bring back, they insist on keeping everyone alive, including Mr. Sharpe, or else they won't comply."

Felicia sighed. "Freaking kids."

"Technically we're young adults, and we can hear you," Kam remarked.

Viv smirked at his counter while nudging his shoulder with hers.

"For crying out loud…." Felicia made an exasperated groan.

"I'm here, too, Fi," Sebastian added to the little chat. "And there's something you should know about the rifts—"

"Quiet, Sharpe," Archer growled, not wanting things to get out of hand.

"It's okay, Keith." Though getting overwhelmed, Felicia found herself drawn in more when she heard Sebastian's voice. "Let him speak."

Surprised by the turn in the conversation's direction, Sebastian took a tentative step forward. "From what I've discussed with others, there are more and more unanticipated rifts popping up. It's possible that what we're doing—" He cut himself off, remembering the unorthodox way he got fired. "What SauraCorps is doing could lead to destroying the world with time-space energy."

Slightly confused and troubled, Kam whispered to Viv, "What's he going on about?"

Shuffling sounds came from the present time's side. "You may be onto something, Seb. I'm about to talk to the board about what's happening."

Sebastian stared at the radio, shocked that she would agree. "Uh, okay then. Great."

"Meanwhile, I'll be updating some clients on the Giganotosaurus' status." Felicia shifted back into business mode. "Keep me informed."

"Y'all heard the lady." Nodding, Archer stood back up. "Time to catch some dino-cash."

A COUPLE OF MINUTES EARLIER – PRESENT DAY

"So he's dead?" Felicia sat by the high-tech radio in the SauraCorps facility. Her cellphone buzzed beside her, prompting her to pick it up.

"Even better," Archer responded.

She unlocked the phone's screen to read a message. "Better than being dead?"

"He knows where to find Giganotosaurus'."

The news from the past made Felicia physically pause, but her eyelids opened wide at the information she'd just received.

Rift just opened up in San Francisco a block wide. Trolley of civilians and two vehicles crashed through. Local police are at the scene & Feds are on the way.

How do you want to address this?

"Uh, Felicia?" Archer stirred her from the disconcerting predicament. "Are you still th—"

"Sorry, something else came in." Felicia cleared her throat. "So we're using Theo for his knowledge of the dinosaurs and terrain? What if he's lying?"

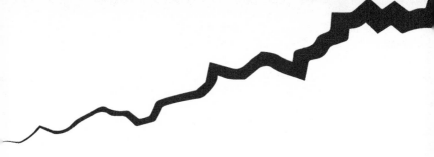

THIRTY-EIGHT

FELICIA SAT in front of her laptop at her desk a couple of minutes later.

Voices came from the computer, greeting ones back and forth and making chit-chat. SauraCorps board members had been contacted for an impromptu meeting.

"All right, we might as well get started," Felicia spoke up, getting everyone's attention. "Thank you all for sacrificing some time out of your day. For those of you who were sleeping, my apologies, but what I have to discuss is something that we cannot put off any longer."

Knock-knock-knock.

Felicia turned her head to her office door. "Come in."

Anthony Bartelloni strolled in, sporting one of his sharpest suits. He heard the voices of his fellow board members and sat down in a chair across from Felicia.

As for Felicia, she'd never dealt with Bartelloni in this environment and wondered how he would act. "Now that we're all here, we need to discuss the rift situation."

"Is this related to the incident in Singapore?" Mr. Xing inquired, sleepy-eyed. "Our men have contained the arthropleura. Injured are having their treatments covered by our contingency funds."

The Norwegian Tómasson piped up, "Three men died, correct?"

"There's been another incident near the heart of San Francisco," Felicia brought up, which induced multiple faces staring at her in alarm. "The rift closed up, trapping almost thirty people in the prehistoric time."

A few gasped.

Miss Favreau, the French woman spoke in apprehension. "They are getting bigger?"

Mr. Xing rubbed his forehead. "They are getting worse."

"So we'll just keep monitoring them as closely as possible," Bartelloni suggested, skimming through the e-mails in his phone. "Keep business going as usual."

The other board members within Felicia's screen uttered bothered noises.

"And what if a rift engulfs an entire city?" Another member inquired, which made quite a few realize the perilous ramifications.

"Then we'll have even better access," Bartelloni countered, nonchalant with an ounce of smugness. "And as long as we have access to what makes all of us an excess amount of money, I don't see what the problem is."

"The *problem* is that the rifts keep getting bigger," Felicia threw back as professional as possible. Everyone else seemed to be getting the idea except for her new colleague. "Forget city blocks or even cities. By our analyst's calculations, they could grow at a rate of possibly spanning entire continents by some point. More people might get trapped in the past, leading to possible casualties. And who knows what screwing with time will do overall."

Bartelloni let out a small chuckle. "But with the right perspective, or should I say *motivations*…." He clicked some buttons on his cellphone. "…it's no longer a problem."

One of the board members received a notification.

Within seconds, more cellphones dinged and beeped.

Miss Favreau received an e-mail right before Tómasson did.

Mr. Xing's eyes opened wide as he opened his e-mail to find a video of a familiar hotel room. The door to the room opened. He walked in, along with a woman who wasn't his wife. "Mr. Bartelloni, *what is the meaning*—"

"It wasn't difficult getting dirt on each and every one of you," Bartelloni remarked, victorious in his delivery. Up and out of the chair, he made his way over to eventually glare into the laptop screen. "Especially since this little close-knit SauraCorps family you've got going here did most of the digging on each other. I have two words for everyone—better firewalls."

Flabbergasted, Felicia had backed up in her wheeled desk chair as she stared at her phone in utter disbelief. "Anthony, this is—"

"As long as dinosaurs are coming through those rifts, there are no issues." Determination smothered every single one of his words. "And if anyone here at SauraCorps blows even the faintest whistle, I will destroy SauraCorps."

Felicia simply let her hand rest on her skirted thigh. It dumbfounded her how blinded Anthony Bartelloni had become with his greed. Admittedly, she'd more than appreciated what she'd been able to make of herself with dinosaur sales.

Now she'd seen one of the ugliest sides of all face-to-face.

"Pleasure chatting with you all." Bartelloni closed the laptop before perching on the edge of Felicia's desk. "Now, let's discuss those giganotosaurus', shall we?"

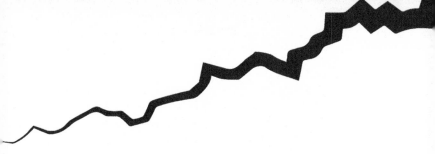

THIRTY-NINE

MINUTES LATER, five SauraCorps vehicles tore through semi-dense forest.

So far it had been a quiet trip for Theodore and Emily-Ann Lewis in the back of one of the army-style jeeps. After all the time of being apart and missing each other, they met an emotional impasse.

Over in another bumpy vehicle, Kamren and Vivienne had also been sitting in silence. Though they didn't talk about anything, their eyes had connected more than a few times.

Kam arched his eyebrows and leaned his head at her as if to say *'Are you okay?'*

Viv grinned and nodded, then bobbed her head in response. *'I'm good. You?'*

His smile reached almost from ear to ear. To utter the words 'I love you' behind a couple of random people didn't seem like the right moment. He wanted to give her a sign of affection, but a kiss—even on the cheek—also didn't seem appropriate at the time.

Then he reached into his pant pocket.

Viv's cellphone slid into the side of her hand.

Surprise took over her face. "You've had it?"

Again, he nodded. "You dropped it before heading into the river. It was all I had of you while I thought…." He started to take his hand away.

Viv caught him by the wrist. "I get it."

Both of them looked down at their hands.

Gently, he turned his palm over, letting her fingers glide toward his.

A fiery heat engulfed them when their digits intertwined. The residual heat licked up their arms, eventually inflaming every bone and cell within them. When they were little, they'd innocently held hands plenty of times.

This time, it set both of their hearts blazing for each other.

At that moment, Kam recalled what E-A had said to him early on. *'A fire doesn't know it's a fire until the spark has been lit.'*

Their hands being clasped tight reminded Viv of when they'd locked hands together in the chaos of the river. That also brought to mind the words she'd only been able to partially tell him. It was as if her heart nudged her chin downward to speak. "Kam, I—"

Screech!

She jostled forward along with Kam as the jeep came to a halt.

Creatures scattered from a riverbank as the vehicles had passed the forest's edge.

Both teenagers unclipped their seatbelts as they noticed the other jeeps had already arrived and had started unloading equipment and their occupants.

Sebastian—still cuffed with zip-ties—passed by, being led along by two SauraCorps troopers.

At the riverbank, Theo and Archer approached a gangway leading to another form of transportation.

Archer called over to two of his men. "Get that apex predator trailer rig hooked up." Then he snapped his fingers at others. "Stowell, Katz, make sure we've got enough ammo for this trip. Don't need any surprises."

Theo noticed a few large claw slashes up and down the side of the hull. "Remember that time you had a Spinosaurus family attack this thing?"

Halfway across to the riverboat, Archer stopped mid-step. "You were there for that?"

Smirking, Theo began his embarkment. "I most definitely was."

Over on solid ground, Kam and Viv caught up with E-A.

"Your dad has a plan, right?" Kam couldn't see her facial expression as he just came up behind her. "I sure hope he does."

E-A didn't say a word. All she did was carry on walking toward the boat.

Viv tried to match her stride. "He's going to help us get back home, right?"

Still, E-A didn't respond.

Running ahead, Kam made it past her and turned around to walk backward. "E-A, are you okay or—"

"Boy, I am *the least bit* okay." E-A's voice rose as she spoke with both feet planted to the ground. "I risked *my life* going to SauraCorps, got hurled through a *freaking* rift, I've had to eat *disgusting* bugs, take care of you two googly-eyed, hormone-raging *twerps*, walk miles in a God-forsaken dinosaur world—only to have my father tell me he *does not want* to come back home."

The mouths of both teens gaped open.

From the boat, Theo had heard everything his daughter had just spewed.

Every SauraCorps employee within earshot had also paused to watch the show.

All Kam could do was stare at her wide-eyed, realizing the hurricane he'd just unleashed from within her. "Whoa."

E-A turned every which way to realize she'd become a spectacle. Embarrassed and fuming, she let out an aggravated roar before stomping away into part of the forest.

Theo had almost made it to the teen's position. "Emily, honey, let me—"

"Hold on, Theo, give her space." Viv got in his way, her tone equal measures of firm and gentle. "And time, she needs that."

"But I...." Scratching at the stubble on his face, a reluctant Theo gave in. "Okay. You're right."

Once Viv had observed him start to head back to the boat, she turned and didn't find her friend anywhere. "Uh, Kam?"

One of the guards turned to go after the fuming Lewis girl.

Another employee stopped him. "Dude, you sure you

want to deal with that?"

Kam had followed E-A into the dense forest. Tree roots and jagged stones made a difficult path. Eventually, he found her nestled up against a mossy boulder, hugging her duffle bag as if it were her childhood teddy bear.

She'd been sobbing into the fabric of the bag. Everything she'd been holding on to seemed to have been nothing but wishful thinking.

"Hey, Em." Kam noticed the streaks running down her cheeks as he approached and planned on soaking his words in warmth. "I'm sorry, I didn't mean to push—"

"No, Kam...don't be sorry." E-A pulled her face away from the duffle bag to look at him as he came up beside her. "I was about to explode anyway, and you got caught in my crossfires."

"Yeah, well...." He kicked a twig to the side before plopping down beside her. "To be fair, I'm kinda used to you telling me off by now."

After a sniffle, she snorted.

"Don't feel bad for yelling at me either," he continued, not looking her in the eye but directing his voice to her. "Let your emotions be what they are. When you try to deny them, even if you think you need to 'push them down' or 'be strong', you're denying yourself of getting past those emotions. And you're also denying yourself of being you."

E-A sucked in a deep breath. She wiped all tears from her face before looking at the teenager beside her. In the beginning, he'd been nothing but a nuisance. As for the last few hours, she'd seen who he really was and had grown to actually like the young man. "Thank you, Kam." Her shaky right hand patted him on his nearest forearm. "You're just a sweetheart underneath all that snark, aren't you?"

He chuckled. "I have my moments."

"And it's nice to know you care…" she added, finally meeting his gaze. "…lil Bro."

Surprised and amused, Kam rose an eyebrow. "*Bro,* huh? Does that mean I'm allowed to annoy you even more now?"

E-A snorted again. "Don't make me retract that."

"Nah, I wouldn't want you to do that," he responded with a grin. Considering how things had been in the beginning, he embraced their buddy-buddy relationship. "Besides, if you're going to be my *Sis…*" After he'd stood, he extended a hand to help her up. "…I'm going to need some advice from you on talking to girls."

Her hand clapped into his. "In that case, you'll need all the help you can get."

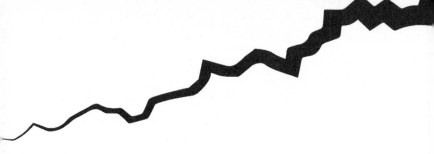

FORTY

IT DIDN'T take long for SauraCorps' heavy-duty boat to get loaded up and heading down the river. They pulled a floating cage specifically shaped for large predators behind the vessel. In the front cockpit, Theodore Lewis directed the captain and Archer of where to go, points of interest, and how long it should take.

Sebastian sat in one of the corners.

Up and down the vessel, Archer's men remained armed and cautious. For those who were used to it, the weapons were of no bother and served as protection.

Vivienne leaned against the left-side railing. "Wish there weren't so many guns around us. Freaks me out."

Kamren stood beside her, enamored at how the sunset's light made her hair gleam in shades he never knew existed. "Pretty sure you'd be singing a different tune if we were surrounded by bugs, though."

"If that were the case, then I'll ask for the biggest gun

they've got," she remarked with a confident smirk.

"I don't doubt it." He slid closer so their arms brushed against each other's. "Speaking of singing tunes, I uh… I found *the playlist*."

At first, she squinted at him.

Then she recalled he'd returned her cellphone.

Red immediately flushed her cheeks. "Oh, you, uh…." She began picking at the cuticles of her fingers. "You did, huh?"

Her bashfulness only encouraged his endearment for her. "There's a lot of good artists on there. The song titles were interesting, too."

"Really subtle, huh?" She chuckled to herself, realizing there was no turning back now. She'd anticipated and imagined this moment, and it had finally arrived in the most unconventional way and circumstances. "It was nice holding hands with you in the jeep."

"Hope I don't embarrass you by asking this, but…." Stiffness seized his throat as he looked across the boat in thoughtfulness. "How long have you thought of me in *that way?*"

Viv twisted her pouted lips to the side. "I've been…*fond* of you for a while now."

Her word choice made him laugh. He put on an old-timey voice. "Fond, Lady Lancaster? I reckon that means you've been waiting for me to clue in for a while now."

Warmth from his arm trickled into hers, which made her nestle into him more. "I've had to exercise *a lot* of patience."

"Viv, how come you never said anything?"

His question brought on a queasiness that she'd thought

the boat would've given her. "Well, we've been such good friends for so long, and… I didn't want to ruin that—"

"Don't use that cliché on me, girl," he countered, giving her a playful nudge before reaching an arm around her shoulders to pull her in even closer. "Better question, when did you realize that you knew?"

She spun on her toes just enough to angle her face up and gazed into his eyes. Many instances came to mind. To choose which time she fell for him, or fell all over again, became impossible. "I don't think *when* was ever a variable. Ever since we were young really. You've been by my side almost every day, had my back on rough days, even helped me out of those rough days by making me laugh until it hurt in the most incredible way. Along with random science trivia, there's so much in your brain that amazes me and keeps me on my toes." As she poured everything out of her, she kept squeezing his hand as another sign of affection. "Remember the first time you ever read me one of your stories?"

Kam took his gaze off her eyes for a moment. "You mean my Dino-man book? Oh jeez, that one was absolutely *horrible*—"

"But of all people, you chose to let *me* into the world you'd created. Since then, I've wanted to be a part of your world in every sense of the word." Viv couldn't stop smiling as she spoke. "And I want you to always be in mine, because…how could I not love you?"

For the first time, Kam thought his heart would beat so hard to the point of breaking a rib. "And there's no other world I'd rather be in."

His charming line made Viv grin so hard she thought she'd crack a tooth. Then she growled and folded her arms together. "Dammit, *Kam.*"

"What?" Confused, he stepped back. "What did I do?"

Leaning away from the railing, she shook her open hands up and down. "It's…" She huffed out loud. "You can't go saying things like *that,* making me want to *kiss you,* when there are *weirdo* dinosaur hunters all around us."

"Um, sorry?" Back into the boat setting and not the romantic scene in his head, he understood her concerns. "Pretty sure there isn't a private spot on this thing."

A SauraCorps employee strolled by with a hand on their rifle.

Kam shook his head. "Wish these Saura-Morons weren't an issue."

The armed man had still been within earshot and spun on a dime. "What's that you sayin' *boy?*"

Quickly realizing his mistake, Kam tried to deflect. "I didn't mean to offend. Though I get you all must be trigger-happy and just want to shoot something because that's what you do, right?"

Provoked, the guy threw his open hand out, snagged the teenager by the neck, and pushed him against the rail. "Want to see me shoot somethin' huh? Your little girlfriend may not like the target I pick."

Terrified of what might happen, Viv stayed back a couple of feet while shouting, "Get off him! Let him go!"

Kam placed his hands around the guy's wrist. "Pretty sure your…superior needs us *alive.*"

The man smirked. "That still leaves room for *wounded.*"

Splash!

A wet creature barrelled through.

Hissss!

Ka-thwack!

Kam half-stumbled as the SauraCorps antagonist slammed sideways into the deck.

The man tried to defend himself by throwing an arm up.

A blueish crocodilian dinosaur chomped down on the exposed flesh of the forearm.

Both Kam and Viv stood in shock and spoke nearly in unison. *"Nandy?"*

By now, Archer and Theo had bolted out of the cockpit due to the commotion. Even E-A had rushed over.

"Nandy, leave him alone, buddy." Kam pulled on the nundasuchus' shoulders, easing it off the injured man. "Easy, *easy* now."

A side-glance let Nandy know that its friend was no longer in danger. It hissed once more at the armed man before being led to the side.

"What in all heck is going on down here?" Archer shouted as soon as he noticed one of his men injured and laying on the deck. He unholstered his gun and pointed it at the uninvited dinosaur. "Did that thing do that to—"

"Kam, do you know this nundasuchus?" Theo pushed Archer's gun downward as he took a step closer. "Have you...bonded with it?"

"It's taken a liking to me, yes," Kam responded, wary of all the guns pointed at him and the dinosaur.

"Me too," Viv added shortly before Nandy hobbled over and rubbed its snout against one of her legs. "I've even grown fond of the crazy ninja-dog."

"Kill it!" The SauraCorps trooper stood up, holding his bleeding limb. "That thing tried to rip my damn arm off."

Before anyone could take aim, Theo stood defensively in front of the nundasuchus and the teens. "Now hold on, this behavior is *exactly* what I've been studying." Once he figured he had a full audience, he continued. "Every dinosaur that I've come across in this time is easily taught what is friend or foe. Treat it as a friend, they'll view you as a friend. Shoot it with a gun or injure it in any way, it will see you as a threat."

As her father spoke, E-A thought back to the time she'd greeted the utahraptor in his farmhouse basement.

"SauraCorps didn't want those findings leaked, because what's been perceived as being carnivores for so long would lose extreme monetary value." Theo stared directly at Archer. "Which, in relation, is why I've been wanted dead, correct?"

All Archer did was cross his arms and nod.

"Keep people misinformed as long as it fills your wallets, right?" Theo added, drenching his words in utter repulsion. "As for those giganotosauruses I'm leading you to, I can't wait to see how they react to you all."

FORTY-ONE

FELICIA SWIRLED the half-full glass of seven-hundred-dollar Tuscan wine. She sat on a plush barstool at the island of her kitchen. Unwinding after a stressful day, she hoped every sip would magically whisk the problems away.

Anthony Bartelloni's threats still loomed.

Rifts were probably popping up in other parts of the world, creating chaos that SauraCorps would have to clean up yet again.

Another sip of red liquid entered her mouth. She let the berry notes linger among her tastebuds until the dry tannins had coated everything.

Buzzzz.

She gulped down her drink before collecting her phone from the marble-top counter.

Xing's contact information popped up.

Felicia answered, "Thought you would have gone back to sleep."

"After what I heard and saw from Bartelloni, that was no longer a luxury."

She picked up on the disturbance in his tone. "He's probably tracking this call—"

"This is an encrypted line." Xing cleared his throat. "Others are on the fence, but I wanted to discuss more concerning the rifts with you."

She nodded, pouring herself another drink as something she never thought she'd say came out, "We can't let SauraCorps go on like this anymore."

"Agreed."

This had been the only time she'd ever heard him terrified of something.

"My proposal, is that we *destroy* them."

His solution brought her eyebrows together in puzzlement. "How exactly are you expecting to destroy time-space energy?"

"Since we began this endeavor, I've had my own scientists working on manipulating the energy on an atomic level." He'd spoke in an everyday chitchat manner. "We have found a way to contain an inverted form of the energy. Although tested on a small scale, we believe that if exposed to the rifts, it could be used to…."

Felicia hung on every word. "To what?"

Xing paused, considering everything he'd built with the means he'd taken from the gateway to the past world. "To close them, and perhaps *destroy* them."

Felicia stopped her hand from bringing the wine glass to her lips.

No more rifts. No more unruly threats to either time.

It also meant no more dinosaurs.

And would lead to no more job.

But the world would hopefully still be intact.

"Miss Voorhees?"

Felicia set her wine back down and collected herself. A decision had to be made. "Let's do it. Contact the others, except Bartelloni." Mention of his name made her glance around. "And let's hope our places aren't bugged."

FORTY-TWO

OVER HALFWAY to the giganotosaurus grounds, the SauraCorps vessel entered a swampy area. The sunset had almost disappeared, giving the night one last caress of colored light.

"Anyone got any food on this rig?" Kamren asked out in the open with Nandy by his side. "Couple of teenagers here, you know, trash compactors."

Vivienne chuckled at his quip. "Hope they don't serve bugs on this cruise."

"You two talking about food again?" Emily-Ann sat down beside them near the rear of the boat. She started unzipping her duffle bag. "At first they confiscated this from me, but thanks to the change in circumstances, my dad got them to give it back." One after another, she handed out the fruit they'd collected on their travels.

"Oh man, I've missed these apples." Viv took a juicy bite out of hers. "All I had for lunch was green onions."

Kam smirked. "Thought your breath smelled funky—"

"*Bogey* port side!" one of SauraCorps' men pointed his rifle down to the water. "I count one—"

"Make that three," someone from the other side added. "Two more on starboard."

Everyone with a weapon lined up along the railings.

Even Archer picked up his modified elephant rifle and rushed over to his men on the boat's port side.

Theodore placed his hands on the railing next to the teens, who separated him from his daughter further down. He glanced over to E-A, who looked away when their eyes connected. *Still needs more time.* Then he studied the approaching thirty-foot-long floating creatures. "Can this boat go any *faster?*"

Gripping his rifle tighter, Archer didn't like the scientist's inquiry. "What does that mean?"

"Those are deinosuchus." Theo recoiled from the railing. "And they're extremely territorial."

"Then let's give these dino crocs a reason to back off." Archer snickered, pointing the weapon down to the swamp waters. "All right men, fire off some rounds to scare—"

Snap!

"Aaaauuuughh!"

Splash!

Archer spun around.

Where three of his men had stood, only two remained.

Near the middle of the boat, Kam held Viv close. "Did that poor dude just Wilhelm scream?"

"Damn dinos." Archer turned to aim over the railing he

stood by. "Give 'em all—"

Banana-sized teeth shot out of the swamp, attached to a six-foot-long snout. It chomped onto the rifle of the SauraCorps employee beside the superior, pulling the man down and under the churning water.

"Get back from the railing!" Theo suggested, understanding the creature's behavior. "With bigger threats, they attack what looks like appendages."

With their forces down two men already, Archer agreed with Dr. Lewis. "Fall back, men! And get this rig going fast—"

CRRRRACK-ACK-ACK!

"Oh jeez." Kam recognized the sound as blue light glowed in front of him. "Not again."

ZAP! CRACKLE! SNAP!

Half-submerged, the effervescing right side of the rift shredded a section of the vessel's front port side. The strike pushed the boat over, giving most a view of the rift's future side.

Water poured down into the local movie theater of Kam and Viv's hometown.

Screaming people clamored out of their seats.

The only direction most moviegoers could go was down, closer to the screen.

E-A stood up alongside the teens. "Oh god."

One after another, two deinosuchuses swayed their muscular tails and passed through the rift. As the crocodilian dinosaurs thrashed about and descended into the theater, louder screams erupted.

Viv looked down to her left hand, which had been

grasping Kam's shirt. It appeared that he didn't mind, so she pushed herself closer into him.

"There's kids from our school in there." Kam even recognized ones that had bullied him in school. No matter what others had done to him though, he didn't wish any harm to anyone. He wanted to reach out and help but knew there was nothing he could do.

CRRRRACK-ACK-ACK! ZAP! CRACKLE! SNAP!

On starboard, another space-time gateway ripped open.

Without any chance of stopping, a transport truck barrelled through and crashed into the swamp, grazing enough of the boat to push it closer to the first rift. Cars behind it managed to slam on the brakes before reaching the second rift.

All of SauraCorps' men helplessly watched.

Archer's jaw subconsciously dropped.

Up in the boat's cockpit, Sebastian shook his head.

Z-Z-ZAP! ZZZZEEEEUUUU-POP! POP!

Tiny bits of energy static fizzled as both rifts disintegrated into nothingness.

Nobody on the large vessel said a word.

Among the silence, a few of Archer's men stood in disbelief.

Theo opened his mouth to make a snarky remark, but opted not to as he witnessed shame on the faces of every gun-toting person on the top deck.

After rubbing his face, Archer turned and coughed into the air. "Um…. Let's…keep moving on, men." He mostly stared at the deck as he made his way back to the cockpit. "Someone get me a status report on the rift's damage to the hull. Don't see the driver coming up, probably died on impact."

Around the middle of the boat, Kam helped Viv to her feet. "Guess the rifts are getting worse. I can't believe...." What they'd just witnessed replayed in his mind. "Hopefully no one got hurt. That would've been a horrible 3-D experience."

Viv rubbed her cold arms. "I've never seen so many scared faces at once."

"After seeing that, looks like these SauraCorps goons are getting a conscience check," E-A mentioned as she glanced around. Her eyes met her father's. Tucking her hands into her pant pockets, she moseyed over to him. "Hey, Dad."

Theo gave his daughter a small grin. "Are you okay, sweetie?"

She pulled one of her hands out to rub an elbow. "Other than still getting my sea-legs, I'm good."

"Good," he responded, happy to have some kind of conversation with her, even if it was awkward. "Glad you're good."

E-A looked out over the swamp, which reflected pockets of stars and the moon's grace. "I'm guessing you heard my outburst earlier."

"And you're entitled to your feelings." He'd taken a step closer, hoping he could give her some kind of comfort. "I'm sorry you went through all the trouble of—"

"How could you...." She faded into a quieter level and tried to reel in her exasperation. "I mean, I get why you would want to stay here. But...Dad, *why?*"

Theo scratched at the stubble on his chin. "There's times when life presents a door to you." Taking himself back to the moment he'd been banished, his momentary scowl morphed into a smile. "Life also gives you the option to walk, run, or drag your feet across its threshold. Sometimes, it doesn't even give you the option and *throws* you right through it, and you can't do anything about it no matter how hard you may try." Another step closer to her, he found it easier to connect with her gaze. "Even if that door closes behind you once you're through, it's what you make of the other side that matters."

"There are more rifts opening up, though," she countered, hoping the softness in her voice would convince him to go home with her. "Doors are opening again."

"Which will only take me back to a world of hypocritical, selfish, war-torn humanity that keeps searching for peace, but is always failing to find it." Slipping an arm around her shoulders, he gave her a gentle squeeze. "Plus, if I go back to the present, SauraCorps and the paleontology community still have a hit on my head. Unless my findings fit the narrative of what general science—and in this case, paleontology—has going, my research is null. I would rather live somewhere that's far away from all that. Or in this case, some*time*."

E-A completely understood his logic and reasoning, though she still didn't want to accept it. *He thinks he has no future in the future.* At this point, she figured there wouldn't be much she could say to make him change his mind.

Taking her fully into his arms, he kissed her forehead.

"This prehistoric world, as ominous as it may appear, this is my paradise."

Sniffles came from her nose as she used a free hand to wipe at her tear ducts. "As for mine, it will never feel complete without you in it."

Unprepared to hear that, Theo wrapped her right up in both arms as his chest tightened. He never thought he would or could hurt his daughter in any way. It warmed his heart to have her by his side, but her disagreement with his choices made his arms ache. "Wherever and whenever you are, I will always love you."

With her face in his chest, she managed to respond, "I love you, too, dad."

The embrace continued for a few more seconds until he angled his head down to whisper, "Now, go tell your friends that I'm leading SauraCorps into a trap."

The sudden swerve in conversation made E-A try to pull away. "Wait, what are—"

"*Please,* sweetie." Theo kept a firm grip on her. "Don't make a scene and trust me. I'll get you all out of here, but to do that, we need the giganotosaurus."

FORTY-THREE

FINISHED WITH their fruity dinner, Kamren and Vivienne had been reminiscing about times they'd spent together in the past, and in this dinosaur past as well. They tried their best to not think about their surroundings, the boat, and the armed people.

At one point, something dawned on him. "Wait, you took your sweater off in front of me *on purpose,* didn't you?"

Viv flicked his nose with a finger as she snickered. "Should've seen your face when I caught you looking. It was the cutest thing I've ever seen you do."

"I, uh…." A cough sputtered out of him. "Oh gosh, um…. How do I even respond to that?"

Her smirk grew bigger as he squirmed. "Choose your words wisely."

"Gonna put me through that, huh?" Chuckling, he composed himself as he looked her up and down, then focused on her cute face. "You'd look even better without the bug guts. Mostly, though…" *Never thought I'd say this.* "…I'm attracted to your kindness, your brilliance, and since you've been waiting a long time for me to clue in, your perseverance."

She delivered a slap to his shoulder while laughing before holding up her index finger and thumb apart by a smidge. "I'll admit, I had this much patience left in me."

Glancing away for a moment, he turned back to gaze straight into her dazzling teal eyes. Everything about her in that moment captured him. Having her seize his heart with just a look didn't bother him at all. "I should apologize then."

In the hopes of making him feel better, she took one of his hands into both of hers. "Apologize? For what?"

Now that she had his hand, he pulled hers closer to his face. "I'm sorry that it took getting thrown into the past to realize I could have a real future with you."

Viv opened her mouth to speak, but all words seemed jumbled up in her mind. The last thing he'd said made her want to bombard his face with her lips and everything she'd been holding onto for so long. Before she could even think about leaning in, the SauraCorps situation returned to her thoughts. "Really know how to put on the cheese, don't you?"

Kam picked up on her shy demeanor. "I thought it was pretty good, gonna have to remember it for a book sometime."

"Hey, you two *lovebirds.*" Emily-Ann had seen them holding hands from a distance. "Can I officially call you that?"

Rosiness claimed victory over Viv's cheeks. "Well, we're

definitely connecting on a new level now."

"Excellent." Making cautious glances all around, E-A got close enough to them so she could keep her voice low. "Hate to burst the love bubble, but my dad is planning something that will maybe get us back to safety."

Puzzled, Kam let go of Viv's hand. "But he made the deal with them. Give them the dinosaurs, we all go *free.*"

E-A flexed her fingers as she sighed. "My dad and I know SauraCorps. They…aren't the most trustworthy of business partners."

Fear and exasperation intertwined in Viv's stomach as she exhaled into the cool night air. "So you're saying we were *doomed* anyway?"

To try and keep her calm, E-A placed a hand on the teen's shoulder. "I'm saying you need to stick close to me and keep your eyes and ears open." She lowered her voice even more. "Whatever my dad's leading them into, we will still get you two home."

Up in the boat's cockpit, Archer stood a short distance away from the driver. Periodically, he would check his peripherals to keep an eye on Sebastian sitting in a corner. "Cheer up, Mr. Sharpe. Once we get these dinos, you're a free man."

A stifled laugh came from Sebastian. "Even multi-millionaires know words are cheap."

Archer chuckled through his nose. "Surprised you're willing to give up that life."

Still restrained at the wrist by zip-ties, Sebastian let them rest on his thighs. "It isn't much of a life when you're paying lawyers and an ex-wife just to see your kids, and you never get to see them."

Once Archer had registered that, he had nothing left to say to him.

The door opened and Theo entered. "This is a good enough spot to dock."

A quick once-over of the scientist's rudimentary map gave Archer enough to agree. "Set her over on the left." He reached over to pick up a receiver for the vessel's P.A. and brought it to his mouth.

"Actually, I wouldn't do that if I were you." Theo extended a warning hand, then emphasized it with an index finger. "It'll be easier to take them when they're sleeping."

Archer gave him an impressed grin. "If you say so. Sounds like you could've been a decent member of my unit."

Halfway back through the door, Theo paused to remark, "I'd rather appreciate nature than desecrate it." He made it down a set of stairs and passed by the unit members before making it to his daughter and the kids. "Everybody ready for some fun?"

As the boat neared the river's edge, Nandy became excited and headed for the railing. It grew eager to explore a new area.

Kam piped up. "That all depends."

Viv added, "Does the definition of that include bugs?"

Amused by their replies, Theo patted Kam on the back. "You kids are a hoot. I'm going to miss you both when you get home."

The three young friends exchanged confused looks as Dr. Lewis walked away without any other information.

A somewhat alarmed Viv called out, "That doesn't answer my *very important* question!"

FORTY-FOUR

MASSIVE GATES closed behind Felicia as she pulled into her parking spot back at the Utah SauraCorps base.

A few vehicles remained, but she recognized most of them belonging to cleaning staff and a couple of their scientists. Sometimes they'd stay late when big projects were happening, or in this case, big disasters.

Felicia heard her phone go off as she got out and shut the door to her Porsche. Once again, the screen showed Mr. Xing. "I just arrived. What's the status on the explosives?"

"We've already sent some off to the main rifts around the world," Xing remarked with intense urgency. "Thanks to our jet-drones, one had already made it to the rift in Liaoning five minutes ago. Another is off to the Netherlands, while one is heading to Argentina." He checked his tablet for an update. "Yours should arrive in less than ten minutes. Calgary should receive theirs fifteen minutes after. There are still more to go out."

His mention of one making it to a site made her curious as she leaned against her car. "Did it work in Liaoning?"

Xing cleared his throat. "It did."

She wasn't fond of his short answer. "Care to expand on that?"

"The space-time bomb succeeded in imploding the rift," he reported, tapping on a file on his tablet. The video surveillance replayed the events. "Because this particular energy is so unique and requires more research, we had no idea of certain *side effects.* Sending you the video now."

"Not sure if I like the sound of—"

"Make sure you are up on the roof to obtain the package." Xing said some words to his employees, then returned to the conversation. "It will work, Felicia. All rift energy in Liaoning is gone."

Hearing of success gave her some sense of peace. A few variables stuck out in her mind, one of them being Sebastian. "What about our people on the other side? And those kids—"

"The longer we wait, the longer we risk losing everything," Xing countered with absolute firmness. "Maybe by tomorrow morning, we'll have the world back to normal."

"Let's hope." Felicia hung up, only to turn around and see Bartelloni fifty feet away and about to get into his car.

Their eyes connected.

"Felicia?" Anthony closed the driver side door. "What are you doing back here?"

"Dammit." She hung around her Porsche for a moment longer. "I...forgot something up in my office."

Straightening his fancy suit, he strolled over. "Heard we sent a team for some giganotosaurus. Should we be expecting the delivery this morning?"

"Possibly." Felicia scratched the back of her neck, hoping to keep the conversation short. "I'll let you know as soon as I know."

"Sounds good."

"Okay, see you in the morning, Tony."

"Oh and, Felicia?"

She'd only taken two steps. Everything within told her to get out of there and book it to the roof, but she tried to keep any suspicion at bay. "Yes, Anthony?"

He smiled. "How about we go grab drinks sometime soon?"

Immediately, her eyebrows shot up. "You're seriously going to ask me that after you sent me the blackmail earlier?"

A single chuckle left his mouth as he shrugged. "Thought it was worth a shot."

Felicia maintained a good pace toward the facility's door. *What a frigging creep.*

Bartelloni made it halfway to his car when he came to a slow stop and squinted. Swinging his gaze around, he perked up his ears. "Do you…hear that?"

On full alert, Felicia had just tapped her keycard to the reader. All of her muscles tightened at once. "Hear what?"

Mechanical whirring came from above.

Both of them looked upward to the night sky.

An unidentifiable object flew in and descended overtop

of the SauraCorps building.

"Did that just land—"

Clang!

Before Bartelloni could finish his sentence, Felicia had already disappeared into the building. "What the heck is going on?"

FORTY-FIVE

UNLOADED FROM the boat and armed to the extreme, Archer's unit followed Theodore Lewis through the thick prehistoric forest. A few among the group hacked away at fronds and young trees to make a recognizable path back to the river. It also helped two large jeeps pulling trailers to follow along.

Between the treetops, some light from the moon and stars made its way through. Everything else was being lit up by swinging flashlights or headlamps worn by SauraCorps operatives.

Sebastian kept in stride behind Archer—the man he currently disliked—and Theo—the man who more than likely loathed him. Along the way, he reflected on each and every relationship he'd ruined.

Archer glanced back to his men to check on their collective countenance. "How much farther to go, Theo?"

Theo took in what he could see with his flashlight,

which he'd stolen from the camp a couple years ago. "We're almost there."

Those three words failed to resonate with Archer. "You better not be leading us somewhere totally—"

"Calm down, Keith." Theo didn't even look back as he replied. "And don't worry, you'll get your giganotosaurus. Maybe even a couple of them."

In the present, Felicia pushed her way through the roof access door. Making her way up a ramp to the helipad area, she noticed the small aircraft right away.

The idle smart-car-sized drone sat roughly ten feet from where she stood.

Attached to its underbelly, the space-time bomb glowed a menacing, unearthly blue.

A million thoughts burst into her mind. *This is it. Is this the right move? What if we're making a mistake?*

As she twisted the bomb away from the carrier with both hands, she thought it looked twice the size of an industrial mail canister. She tucked it into her like a swaddled baby and returned to the access door.

Opening it, she took one step in.

Slam!

Another door somewhere below within the stairwell echoed.

Alarm bells replaced all the doubts in her head as she closed the metal door behind her to make the least amount of sound possible.

Emily-Ann, Kamren, and Vivienne stayed close to the group's rear.

A pair of SauraCorps men kept them in their suspecting sights.

Without any cares in the world, Nandy trotted along beside its human friends. It sniffed the air a few times as it weaved between everyone. Slight noises made it halt and gaze around.

Kam hiked beside his newly appointed girlfriend. "Think these bozos will let me take a bathroom break?"

Viv sighed. "Really? You had a chance back at the boat."

"I didn't have to go then."

"That was literally less than three minutes ago."

"It doesn't really matter now, does it?"

E-A cleared her throat louder than their chatting. "Didn't take you guys long to reach marriage banter, huh?"

Kam smirked. "Does it make you uncomfortable?"

"Hey." One of the SauraCorps personnel called over. "Go take your leak." Then he spoke under his breath. "Can't stand this kid."

About to step away, Kam raised a finger. "Excuse me, Private Ryan, mind if I borrow your rifle in case something tries to, you know—"

"Go now before I shoot you."

Both hands up, Kam tried to suppress a laugh. "Loud

and violently clear." He headed left, slapped away some low-hanging branches, hopped over a mossy, fallen log, then finally found a spot worthy of relieving himself.

Yawning, he unclasped his belt.

Snap!

His fingers had just touched the zipper pull of his pants when he heard the twig break. "Uh…Viv? That you?"

Looking left, he kept unzipping as he turned his head to the right.

Hiss!

"Gah!" Kam stumbled back a step as he identified the reptilian face. "Freaking Nandy, don't do that to me, you dumb dino."

Snap! Crack!

Already mid-stream, Kam and the alert Nandy reacted to the noise that neither of them had made.

"Um, hello?"

Felicia had made it to the elevator which led to the basement. Thankfully, she hadn't come into contact with any of the janitorial staff on the way. Every footstep brought her closer and closer to the possible end of SauraCorps.

Ding!

The elevator doors whooshed open.

A half-second of hesitation went by before she boarded.

Repositioning the explosive, she stuck a hand out to press the button for the rift's level.

Ding!

As the doors began closing, she stared straight ahead.

Bartelloni came into view. "Felicia, what are you doing?"

Her eyes flew open in panic.

Running up to the elevator doors as they closed completely, Anthony slammed a closed fist into the shiny metal. "Goddammit, what's she up to?"

Meanwhile, at the front of the caravan, Theo peered ahead.

Archer had his head turned and nearly bumped into the back of the scientist. "Hey, watch where you're stopping—"

Theo's right arm sat at ninety degrees with a closed fist in the air.

The crew recognized the signal to hold their position.

To make sure they all knew what to do, Theo slowly spun around and shone his flashlight under his face. *"Go…slow."*

Everyone down the line stepped through the brush with extra care, including the jeeps as they decreased in speed.

E-A and Viv also complied, who had been cognizant of Kam still being a bit behind.

"Should I go see if he's okay?" Viv subconsciously picked at her thumbs again. "Or maybe he's… Maybe I don't want to go near that."

E-A's snort morphed into a laugh. "Girl, trust me, after what I had to deal with after eating that dragonfly, you don't want *anything* to do with that."

Entering the cave-like room, Felicia used her keycard to bypass the metal safety wall's door. On the other side, she gazed at the swirling, electrifying rift she'd protected for so long. At that moment, she reflected on its significance.

The rift had been a part of her life, her livelihood.

Now, it threatened the world she lived in.

Increasing warmth tingled within her arms.

A reinforced glass partition of the bomb glowed with excitement the closer it got to the window of space-time.

Every step Felicia took made the explosive vibrate within her arms. It was as if the energy of the rift itself and the reversed energy were calling to each other.

Ten feet away, she took one last look at the picturesque prehistoric time. *Here we go—*

"Felicia, what in God's name are you doing down…."

She spun around when she heard the voice.

Bartelloni had charged through the metal door. His eyes focused on the unfamiliar tech in her clutches. "What is *that?*"

Mere steps away from the nest, Theo grinned from ear to ear as he veered off to the right. He directed his light to small bodies within the flattened sticks and greenery that had been torn from trees. "Aren't you two beautiful specimens."

Archer finally got into a position to peer into the nest. "Wait, there are actually…."

"Babies, yes." Admiring the infant giganotosauruses, Theo hopped into the nest. "You know what that means, right?"

Sebastian took one look at the babies and immediately thought of his own children. "Oh…*crap.*"

All Archer could see were dollar signs as some of his men came up beside him to observe their findings. "Other than a full bank account, I'm not sure I follow."

Crouched beside the infants, Theo flexed his hand before making a flat palm.

Smack! Slap!

Both baby giganotosauruses woke from the strikes and cried out.

Archer's face went slack. "Theo, *what the heck—*"

"Yup." Theo sprang back up. "You just came between them and their parents."

RRRROOOOOOOOOOOAAAAAAAAARRRR!

"Is that what I think it is?" Bartelloni took a deep breath, trying to catch it as he had rushed the entire way to the basement. "Is that…some kind of bomb?"

Felicia noted his small steps toward her. "Stay *back,* Anthony."

"What are you doing down here?"

"We need to close it and end this," she answered,

attempting to steady her shaky voice. She took the weight of the bomb in her right hand and held it closer to the crackling rift. "Don't even try to—"

CRRRRACK!

Blueish time-space energy shot forward and lit up the room, taking both humans by complete surprise.

By the time Felicia had uttered a gasp, a pair of hands caught both of her wrists.

Bartelloni blocked a kick with his leg before shaking her around. "Give me...the bomb!" He overpowered her enough to throw her to the ground.

She yelped as her back hit the concrete floor.

The canister of unstable energy rolled out of her hand.

Still standing, Anthony darted for it.

His fingers barely grazed it when multiple lightning-esque currents stretched out from the rift's edges and clinched the tech.

The rift glowed brighter than it ever had before. Electric-like currents of the space-time force swirled and sparked like a storm on steroids.

Right in the center of it, the energy bomb hovered with the help of sizzling bolts.

Bartelloni managed to tear his stare away. "You need to tell me what—"

Clang!

On the safe side of the protective wall, Felicia locked it from the only side which could be accessed with a keycard. "I'm trying to redeem myself."

FORTY-SIX

RRRROOOOOOOOOOOAAAAAAAAARRRR!

Thunderous footsteps seemed to emanate from all around.

Archer fumbled to clip his flashlight to his rifle. "Theo, did you just make us frigging sitting ducks?" He called out to a pair of his cohorts. "Net the younglings before they run."

Theodore bashed into the SauraCorps unit leader, which jostled the rifle out of the hunter's hands. "You should've stayed out of this time!"

Weighted nets shot out and expanded over the babies, restricting their attempt to flee.

Archer charged at Theo, grabbing him by the shoulders and sinking a knee into his gut. As the scientist writhed on the ground, Archer growled. "You should've died out here a long time ago." Then he barked at his men. "Get those infants tranqed and rigged up. The rest of you, keep an eye out for Ma and Pa."

One of the jeeps pulled up to load the baby dinosaurs.

A couple dozen SauraCorps personnel had formed a perimeter around the nest, as it had become a possible ground zero of a parent giganotosaurus attack.

Distressed by the hidden cry, Emily-Ann stayed close to Vivienne. "Wherever Kam is, he better—"

"Momma's...coming...through!"

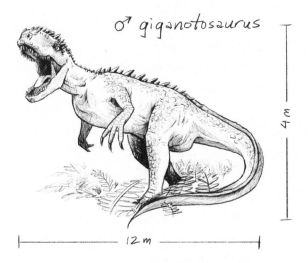

♂ giganotosaurus

4 m

12 m

A massive giganotosaurus head broke through trees. Another deafening roar bellowed out of its jaws lined with serrated teeth.

Nandy galloped out of the forest toward the others.

Kamren dashed through overgrown fronds and booked it as fast as his legs could take him to Viv. "Get outta the way, she's furious!" Back in her arms, he sucked in a hard breath. "Might be poppa, I didn't actually check."

Almost to the group of armed humans, the railroad car-length, eight-ton adult giganotosaurus didn't decelerate. It slammed its giant feet into the brush beneath it.

Some aimed their weapons at the behemoth of a dinosaur.

RROOOOOAAAAARR!

Crash! Crunch!

Another parent giganotosaurus barreled through from the left. It knocked the jeep over without much effort, sending the passengers inside tumbling like laundry.

The force of the mangled vehicle slammed into other SauraCorps bodies.

Theo and Archer pushed themselves away from each other, just getting missed by one of the huge, clawed reptilian feet.

One simple chomp completely encapsulated a SauraCorps employee. A limp arm stuck out from the second dinosaur's maw before slipping down its throat along with the body.

Alarmed operatives clipped regular bullets back into their guns and started taking shots.

The first giganotosaurus pinned one of the shooters inside of its mouth. It knocked a second man over as it shook the first like a ragdoll. It tossed the corpse into a group of men about to fire.

Terrified, Archer screamed out, "Give 'em everything you've—"

KRAAAA-KOOOOOOOOOOOOOOOOOOOOOOM!

Each and every human and animal turned its head toward the distant noise.

Cobalt-blue firework-like streaks lit up the night sky.

Some of them swirled and sputtered into nothingness.

"Was that…" Something within Viv constricted her gut. "…the rift?"

A snap right above E-A's head made her gaze up and turn to view it.

CRRRRACK-ACK-ACK! ZAP!

Bursting outward from a blueish core, a rift manifested.

A speeding black pick-up truck from the present careened and fish-tailed as the screaming driver had slammed on the brakes.

E-A didn't have time to move.

ZZEEUU-POP!

The rift collapsed in on itself, slicing the truck's engine away from the windshield.

Sebastian whipped past, snagging E-A's shirt with his fingers.

An awkward roll made the truck's partition slam into the parent giganotosaurus's leg.

The powerful dinosaur staggered, crushing another SauraCorps unit member as its thick, muscular tail thrashed around. It took out another two men before getting back up to kick the damaged truck parts out of the way.

On her side, an alive and well E-A rolled over.

Unable to stop himself with his zip-tied wrists, Sebastian winced beside her as his hip had struck a small boulder.

Stunned by his heroic act, she stammered, "Seb… Sebast… You—"

His grimace turned into a half-smile. "Thank me when we get back home."

Archer aimed at one of the adult dinosaurs. "Got you now."

CRRRRACK-ACK-ACK! ZAP!

Behind Kam and Viv, another rift materialized.

They discovered a decrepit city on the other side.

About fifty feet away, a figure covered in high-tech armor pointed one of its arms at them. A mechanical voice uttered, "Unidentified civilians. State your name and—"

One of the giganotosauruses rammed its head into a bolting SauraCorps employee, sending them through the anomaly. The machine-like being didn't even flinch as it shot an orange beam at the employee, disintegrating them before they hit the cracked asphalt.

Then it aimed it at the teens. "Threat detected—"

ZZEEUU-POP!

The residual wind from the rift closing tousled Viv's hair as she stared in disbelief. "Was that…a robot?"

A few SauraCorps men had taken cover underneath the empty trailer. Though they'd taken down large dinosaurs before, nothing had prepared them for the ferocious surprise.

Simple bumps from one of the giganotosauruses snouts made the cowering humans yelp and cuss. Its lower jaw slid under the trailer and clamped shut.

Kam grabbed Viv by her arms, pulling her out of the way of a charging giganotosaurus as two SauraCorps men tried to high-tail it. "Why are all these rifts popping up?"

Theo met up with his daughter and helped her dodge a swinging dinosaur tail. "My guess is something happened to the main rift."

"Something bad?" E-A caught her breath, resting her hands on her knees. "Judging by the noise it made, almost sounded like—"

CRRRRACK-ACK-ACK! ZAP!

"—it exploded."

The new rift opened by the trail they'd made from the boat to the nest. It gave everyone a peek at a dark, rocky skyline lit up with violet lighting.

Sebastian held his side as he hobbled over. "These must be residual rifts, like water droplets spraying out."

"If the space-time energy is unstable enough, it could do anything." Pulling out a knife, Theo grabbed Sebastian's forearm and slipped the blade through the zip-ties. "And thank you for saving my daughter."

Ashamed of his past mistakes, Sebastian rubbed his wrists. "I more than owed you."

Kam pointed to the other side's upper atmosphere. "Whoa, there's three moons in the sky—"

"Look out!"

The front end of the trailer flew out of the wrathful giganotosaurus's maw.

As the group split up to dodge the hunk of metal and wood, half of the trailer entered the otherworldly side.

ZZEEUU-POP!

Among the chaos, Archer stumbled into the forest and finally found cover as he readied his rifle. Tranquilizer darts had been loaded. He wiped his brow before aiming at one of the adult giganotosauruses and placed his finger on the trigger. "Now you're mine."

CRRRRACK-ACK-ACK! ZAP!

"Son of a—"

Water flooded toward him.

Caught in its wave, Archer flailed until his back connected horizontally with a tree. His arm smacked into another trunk, knocking the rifle out of his clutches.

A stone's throw away from him, Nandy perked up and sniffed the air.

The man's scent mixed with water became familiar.

Stepping toward him, Nandy recalled a traumatic experience thanks to the odor.

Most of her pack of nundasuchuses had been attacked less than a year ago. Their helpless cries and fearful hisses had added to the mayhem of SauraCorps trying to capture as many as possible.

Her hatchlings had also been taken.

They'd struggled to escape small sacks in Archer's very hands.

Sprawled on the forest floor, Archer couldn't move his dazed head. Searing pain encompassed his undeniably broken back. After screaming out in agony, he noticed a creature in his left eye's peripheral.

Nandy approached with rage-filled eyes.

Every twitch of Archer's back muscles made him shriek. "No, Go-*ow*-God, *please no*—"

Hissss!

"What about getting home?" Viv yanked Kam out of the way as yet another space-time gateway expanded nearly right beside him.

One of Archer's men didn't even realize as he'd been running away from the protective parent dinosaur. He hustled into Times Square of New York City and knocked a couple of people over.

Some on the opposite side saw the giganotosaurus and screamed as the rift closed back in on itself before the dinosaur could storm through.

"Jeez." Unsure of their odds, Kam looked at Viv's distraught demeanor, then pulled her in close. "Viv, listen to me."

Wrapped up in him, Viv let her agitation wane as he stared deeper into her eyes than he'd ever done before. "Kam, what if we don't—"

"Whatever happens to us, wherever or whenever we end up…" He took a breath which gave him the extra courage to give her his all. *"…I love you."*

A second after he'd said those three words, Viv teared up as she nodded, which brought her unsteady lips closer to his. "Kam, I love you."

Their arms cinched around each other as their lips connected for the first time. In that moment of complete disarray, their feelings for each other synced.

Rifts continued to open and close around the area.

The giganotosaurus duo continued to defend their nest

against SauraCorps men who had the guts to try and shoot them down.

Yet, Kam and Viv's kiss seemed to stop all anarchy, space, and time.

CRRRRACK-ACK-ACK! ZAP!

Across the nest, a window to the present took formation.

The teenagers came out of their passionate kiss and gazed over.

Viv recognized the area right away. "That's...*our* high school."

"Kids, go now!" Sebastian had already started running as best he could. "That's home."

Adrenaline coursed into Kam's legs as he took Viv's hand. "Come on!"

They took off, heading toward the nest where the giganotosauruses had taken up defensive positions. One of them lowered its jaws at the teens.

Kam pushed Viv to the side, helping both of them to barely miss the dagger-like teeth.

Having left her father's side, E-A rushed over to help Sebastian get to the rift faster. Swinging one of his arms over her shoulders, she noticed his shocked expression. "This is me *thanking* you."

Sebastian hurried through the rift, which cued relief to reach every nerve in his body. Swirling around, he reached out an arm. "Let's go, you can do it!"

On the prehistoric side, E-A kept her arms out to the kids. "Viv, Kam, *go go go!*"

Halfway between the nest and the rift, Kam noticed the

outer rim of the anomaly begin to twitch inward. "We can make it, Viv."

Safety became only a dozen feet away.

Viv kept her legs moving against their tired will. "Almost there!"

Five feet.

The rift began shrinking.

Kam propelled Viv forward.

Nandy sprinted behind them as if cheering them on.

Viv's outstretched hand connected with Sebastian's.

E-A gave her an extra shove, pushing her through.

On the present side, Viv grinned as she spun. "Kam—"

ZZEEUU-POP!

FORTY-SEVEN

"KAM?"

Vivienne stood on the solid ground of home.

But the only person around her was Sebastian.

"No." Her fingers raked through the front tresses of her hair. "Kam, he... He *had to* have...."

Street lights lit up the area.

Everywhere she looked, she saw no sign of the young man she loved.

Sebastian had no idea of what to say. "Viv, it doesn't look like...." He didn't want to make things worse for her. "I'm sorry."

Her voice cracked as all strength within her vanished. "But he... He was *right there.*"

"I was...*almost there.*"

On his knees, Kamren had sunk to the grass.

Gunfire could no longer be heard, as most of the SauraCorps people had either been taken out by the protective giganotosaurus parents or had high-tailed it out of there.

Kam waved an arm out in front of him in the hopes of willing another rift. "Open again."

Off to the side, Emily-Ann struggled to think of any proper words of comfort. "Kam, I'm so sorry."

"Open..." Kam didn't register her voice as he raised his own. *"...again."*

E-A had started walking over to him when she noticed one of the giganotosauruses turning to stare at the teenager.

Theo had just finished pulling the weighted nets off the dinosaur babies, showing that he wasn't a threat. When he saw the one turn toward his daughter, he froze. "Sweetie, stay calm, okay?"

But the giganotosaurus didn't focus on her.

Kam didn't care that tears had been streaking down his face. He'd finally realized his true feelings for Viv, and now something as complex yet simple as time kept them apart.

He took another swing at the empty air. "Please.... *Please,* open—"

A large nostril bumped into his back.

"Oh jeez!" Startled, Kam awkwardly turned and came face-to-snout with the huge, intimidating giganotosaurus. There was nowhere for him to go. Nothing he could do would get him away from the dinosaur's toothy jaws.

A vocalization reverberated up from its chest and through

its closed mouth as if it had sensed his misery. Slow and gentle, the giganotosaurus nudged its broad nose against Kam's torso.

Nandy exited the forest and saw the larger dinosaur tuning in to the boy's distressed demeanor. She trotted over, getting the attention of the mother giganotosaurus for a moment, then laid on the ground beside Kam and set her head in his lap.

"Oh my God." E-A couldn't believe what she had been witnessing.

"This adds more confirmation to my research," Theo remarked as he walked up to her. With everything he'd studied so far about the prehistoric creatures, this moment offered even more to explore. "This is something the whole world should be witnessing."

Though unexpected, Kam gave in to the dinosaurs comforting him. He raised his left arm to pet the giganotosaurus's gigantic head. His right hand rested on top of Nandy's head and brushed his thumb against her scales.

Kam noticed the others watching. "Didn't…this thing just eat a guy or two?"

"To defend its young," Theo answered, relying on his experience. "A mother elephant would do its utmost to save their baby, too."

Completely in awe, E-A left her mouth half-open. "It's incredible."

"By acknowledging our humanity and the true meaning of acting humane, we can understand each creature better, therefore bringing more balance and peace to the world,"

Theo waxed poetic, bringing his daughter closer to him with an arm around her shoulder. "I noticed you didn't exactly *jump* at the opportunity to jump through."

"Yeah." She nodded, fully aware that she'd had the perfect chance to be back in the present. "It wasn't the right time for me."

Puzzled by her statement, he looked her in the eyes and noted her smirk. "Ah, the right *time*, I see now." He kissed her on the forehead and grinned. "I love you, Em."

"Love you, too, Pops."

Unable to keep herself fully upright, Viv managed to reach the curb and sat down. She couldn't fight back tears any longer as they washed over her cheeks.

Over the last couple of days, her and Kam been through so much together.

They had discovered a lot about each other.

More than anything else, they'd learned to truly love each other.

Taking a spot beside her, Sebastian placed a hand on her shoulder. "How about we stay here until your family comes here to get you, okay?" He pulled out his cellphone and found it only had eleven percent left. "What's your parent's number?"

The mention of phones made Viv slip her own out of her pant pocket.

Clicking the side button, she noticed the standby screen

showed only six percent battery life. The front camera unlocked with her facial biometrics. About to press her thumb to the 'phonecall' app, she realized a different application had been left open.

Voice recordings.

She clicked on the last file that had been created earlier that day and turned up the volume.

"Hey, Viv."

The sound of Kam's voice both crushed and warmed her heart in equal measure.

"This is weird, talking to your phone without you around, but anyway."

Since there were no headphones in the cellphone jack, Sebastian could also hear the message.

"We're preparing to head out and try to find you, I'm currently sitting in front of a snoozing quet—uh, quetzal— you know what, that doesn't matter right now."

His stammer helped Viv to giggle though she still cried.

"What matters, is that I should've been able to tell that you liked me a long time ago. I feel like such an idiot, never noticing it before. As soon as I heard you say the word 'love' *in the river…"*

Clutching her phone harder than she meant to, Viv hung on his every word. To her, she wondered if these would be the last words she'd ever hear from him.

"…that's when I realized that I, um… I've loved you for as long as I can remember."

Viv's throat closed up, trapping every ounce of air within her lungs.

"It wasn't clear to me for so long, and again, I feel incredibly stupid for not realizing sooner. Everything about you has always made me happy. Your laugh lifts me up on a bad day, your smile has always healed my wounds. And for crying out loud, every time you slapped me on the shoulder for being a turd, I realize now that was your way of telling me that you loved me, even though I was being a turd."

About to comment on the word 'turd' being used in a love declaration, Sebastian opted to say nothing. He couldn't restrain his heart from being affected by the emotional circumstances and let a few tears roll down his cheeks.

Viv leaned her forehead forward, touching it to the top of her phone as drops from her streaming tears fell to the present-day asphalt.

"I just want you to know that whatever happens to you, or me, or us together, if we make it home or not..." Kam had taken a shaky breath. *"...that I love you, Viv. Past or present, the time we've spent together is time I'll always cherish."*

The recording finished.

By the end of it, Viv squeezed her phone and held it close to her chest. She wanted his words to be as close to her heart as possible. Putting her fingers to her lips, she lingered on the sensation of having their first kiss—and their last.

After giving her a moment, Sebastian gave her back a light pat and opened his phone to the call screen. "Let's, um… Let's get you home, Viv."

FORTY-EIGHT

ABOUT FIFTEEN PREHISTORIC MINUTES AGO

DARKNESS.

A grittiness hung in the air.

Anthony Bartelloni coughed before inhaling a deep breath.

Something likened to the sound of sticks cracking and rubbing against each other echoed all around.

Migraine-like pain throbbed through his head. "The heck… Where am I?"

Still waiting for his eyes to adjust, he pulled his cellphone out of an inner pocket in his suit jacket. He set his left hand down beside him, which helped him identify the ground he'd been resting on.

Anthony brought a fistful of it to his nose.

Dirt.

Another smell offended him.

Decay.

Letting the clumps fall back down beside him, he stretched his hand out again to help him sit up. His fingers brushed against a long, smooth object.

As he turned on the flashlight of his cellphone, he brought the item to his face.

A femur bone. Some flesh still clung to one of the ends.

Looking up, he couldn't see stars of any kind or even the moon. Only absolute darkness.

Crick-crack-crick-crack-crick-crack.

"What in the...." Swinging his tiny phone light around, Bartelloni discovered he wasn't the only body down in the cave-like chamber.

Except, the other bodies weren't among the living.

Small dinosaurs and animal corpses were mangled, heaped, and some only had half their substance torn from their carcasses.

He shifted in the dirt and directed his phone's light behind him.

Hissss!

A creature pulled its front end behind one of the piles of bodies to hide.

Bile crept up his chest and almost into his throat until he noticed tunnels dug into the bottoms of the dome-shaped space.

The more he discovered, the more he kept telling himself, *I need to get the heck out of this frigging—*

Hissss!

A creature darted out of a dark opening near his feet.

Before he could pull his legs back, it clamped its mandibles around his ankles.

"God sakes." Anthony whacked the femur at the arthropod's head. "Get off me you piece of—"

The end of the bone glanced off the giant millipede's armored head, making it even angrier and more forceful with its strong jaws.

Hisssss!

Another giant millipede entered the space from another passage. It arched the front half of its overgrown body and knocked the club-like bone out of Anthony's hand before latching onto his bicep.

"No, no no this can't—"

Crunch!

The fingers of his right hand entered the mouth of yet another arthropleura.

All three giant millipedes forced him back down to the dirt floor of their burrow.

Hissss! Hissss! Hisss!

In short succession, younger ones exited other tunnels into the main chamber with incredible speed to have some human dinner.

"Noo-aaaaaaahhhhhhh!"

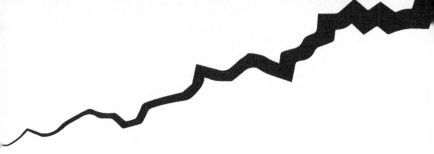

FORTY-NINE

PRESENT TIME – IN THE PAST

DONE WAITING, Kamren rubbed his face, wiping tears from his cheeks in the process. He'd held on to hope for a couple more minutes, but nothing happened. A deep breath left his lungs before he spoke. "Guess that's it then."

"Oh, Kam, I can't believe that happened to you guys." Disappointed, Emily-Ann walked over and took the boy in her arms. "I was really rooting for you two."

Theodore had been admiring Nandy off to the side when he chimed in, "I know of a couple more rift sites we could check out." He stood up with a slight smirk. "It would take a bit of a flight, though."

Kam weighed the variables. "The contents of my gut say no, but my heart says yes."

"Figured so," E-A responded with a grin. "Let's go see what we can do."

Theo started for the path that had been made earlier. "Wonder if that boat is still there. Would be a nice gift from SauraCorps."

Side by side with E-A, Kam moved along.

Then he glanced back one last time.

Still nothing.

Facing forward once more, he had Nandy come up beside him and cocked her head to connect her gaze with his. Her presence made him chuckle. "You've been a good buddy, too, little ninja-dog."

"Ninja-dog?" Theo half-turned as he hiked on. "That's a nundasuch—"

"I know," Kam answered, sadness in his tone. "It's just… what Viv called it."

Theo took that as his cue to remain quiet for the next while. Instead, he got lost in his thoughts of what he'd observed a few minutes earlier. A massive giganotosaurus had shown concern for a young human. It had responded like a dog or cat would to its distraught owner. Overall, it gave his research more fuel for its fire.

All Kam could think about was Viv. The moment the rift closed kept replaying in his mind. He'd been inches away from home, from her, and love. Though his mind filled with numerous thoughts, he glanced over at E-A, who had been mostly staring down at the ground. "Decided to stay with your dad then, huh?"

E-A's grin diminished as she walked. As much as she loved her father, part of her wondered if she'd made the right decision. "I'll admit, leaving the future behind…" She cleared her throat. "…it took a fair bit to make that decision."

Kam smirked. "The giant millipedes sealed the deal, didn't they?"

Bursting with laughter, E-A hadn't expected his remark. "Oh yeah, I love being dragged to my death." She pushed on his shoulder just enough to almost knock him off stride. "Nah, as much as I had more of a life in the present, I didn't want a future without my dad. Even if that meant staying in the past."

Hearing her endearment toward her father made him smile. "Now that's one of the most timey-wimey sentences I've ever heard. Mind if I use that for a—"

Reality checked him.

"Oh, right. There's no books to write in here."

They walked in silence for a couple seconds and watched Nandy trot ahead of them, veering off to parts of the path that made her curious.

Kam found something else to talk about that meant a lot to him. "Thanks for helping Viv get through, by the way."

E-A nodded. "Wish I could've helped you both."

"There was so much going on back there."

She brought her hands to the sides of her head as if her mind had been blown. "Some of those rifts weren't all leading to our present earth either. I wonder if we may have seen other planets, or even dimensions."

Kam raised a finger to add, "You saw the one with the purple sky, right? I'm pretty sure I saw something like a *large moth* of some sort flying by."

"Is that what that was?" E-A recalled the details. "It's red eyes were pretty freaky."

"Right? I was hoping it wouldn't...."

E-A took a couple more steps before stopping. "Kam? Are you—"

He shushed her. "Do you hear that?"

Snap!

Kam froze, trying to channel all his senses to pick up on where it came from.

Crack-ack-ack!

Up ahead, Theo tilted his head. "Is that—"

CRRRRACK-ACK-ACK! ZAP! CRACKLE! SNAP!

A one-story diameter ring of blue space-time energy took form about forty feet behind them.

Everyone turned to try and identify where and when it led to.

"The other side...it's dark." Kam had started taking subconscious steps toward it. Although he knew something within himself had taken control. "I can't see much."

"That might take you home." E-A began walking over to the anomaly to see for herself. "At least, I hope it does."

Twenty feet away from it, Kam added some oomph to his step. "Even if I end up in Africa, it better."

Only ten feet remained when Nandy came up from behind and brushed against his leg. She circled him a couple of times while looking up at his face.

"Aw, Nandy," Kam cooed as he crouched down. Of all the things he'd expected to happen to him in the last two days, he never thought he'd befriend a dinosaur. "I have to go now, okay?"

The nundasuchus angled its head, giving him an inquisitive stare.

Kam placed a hand on the side of her snout while stroking her tough, crocodilian-like back scales with the other hand. "Make sure you look after E-A and her dad for me, all right?"

Once he'd finished his goodbye, he marched on to the rift.

Kam arrived at the space-time window.

He still couldn't see much.

The other side contained eerie darkness and shadows.

Lifting one of his feet, he paused. *Is this the way home?*

"Hey, Kam," E-A called over.

He turned to look at her and her father. "Yeah?"

"You'll find her." She gave him a confident grin. "I know you will."

Kam nodded, then took his first step through the rift.

Another step further in helped him gain a better adjustment for his eyes.

ZZEEUU-POP!

Gone.

The rift behind him vanished.

Its sudden disappearance made him spin around.

Large teeth were inches away from his face.

Freaking out, he backed up into a cordoning rope and tumbled to the ground. Metal poles fell from either end of the rope, clanging against the floor.

His hands touched a smooth surface like tile. "Where… am I?"

As more of the environment took shape around him, he

gazed up at a utahraptor skeleton in a leaping pose.

Among the shadows, a voice asked, "Who are you?"

Startled, Kam managed to pull himself up and out of the tangled equipment. "I'm sorry, I uh… I, um…."

A woman entered the room from a connecting hallway. Upon coming closer, she took a good look at the teenager. "Are you…Kamren Eckhardt?"

Shocked to hear someone he'd never met say his name, he cleared his throat while taking a step back. "Yeah, that's me."

Incredibly relieved, she stopped within a couple feet of the boy and extended a hand out to him. "Felicia Voorhees, I'm happy you've made it home."

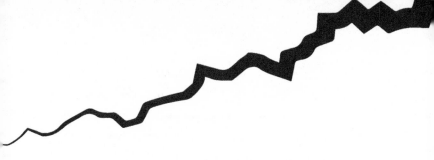

FIFTY

ALMOST HOME.

To Vivienne, the taxi ride home had started to feel like an eternity. Inside of her, a dullness seemed to overpower excitement. All the familiar streets that passed by should have given her comfort.

Nothing could fill the expanding void in her heart.

She wanted to hear the recorded message from Kamren again, but she didn't want to annoy Sebastian or make things awkward with the taxi driver.

On the opposite side of the vehicle, Sebastian hadn't said a word since they hopped in. As much as he longed to go to his own house, he wanted to make sure Viv would get home safe and sound first.

The taxi slowed to a stop in front of Viv's house.

Inside, none of the lights were on.

Only the front door light illuminated the front walk. Her parents had always left it on whenever she'd been out late.

She recognized it as a sign of their hope.

"Well…." Sebastian gave her an empathetic grin. "I'll take care of this, Viv, you go on up." He tapped on the fabric of the driver's seat. "Keep the meter running, I'm over on the other side of town."

Viv placed her hand on the inner door handle. Somehow everything didn't seem real. All the circumstances that had happened after she'd left her house a couple days ago to be with Kam seemed imaginary. Now she would no doubt have to explain it all to her family. "What do I even tell them?" Her question came out timid and lacking confidence.

Perplexed, Sebastian rubbed his wrists. "Whether they believe you or not, you know everything was real."

Her last moments in the prehistoric time were still the freshest in her mind. Especially the image of Kam reaching out to her as the rift collapsed. "I wish it wasn't."

The ache in her voice made Sebastian look away from her and gaze out his window. Instead of focusing on the houses on the other side of the street, all he could see was his regretful reflection. "Me too, kid."

Viv sucked down a deep breath before opening the taxi door. She finally exited but popped her head back in before leaving. "Oh, and I hope you get to see your kids sometime soon."

He turned his gaze away from the window and smiled at her. "Thanks, Viv."

She nodded, closed the door, then took her first steps onto the front walk. She didn't have her keys on her, since she'd left her purse in Kam's truck. *Who's going to answer?* Telling her parents everything would be easy and challenging at the same time.

Over halfway to the house, she realized an even more difficult task would eventually come up. *I'll have to tell Kam's parents about him.* As that slammed into her like a freight train, she slowed her stride. *That just might break me.*

As those thoughts weighed on her mind, she made it to the white front door.

The taxi driver put the vehicle into gear.

"Wait." Sebastian leaned forward to pat the man's seat. "I want to make sure she gets inside okay."

Viv lifted a fist and expelled a deep breath.

Knock-knock-knock-knock.

No one seemed to stir within the home.

She placed a finger against the doorbell and closed her eyes.

Ding-dong.

Three seconds went by until the living room light went on and shone through the front windows. Someone came closer to one of them to see who was there.

Viv turned and made eye contact with her father.

Andrew Lancaster shouted further into the house, "She's home! *Viv's home!*"

He whipped around to the front door as other rooms became illuminated. His hands trembled so much from elation and excitement that he couldn't unlock the door fast enough. Once he opened it, he lost all breath as he fell to his knees and wrapped his daughter up in his arms.

Pleased to see a reuniting family, Sebastian sat back in the taxi and smiled. "We can go now."

On the front step, Viv could hear her mom and little brother clamoring down the stairs as she held her father's head close to her chest. "Dad, I'm so sorry, Kam and I…we shouldn't have—"

"Viv, oh my God, you're here!" Cassie Eckhardt came to the door just as thrilled as everyone else. She let Denise pass through to embrace her own daughter before noticing that only Viv had arrived. "Honey, where… Where's *Kam?*"

In the comfort of her mother's arms, Viv managed to turn her head and glance up at Cassie. "He's, um… We should probably go inside."

Evan Eckhardt stood beside his wife.

Only seeing Viv made his chest tighten.

Arty hugged her just as she crossed the threshold. "Where have you been?"

She rustled the hair on the top of his head. "Buddy, you're not going to believe—"

"Hey, what's everyone crying about?"

Viv's hand still held the doorhandle.

The voice had come from behind her out by the street.

It gave her chills of an amorous nature.

"Did someone get trapped in a prehistoric time or something?"

Smiling the biggest she'd ever made in her life, Viv spun around and immediately leaked ecstatic tears as she bolted back outside.

Kamren sprinted toward her while grinning so hard that it hurt.

Out in the street, Felicia drove off, letting the teenagers have their moment.

Right before they met, he braced himself as she collided into him. He kissed her cheek and embraced her with all he had. Having her so close to him made his legs weak and his heart pump overtime. Considering he'd lost all hope just a matter of minutes ago, he'd been revived by simply being in her presence.

Viv let herself melt into him. She raked her fingers through his hair, pushing his head into the side of hers. The combination of having his words from the recording in her mind and having him safe in her arms put her in an emotional state she couldn't even begin to explain.

Out of all the things she felt in that moment, relief and love trumped them all.

"We made it, Viv," he cooed in her ear before giving her another peck on her soft, misty cheek. *"We did it."*

She pulled her head back to gaze into his eyes. Cradling his face in her hands, she struggled to come up with much to say. "How… *How* did you even—"

Urged by his affection for her, Kam pushed his lips into hers.

She more than accepted his kiss, letting him press against her trembling lips again and again. Every time he gave her another, her love for him swelled to the point she thought her heart would explode into a rift of passion.

Kam and Viv caught their breaths.

They gazed into each other's eyes, taking in every inch of their blissful expressions.

"Don't take this the prehistoric way, but…" He kissed her one more time. "…we should've done that *a long time ago.*"

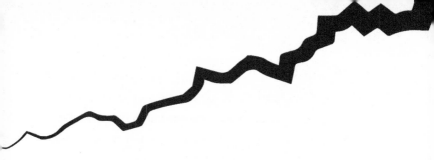

EPILOGUE

THREE MONTHS LATER

"TOMORROW AT two o'clock?" Sebastian Sharp held his cellphone to an ear as he stood out on the front porch of his new home. "Sounds good to me. Oh, and make sure the baby stegosauruses have enough food before they arrive. You'd be surprised how much they can pack away…. Okay, take care."

Ending the call, he nodded to himself.

SauraCorps no longer operated with the aid and use of space-time anomalies.

Legalities and red tape had all been taken care of over the past couple of months. All SauraCorps would be known for from now on would be simple dinosaur museums.

"Hey, Seb?" Felicia stepped out from inside the house holding her phone. "Peirce is wondering if they can deliver Trudy's new troodon friends on Thursday next week."

Sebastian scratched the back of his head. "Ask if they can come Friday, I forgot to tell you a young adult brachiosaurus is on its way from Oregon. Someone found it injured, I'm hoping we can help it." He went to scroll through the contacts in his smartphone. "Which reminds me, I need to call Beaumont so she can come and take a look at it."

Felicia brought the receiving end of her phone back to her mouth. "Friday works better if that's all right with you…. Okay, great, we'll see you guys then." By the time she'd stopped the conversation, she came to Sebastian's side.

After taking a deep breath, he turned to look at her in her stylish early-fall black sweater. "I sure hope taking over Bartelloni's property works out."

"It will." She held a hand out to him, which he took while giving in to a grin. "It may not be SauraCorps, but this is a good new start for both of us."

Again, he nodded as he looked out over the nearest domed enclosure where diverse dinosaur species roamed in peace. "I definitely needed it."

She layered his hand between both of hers. "Aiden and Olivia are still coming over this weekend, right?"

"That's right." Sebastian smiled at the mention of his kids. "Speaking of kids…" He gazed over at the front gate. "…I'm surprised they aren't here yet."

"Should be any time now, right?"

Ding!

A notification sang its tune on his phone, and he read the text message. "Ah, they just turned onto the road. I'll go meet them at the gate."

About two minutes later, a modern pick-up truck drove past the open gates and onto the bridge. As soon as the young driver noticed Sebastian, they parked and hopped out. "When you said secluded, you really meant it, huh?"

"Nice to see you made it, Kam," Sebastian responded, coming over for a handshake.

"It made for the perfect trip with tunes." Vivienne exited the passenger side and came over to them. She also shook the older man's hand. "It's good to see you, Seb."

"I'm happy you were both able to make it," Sebastian remarked with a big smile.

"So what is this place?" Kam glanced all around, then he noticed the long necks of certain creatures off to his left and stepped over to the stone railing. "Wait, you have—"

"Dinosaurs?" Viv wore an excited grin as she also walked over. "How did you get them here?"

Sebastian crossed his arms as he also gazed over his new endeavor. "This used to belong to someone who abused the privilege of owning dinosaurs. His practices were underhanded and unethical. But since his disappearance when we destroyed the main rift here in Utah, I've taken over all of it."

Kam looked over at the refined businessman. "Is it going to be like a dinosaur *park?*"

Sebastian leaned his head side to side. "More like a reserve of sorts."

Viv smirked. "Good, because there may be *trademark issues* if you made it into a park."

Laughing at his girlfriend's quip, Kam nudged his shoulder into hers. "You beat me by two seconds on that one."

Even Sebastian chuckled as he placed his hands on the railing. "I have something to show you two. Come with me."

Kam squinted at him. "You're not going to lead us to a time rift and throw us through again, right?"

A slap came from one of Viv's hands. "Jeez, Kam."

The insinuation made Sebastian snort. "No. Those days are behind me."

Nodding, Kam began following him. "Just checking."

After a small hike into one of the domed enclosures, the three of them came to an opening in the trees which led to a small lake. Side by side on the opposite side of the water, a family of triceratops and a small pack of velociraptors drank together.

For Kam and Viv, everything within the place took them right back to the prehistoric time they'd tried so hard to escape. Yet, they knew nothing here would harm them.

"This is incredible," Viv remarked in wonder. "How long has this place existed?"

Sebastian counted in his head. "Roughly four years now."

"And their presence hasn't affected the time-space energy at all?" With everything that had happened, Viv recalled her theory. "No rifts pop up around here?"

"Funny you should mention that," Sebastian responded

as he looked around the lake. "Our scientists—well, *former* scientists—figure that because SauraCorps had let the main rifts all over the world stay open for so long, that's what caused more to randomly open."

Kam strolled over to the water's edge. "Makes sense."

A few feet away, Sebastian placed his hand above his eyes as he watched the surface of the pristine lake. "Oh, here they come. Almost like clockwork."

Confused, Viv stepped forward. "What's *they*, exactly?" Then she saw multiple creatures swimming toward their position. "Wait, aren't those—"

"You gotta be kidding me," Kam raised his voice in absolute excitement.

Two adult-sized nundasuchus swam up to them and exited the water.

Kam got down on one knee and held his hands out to them. "I can't believe you have some of them here!"

"We just received them last week." Sebastian kept grinning as the teenagers brimmed with elation. "Wait for it."

Viv kept staring out at the water.

Three little nundasuchuses breached the surface before scrambling onto solid ground to join their parents.

"Babies!" By now, Viv joined her boyfriend closer to the shore to pet and enjoy the aquatic dinosaurs. "Oh my goodness, they're so freaking *adorable!*"

"They aren't Nandy," Kam mentioned as he picked up one of the baby dinosaurs. It chirped a little noise as its little arms hung over his cradling hands. "But I'm going to call you Mandy, and that one can be Sandy, and you—"

"Really?" Viv chuckled at him as she had the third infant nundasuchus crawl up her thigh to play. "You're actually going to name all of them?"

"Yup." He gently booped his nose into the baby's snout as it swung its tail back and forth. "And that one you've got can be Nandy Jr."

Smiling at the teenagers as they enjoyed the company of the dinosaurs, Sebastian spoke up. "Just so you know, you're welcome to visit anytime. It's the least I can do after everything that went down."

Viv had Nandy Jr. laying on her forearm. She ran her fingers along its crocodilian-like scales down its back. "We'll definitely be taking you up on that."

Kam looked back at his friends. "Meant to tell you guys, I've been taking notes of the whole thing and started writing about it." He met eyes with Viv and grinned. "I think it'll make a decent sci-fi novel."